Knocking On Buddha's Door

A Novel Memoir

Veda Mata

love
Veda
(Dorothy)

AMITABHA FOUNDATIONAL ENTERPRISES

First Published in Canada 2009.
This paperback Second revised edition 2014.

Edited by Dhyani Jo Sinclair.

Cover designed by author. The cover and first insert photos are from the monastery at Shigatse, Tibet (Tibetan Autonomous Region). All the photos were taken by Veda Mata except those of Amma, Amma's ashram, Thrangu Rinpoche, the Karmapa and the Dalai Lama which have been made available to the public. The author wishes to thank the copyright holders for permission to reproduce their photographs in this book.

ISBN 978-0-9878432-0-3

 The author may be contacted by email at knockingatbuddhasdoor@hotmail.com.

Printed in Victoria, BC, Canada by Printorium Bookworks, Island Blue Print Co. Ltd.

Published by Amitabha Foundational Enterprises

I offer this book at the feet of all my teachers and their teachers . . .

I dedicate this book to my children, and to my children's children.

I acknowledge all those who walked, walk, and will walk with me . . . along the Way.

All the people and events in this book are not necessarily true, nor are they necessarily false.

Knocking
On
Buddha's Door

Jesus said:

"And I tell you, ask, and you will receive; seek, and you will find; knock, and the door will be opened to you."

—Luke, 11:9

"Knock, knock, knocking on Heaven's door . . ."

—Bob Dylan

PROLOGUE

A lone pink rose growing in a brown clay pot with dragons surrounding its base, chasing each other's tails. That's me. I sit out here on my balcony looking at it, while basking in the early July afternoon sun. Solitary. I love solitude, but those dragons persistently penetrate my mind, chasing after me, taunting me, irritating me enough to tell my tale. To tell my story.

I contemplate the possibilities while sipping Dubonnet with lemon out of a new crystal glass (purchased for $2 in the community 'Super Chance' second-hand store) and munching on Triscuits and feta cheese. After all, I have come to realize that I do actually live in the lap of luxury here in Victoria, Canada. The world out there is a very different and at times ugly place. Here we take our safety, all our freedoms, *and* cleanliness for granted! There is all this beauty in front of me—the flowers, the boats, the blue sky, the sea, the Olympic Mountains and the alluring mystique of their snowy peaks. Why push my mind to wander into the past and traverse those other heights and adventures when I sit here amid the beauty and glory of the present?

Oh where, oh where might I begin? Last night watching a video on Beatrix Potter's life, I heard a phrase that caught my attention and thought that's how I should start: "There is nothing more delightful than writing the first few words of a story, for you never know where they might lead you." A bit sappy, but also so true for the first few steps of any journey, since the first few words do set the stage . . .

My venture into the landscape of Buddha and heartland of Tibetan Buddhism started the summer of 1997 when I had my first (and only) experience of what I consider the ABSOLUTE TRUTH! Upon recognition, the moment and the experience vanished. I have been craving to recapture it ever since. Much to my frustration and disappointment, it continues to elude me. As if it lies on the tip of my tongue or just within the grasp of my fingertips, it is there, and yet . . .

Or maybe, I should begin otherwise:

I think I can fairly say that my journey towards the truth began with my very first steps. Time has always been deliberated by my intention towards exactness—getting 'it' right so I wouldn't fall over, ending up off track or flat on my face. Truth for me then relates to two things: a sense of perfection and a middle place where I feel right and true. Maybe my conscience, along with my innate sense of balance, have been the guides that have kept their wits about me, keeping me on my own two feet when I felt I was teetering on the brink of disaster, or throwing me the life jacket when I felt I was drowning in a sea of chaos and expectation to be other than. I have profited by the continuity of my sense of self—a foundational awareness that experiences a sense of security knowing that it exists. So maybe, then, Self is the first point of my truth.

Whether or not a Universal Truth exists also seems to have been an object of my inquiry. At an early age, even before my initiation into the regular Sunday school classes, I found myself obsessed with a conversation with an invisible being that I later identified as God. My first recollection was around four years old, in bed before falling asleep, reaching to someone *out there*, seeking understanding attention. I recognize now those early attempts to communicate with the Divine were actually a desperate attempt for loving attention, as my mother was becoming progressively too busy with her subsequent babies to tuck me in at night. By then, there were already two younger siblings. However, these inner conversations set my stage and established my course in life as a contemplative, dedicated to the pursuit of knowledge beyond the mundane reality of those around me. They also established an ongoing relationship with a higher power (or being) that inevitably surprises me with its immediate answers and absurd sense of humour. At least, that is what I believe. HE, SHE, or IT exists. Whether anyone else believes this, or not, is really irrelevant.

Around age eleven, I remember expounding my philosophical theories to my best friend Joni—theories that are now elaborated upon in books being sold by the millions as the 'power of intention' and the 'law of attraction'! I remember sitting at the end of her bed after school telling her about my latest insight: "Joni, we CAN make our dreams come true. We wouldn't have those ideas if they weren't meant to guide us, to show us what to do in our lives!" At the time, my friend was more interested in playing Barbies and reading romantic comic books! And I was forty-five years ahead of my time!

Later, in my teens, I often took pleasure in extracting phrases out of the books I was reading, words that came close to a universal definition of the human condition. I was obviously seeking spiritual identification. I would leap with excitement when reading the classics and rush to write down some author's definition of the meaning of life or some phrase that captured it.

I think that we have all felt those "Ah ha!" moments when we catch a glimpse at some aspect of preciousness. Such moments are often accompanied by a sense of space, freedom, and joy—delicious feelings that spur us on to experiencing more of the same or that open possibilities of achieving an ideal. Yes, such is this momentous sense of liberation when we may feel that we soar like an eagle on the currents of being-ness. A sacred purposefulness, that waves like the prayer flags blowing on the tops of Himalayan passes, calls to us. Surely, this is something to strive for. My ordinariness loves such reprieve and likes to admit such moments of greatness and divinity into my menial experience. The impulse to reach towards Truth, to search for the Truth, and to find ways to move towards it has become my *raison d'être,* an underlying intention guiding me towards resolution at a time when the crest of middle-age has been traversed and the descent towards the end of this lifetime has become evident and relevant.

So much has happened since those early days. I have remained true to my cause but the question remains: Will I achieve my goal? What are the chances of reaching it when it rests so single-mindedly upon the premise that there is Knowledge to be discovered, that we are all evolving towards THAT which exists for each and every one of us to claim within ourselves? The Hindus call it *Brahman,* the Buddhists the Ultimate Reality or the Nature of Reality, the Taoists the Complete Reality; the Christians and Moslems call it God. Is it possible to meet God face to face, to know God personally and become one with such a 'such-ness'? How to find God? Say, for example, that the journey ended at the end of the rainbow, would it be any more possible to reach it? Maybe these are rhetorical questions. Koans for contemplation.

I set myself upon a journey towards the Divine in order to touch my soul. A task and aspect of Self far greater than any taught within the textbooks of Western pedagogy, which, incidentally, I found rather boring. I ended up quitting university and going travelling, on a quest to follow my star, "no matter how hopeless, no matter how far." I left my family and friends behind. They thought I had sold my soul to the devil by rejecting the 'norm'! They thought I'd become a hippy, that I was doing drugs. Not!

Dorothy had clicked her heels and off she set upon the yellow brick road towards Emerald City to find the Wizard, to ask him how to get back home to Kansas: the place where there is a sense of Home, a feeling that one has finally arrived. I have not achieved that place, neither outside on this earth nor inside within myself. However, I have had a glimpse of it and have once again clicked my heels and taken off at a full run towards the end of my life and my goal. And once again, my family thinks that I am jumping off the edge of a cliff, attempting social suicide at the risk of *their* reputations.

My father would have understood my predicament. But he's dead. He died long before I even took my first trip to India. I don't want to go without mentioning that he was my first spiritual mentor and teacher. He used to wake me up at midnight with

Kentucky Fried Chicken and say: "Get up! Let's talk!" My mother would be sleeping. And we would.

We used to talk about abstract things. He would talk in parables. Unlike my mother, I saw abstract ideas become concrete as he drew analogies to thoughts and things. He fed my unconscious hunger and thirst for spiritual nourishment. He talked about things that nobody else was interested in talking about. He used to say:

"You know and I know that we know. But we just don't know what it is exactly that we know!"

He also said that I would recognize others like us, who also understood, by the mark in the middle of their foreheads. At the time, I had no idea what he meant. Now I realize that he was talking about the 'third eye' and the invisible process of its opening. Whatever. It seemed as if we were side by side looking out the same lens onto the horizon of life, sharing a mutual understanding—a knowing beyond words.

Later, in the last talk before he died, Dad sat in the same quandary that I now find myself. He asked me how he could be free? I replied that he had to take his space and to follow his truth. He told me to carry on the quest. Ten days later he died.

My father had felt that I was rejecting both him and the material world when I would argue that I couldn't pursue a material business life until I had discovered freedom in my spiritual being. At such a point, I would find a business that would match my need to initiate others into this spiritual conversation. When I found Reiki in 1984, I felt that I had at last found this business. But at the time of our final conversation, without any knowledge that there were others who shared this profound interest in the world of the immaterial, I was still searching. I inherently knew that spiritual freedom came first and then, contrary to my father's opinion, material freedom followed.

In the end, my father gave me his acknowledgement and approval. He had achieved his material dream, making his self-designated million dollars, but had found that he was no closer to freedom. On the contrary, he was more tied down to structure than ever. He was working 24/7, his mind caught on the spinning machine of his businesses even while he was sleeping. He wanted out of the rat race that I had never wanted into in the first place. What more could a child wish for? At least one of her parents accepted and understood her.

Dad was a seeker. In that last conversation, he passed on the torch and gave me a directive: "You go find what it is we are looking for. Bring it back to the others. Bring back the 'strength' for the rest of the family. The money will always be here." Little did I know that it would be the last conversation we ever had, and incidentally, the money wasn't there to help me on my quest. It was there for those who wanted houses, cars, and trailers at the lake, bingo, the casino, etc., etc.

Not that I am feeling sorry for myself (or maybe I am), but it would have been nice to have had money to go sit at the feet of all those enlightened beings who I have discovered live amidst us on this planet, to ask them if they had any answers to the questions and problems that I still have left to resolve. I continue to search them out regardless of my meagre budget. The lesson possibly involves doing it all on my own. Just as Milarepa (a Buddhist saint) had his fair share of duress and defeat, so I have had mine, particularly with regards to my attempts at building material structures for the cause!

Coincidently, my Dad's heart stopped on a nudist beach on the initiation island of his paradise, Kauai, Hawaii. Just as he was stepping onto the path off the beach, an artery blocked in his heart; he fell over and died. He must have thought: "I've died and gone to heaven!" as he left his body and hovered over watching as a young, long-haired blonde, birthday-suited nurse came running over, straddling him to give him mouth-to-mouth resuscitation. I shook my head with laughter as I heard the story of his death. If anyone had chosen an exit that pointed the way out of the drama of seriousness, he did!

Grief didn't bypass me, however, as I cried for months and months following his departure and really didn't start smiling again until the birth of my first daughter, almost two years later. I smiled even more when I found out that her name, Oriole (that came to me in a dream a month before her birth), was the female derivative of my father's name, Orville, meaning 'coming from a place of gold', which I have interpreted as heaven.

"Thanks Dad for the verification. Thank you God for your Gift of Grace."

Another way to begin would be to say that . . .

I was born bearing my mother's name, Dorothy. I was always identified in relation to her—big Dorothy or little Dorothy—until I grew taller than her height of 4 ft 11 inches; then I became Dorothy Junior measured against Dorothy Senior. That's how they always identified us on the phone: "Would you like Dorothy Senior or Junior?" Maybe if I hadn't had the same name, I wouldn't have identified so much with the main character in *The Wizard of Oz,* a major myth of 20th-century culture and the generator of the Hollywood song "Somewhere over the rainbow . . ."

Despite her signature film associations, Dorothy Senior was more like the Lion who lacked courage to step outside the bounds of the nest, let alone arrive at Emerald City. Consequently, when I flew the coop at eighteen in search of my dream and womanhood, she stood standing at the door waving her broom in chastisement, threatening to banish me from her brood. There were names for women like me who dared to break the constraints of compliance, names which she did call me in moments of complete exasperation upon realization that I was NOT going to relinquish my dream. And so, to this day.

This Dorothy, coincidentally born within the emerald month of May, has long since clicked her heels and set off across the seas in search of Shangri-La or, as the Tibetans know it, Shambhala. Along the way, she has been given a new name, Veda Mata (this, however, is a story for a later chapter). Will this new name serve to guide her towards realizing the Truth within herself? Follow along as she treads the steps of her personal journey towards the One.

As an observer, I am both the narrator and accompanist on my own journey, serving both as guide and commentator upon myself. As a participant, I share this time with you. Are you ready? Are you with me? Shall we begin? Popcorn anyone?

Back to the present . . . I am experiencing a hiatus in my travels, having just returned from my fourth visit to India, this time venturing further into the heartland of Buddhism—Nepal and Tibet. A time to catch my breath. A time to take a few moments and jot down some notes just in case someone might want to track me down, to prove my whereabouts, to follow a dream into the inner and outer reaches of an extraordinary landscape hidden within one individual's mind. A reflection that might serve to open up doors of other closet identities who share the same cravings and longings for the spiritual path and who might be looking for guidance along the way.

As I sit on my balcony overlooking the sunny, summery sights of the Juan de Fuca Strait and gaze over to the Olympic peaks of America, I allow my mind to wander into the possibility of the mystical reality where reflections of eternal youth and transcendental pursuit just might find their roots. I have been determined to prove my spiritual point and whereabouts most of my adult life. Maybe this recollection of past adventures might serve to validate my present circumstance and win myself a few merit points along the way! Regardless, a story worth living is a story worth telling. May it not fall on deaf ears.

1997
Victory

This is a beautiful story from Rabindranath Tagore, paraphrased by Osho:

I was searching for God for thousands of lives. I saw him . . . sometimes far away . . . I rushed . . . By the time I would reach there he had gone further. It went on and on. But finally I arrived at a door, and on the door was a sign: 'This is the house where God lives.'

Rabindranath says, I became worried for the first time. I became very troubled. Trembling. I went up the stairs. I was just going to knock on the door, and suddenly, in a flash, I saw . . .

If I knock on the door and God opens the door, then what? Then everything is finished—my journeys, my pilgrimages, my great adventures, my philosophy, my poetry, all the longing of my heart—all is finished! It will be suicide!

Seeing the point, Rabindranath says, I removed my shoes from my feet . . . because going back down the stairs might create some noise . . . And from the moment I reached the bottom of the steps I ran. And I have not looked back. Since then I have been running and running for thousands of years.

I am still searching for God, although now I know where he lives. So all I have to do is avoid that place, and I can go on searching for him everywhere else. But I have to avoid that house . . . that house haunts me. I remember it perfectly. If by chance I accidentally enter that house, then all is finished.

A golden, sandy, sequestered beach edged on each side with large black porous volcanic rocks, sheltered by overriding cliffs covered with verdant jungle forests . . . The crashing sound of the waves splashing against the shore overrode the sounds of the jungle and sea birds hovering overhead. Sights of dolphins sounding in the far distant turquoise sea acted as witnesses to the sun rising above the Pacific horizon. Kauai, Hawaii—the sacred island of Kahuna initiation. The nude beach. Secret Beach. The place where Orville Earl Griffeth's heart decided it was time to stop.

A lone woman in her mid-forties, thin, suntanned brown, bare breasted, waist down wrapped in a Polynesian printed sarong, crouched closely to the earth scouring the sands for tiny shells, slowly choosing each precious one, plucking it from the mixture of minute pieces of shells and grains of sand, and placing it in the folds of her skirt. Deliberately, attentively, as if nothing else in the universe existed. Fascinated and held within the gravity of her own deeply penetrating thoughts, she failed to notice the dolphins jumping to herald the arrival of her father's spirit.

As the sun began to rise in the sky, heat began to blanket the earth. She looked up thoughtfully, adjusting the brim of her straw hat to more fully cover her eyes from the sun's radiance. Then she tumbled onto the sand, sitting, stretching her legs out carefully, so as not to drop the precious shells, toes barely touching the remnants of white foam left from the last receding wave. Slightly hopeful that the next incoming one would swish and wash over her feet to offer a refreshing coolant, she was beginning to feel hot. It wasn't yet seven-thirty in the morning.

She had left the two teenage girls back at the hotel sleeping. The last two days of sleuthing for the exact whereabouts of Secret Beach and the discouraging lack of voluntary information from the natives reaffirmed the appropriateness of the name. The younger two had given up the search, not really being concerned. The meaning held significance for the mother only. The nineteen-year-old daughter aligned herself with her friend and elected to sleep in, resting in the comfort of dreams.

The mother was on a mission to lay one of her dreams to rest along with the lingering sorrow and thoughts of her deceased father. She had not had her chance to say good-bye to him over twenty years ago. Child-rearing had prevented her from making the pilgrimage before. The opportunity to come to Kauai, her father's paradise island, to put her grief to rest or bury it at sea on the very same beach where he had died, lay before her as an affirmation that dreams surely could manifest into reality.

"Dad, can you believe it? That I am finally here, on your beach, where you chose to leave us all behind?" Dorothy, the dutiful daughter, had at long last arrived to pay her respects at her father's resting place—or reasonable facsimile, as he had chosen to be cremated and carried home in a metal box, to be discovered by the security metal detector on the way. Most of his remains lay in an urn on her mother's fireplace mantel.

She had a handful of those ashes in her skirt pocket. Dorothy Margaret (gift of God and child of pearl and moonbeams, as her name meant), Orv's eldest daughter, and the only one of eight children who had had an affinity for his mind and spirit, pulled out the plastic film container filled with his ashes and lifted off the lid. She sat there gazing at its contents for a couple of minutes before she rose to her feet.

Undecided as to what to do with the shells, she lifted up the front flap of her skirt and held them as in a basket, while awkwardly raising her other arm to throw the ashes into the oncoming waves.

"I know you have been waiting for me to come. I am ready to begin the quest. The mission you set me on. I haven't forgotten. I have been so busy all these years fulfilling Mother's dream, raising the children. Now it's time for me to find what we were always looking for. I am free now to go my way. The children are ready to look after themselves and have given me their blessing. I am here Dad, asking for yours. You left so quickly; I never had a chance to say good-bye or to assure you that I would never forget what you asked me to do.

"I know, you're probably already swimming with the dolphins which I can't see because I left my glasses in the car, but anyways, Dad, I thought you might like some of your body to be swimming along with your spirit, as I know how much you loved snorkelling and swimming. Here you go! Bon Voyage! Remember, I will always love you and remember you.

"I want to ask one more thing from you. Please STAY with me, walk with me, and be there to guide my way! Bye for now!"

She threw the contents of the plastic cylinder into the huge white-rimmed wave before it had a chance to crash into the shore; she put the vial back into her skirt pocket and took her hat off, waving it to the sky and at the invisible spirit of her beloved father. Then, she carefully placed the shells in a pile beside her, lay down with arms outstretched, breasts bare to the overarching blue heavens, and with her feet touching the frothy waves, Dorothy Margaret soaked up the sun as the sand soaked up the tears streaming down the sides of her burning cheeks.

A month and a half later . . .

As soon as I exited the assembly hall, I spotted her. Standing in the lobby gazing out over the tall grassy fields of August, she appeared like an apparition from some other dimension. Monica—my friend and mentor—is ethereal like an angel, yet practical enough to have staged this unusually monumental event, bringing Gangaji to the Stelly's rodeo auditorium.

"I'm going to INDIA!" I shouted.

She turned to meet my eyes, and hers lit up like the sunbeams streaming through the tall windows beside her. A bit bewildered, she responded to my excitement. "What did you say?"

"I'm going to see Papaji!" I said, so definitely that without argument she reached out her arms to include me in one of her lovely heartfelt embraces.

"When?"

"September. I just know I'll be there somehow. I can't believe it, and yet, there is absolutely no doubt. I have never felt anything so strongly or so definitely. I have just had the most amazing experience of my life in that room!"

Monica took my hand and led me over to the tapestry loveseat against the wall. Sitting down beside me as all the people started streaming out, the satsang meeting being over, she gave me one of her penetrating and engaging gazes, as if we were the only two people in the world. Like a lens zooming in to capture the moment, the outside busyness faded into the background, leaving Monica and me encapsulated completely in the present moment.

"Tell me," she said softly.

"When Hanuman from Vancouver was on stage with Gangaji, talking about being in India last year and feeding milk to the Krishna statues at the puja celebrating Krishna's birthday, something miraculous happened! I had been intently matching my consciousness with Gangaji's because all along I have been skeptical about her authenticity and teaching ability. I've spent the entire weekend scrutinizing her and trying to match her mind's eye every instant. You know that I am not one to hand over my power to gurus; so, I have been suspicious about her, regardless of your raving reports. Anyways, when Hanuman said that the Krishna statue opened its mouth and drank the milk, something shifted inside Gangaji, and I went along with her! At that moment, an extremely clear awareness penetrated my usual stubborn consciousness and for moments' lengths Gangaji, Hanuman, Krishna, and I became ONE! There was no separation and I just *knew* that I was God and that there was no separate Self; that we were all one GOD SELF looking out from different eyes, believing that we were separate and individual, when all the time there is only ONE Self conscious. It is all just a big trick! A lie. There is no such thing as separation. We are all ONE. Just like Jesus said when he stated that 'I and my Father are One' and that we could do all that he could do, and more. Or something to that effect. Monica! I've just had my first REAL spiritual experience. A Satori! I've absolutely no doubt in my mind that this is the Truth. Of course, as soon as I realized what was happening, I jumped back into my usual separate, limited, and frustrated mind. Now I know what all the mystics have been talking about in all those books I have been reading for so many years! It IS all true, and I want to live in that space, that awareness! I am going to see Papaji to see if he can help me get back to that place in my mind, that awareness, that sense of complete unity. I feel desperate to feel it again! Knowing what I now know, how can I continue to live and to act from this place of separateness?"

Monica just gave me one of her deliciously quiet and knowledgeable smiles, one that radiates her genuine understanding and acceptance. How many times have I wished to be like her, so open and so unwilling to compromise her spiritual conviction and commitment towards compassion.

"Is that all?" she said as she gently squeezed my hand with attentive consideration.

I wanted to jump at the opportunity to keep talking to her but noticed that there were other people gathering around us soliciting her attention. I sadly became aware that we were being pulled out of our special bubble. Monica's attention was needed—someone wanting to explain details of something or other concerning the happenings in the lobby, someone manning one of the sale tables.

"There's more, but I'll call you tomorrow and tell you over the phone." I was reluctant to let her go and as she turned away to cross over the room to see what the problem was, I felt an inner wrenching, a sense of grief, and a gush of cold air that rushed in to fill the space her unwelcome departure had left.

"Oh, Monica, you really are a dear and exceptional friend. How I wish I could spend more time with you!" I whispered to myself. Wistful and a bit sad, I left the building to go find my car.

What more was there to tell? Well, for one thing, before the event, I had truly felt that Gangaji was a sham. After all, how could a Westerner profess to be a realized guru? I mean, what history do we have within our culture to be advanced enough to hold the teaching, the ultimate knowledge that has been harboured for at least five thousand years within the cultures of the East, particularly India? No priests or ministers that I have met so far in the Christian religion have had a strong connection to God. Not like that of the Hindu teachers I had been reading for so many years, who all say the same thing: God lies inside of us—we are all harbouring Brahman within the small, encased reality of Atman, or the small self, waiting to be realized. Coming from a Christian background and probably having had the same 'hippie' influence and roots lodged in the sixties, how could an American woman profess to 'know'? But then, she had been to India just as Ram Dass had, and I had had remarkable experiences listening to Ram Dass on tape and in person.

It was important to give Gangaji a fair audience. Consequently,

I had arranged to take a few of my Reiki students to the week-end event just to ensure that I didn't talk myself out of going, as I had done so many times in the past. The first night, I was extremely critical of her teaching methods, finding her particularly insensitive, a bit arrogant and condescending to those who came up on stage to offer their questions. I went home very disappointed and convinced that I had been right in resisting the invitation to go.

However, I valued Monica's opinion and admired her intuition and courage. She had been to see Gangaji's teacher, Papaji, in India the previous year and had returned extolling his virtue and teaching. Papaji was a disciple of Ramana Maharshi (a renowned teacher of the awakened state) from South India. Revered for his knowledge and teaching of non-duality, he promoted a process of Self-inquiry through constant questioning of 'Who am I?'.

Attending the weekend satsangs would give me a chance to find out for myself what the hullabaloo around Gangaji was about. However, not having visited India, I was immediately shocked by multifarious tables of pictures, statues, and all sorts of paraphernalia harbouring Gangaji's image. I felt repulsion. Idolatry! My hackles went up and I felt immediate resistance. Little did I know that this was common practice in India. Once one has become connected to a *satguru* (teacher of truth), it is useful to have an image of him/her to retouch upon the heightened experience of the initial contact. Often such images can be used in meditative practice to calm and concentrate the mind, giving way for the higher Self to penetrate the conscious mind. It is *not* about idolizing the teacher (although it seemed, from my sense of the people milling around the tables, that some of them might have done just that and given their power over to Gangaji).

However, ideally, such images serve as reminders of the higher part of ourselves. Of course, to be effective, the teacher must have first realized this place within him- or herself. Ramana Maharshi's teachings have been so effective because he actually lived and taught from the awakened state, and those students such as Papaji were fortunate enough to touch upon it themselves just from being around him; hence, the necessity of 'sitting at the feet' of a guru. There is a sort of transference or osmosis, so to speak, as the state of pure reality penetrates the visitor's consciousness simply by being in the presence of someone who has achieved that state.

Osho, another renowned Indian master, has said that "Your mind will make you very much frightened of the unknown, it will drag you back. And it is always safer to live with the known; it is familiar, you are efficient in living with it. To move into the unknown, you will need a guide—a guide who has moved into the unknown, who lives in the unknown, who lives in innocence. Just to imbibe the spirit you need the guide—not for any guidance but just to imbibe the spirit of the unknown, the joy of the unknown, the celebration of the unknown . . . It is an energy field, it is a Buddha field. It is communion—nonverbal, heart to heart and, one day, being to being."

This was the rationale behind attending the event—to see if I could 'imbibe' the spirit of Gangaji's realization, to experience for myself this 'thing' beyond the farthest reaches of my imagination. From the looks of the entrance, I had my doubts. By the end of the evening, I was convinced that my being there was a waste of time. I did not feel that I had learned anything important from Gangaji. I arrived home rather late and was determined to sleep in and not go the next day or to any further sessions. I would phone the others in the morning so that they could find another ride.

Very early, after dawn, as I was arising from sleep, I sank back into a dream that seemed clearer than any waking reality. Gangaji appeared as large as life in front of me, laughing her head off. Instead of her usual incredible mane of silver-white hair, she was bald or at least had a shaved head. She was dressed as a punk rocker and appeared quite young. She was playing an electric guitar! Through her raucous laughter, she stared at me and said:

"Don't be fooled by appearances. Come back and see me again!" I awoke convinced that it had not been a dream, that Gangaji had actually appeared to me in the dream state and directed me to come back to give her another chance. So I did.

But I wasn't stupid enough to completely fall for it. I spent the next three meetings with my feet firmly planted on the floor. Neither did I sit in the front row, where I might have been influenced by the strength of her energy. I practiced my observational skills intently, determined to study this as a socially phenomenological experience. I listened intensely and constantly tried to blend my conscious attention into her intentional awareness. Such was the place I found myself on the Sunday afternoon when my consciousness jumped along with hers into God-consciousness. Believe it or not!

I still think that her attitude was rather pretentious and arrogant. I am entitled to my opinion, which doesn't necessarily make it fact. I had expected her to be without ego or personality. I have since learned that every teacher comes with a personality but that the teachings tend to render it transparent, more so in some than in others. However, I do believe that Gangaji is an excellent teacher. She has achieved something far beyond my wildest imagination. I have had my experience and rest with an unshakable conviction that I experienced the Ultimate Truth. I went beyond my normal limits of understanding. I am also convinced that I can and may live and teach from this place. If I am going to be an effective Reiki Master, I feel that I must achieve such life mastery. I would like to be able to offer this example to my students; otherwise, wouldn't I actually be a sham? Yes, I have had my experience but I lost it! Anguish and a sense of powerlessness at times, followed by severe longing . . .

Now determined once again, I have stated my life mission to recapture IT! Will it be possible for me to revive and achieve that state of 'unity consciousness'? In that place, I felt as if I had achieved my lifelong, unstated, unacknowledged goal. I was HOME. Now, how to get back there? Damn, where did I put those ruby shoes?

During the next three weeks, it seemed that a red carpet rolled out in front of me and all I had to do was to step onto it and keep stepping all the way to India! As a single parent, my finances rarely afforded me luxuries let alone a trip overseas. Over the years, however, I had been generous with friends and had lent them bits and pieces of any leftover monies that I might have had. Ironically, those three weeks provided many surprises, particularly when I went to open my mailbox. Every day, a letter seemed to arrive with a note: "Just returning the $100 you lent me five years ago." "Remember the $50 you gave me to get my car fixed, here it is! So sorry it took so long!" "Dorothy, I can't believe how long it has taken me to get this back to you, but finally here is the $150 I borrowed." Et cetera, et cetera. It was uncanny.

Incredulously, I watched myself buy a ticket and pay for my Indian visa all within the first week! I had pledged to have my ticket and a thousand dollars in hand upon departure. Two days before I was to leave, I had my ticket and $800. I was to leave on the Monday morning. Saturday afternoon an elderly Reiki student from a few years before phoned: "I heard you were going to India. I just want you to know that I support your adventure. Would you like $200 towards your trip?"

Such was my magic carpet ride that late August of 1997. It didn't last for long though. I was hit with the REALITY of India immediately upon landing.

Why hadn't I taken the time to read my Lonely Planet *India* guidebook before I got off the plane? Delhi. There it was, right in a side box on the page next to the section 'Getting There': 'BEWARE OF TAXI SCAMS'! Two whole paragraphs advised travellers not to let the taxi drivers take them to the tourist offices across from the New Delhi train station. So what did I do? Just that! How was I to know? Canadians were so trusting and I had been riding on the crest of an exciting wave. I landed at midnight and was a bit freaked by the dark. I was not used to being out alone at night in my own country, let alone in a foreign one. It all seemed very strange to me as I exited the airport. Hit by a very warm, humid wall of pungent air, I couldn't recognize the smells at all. There were people mulling everywhere and men running up to me from all directions trying to get me to take their taxis. And of course, there was a cacophony of sounds—people, horns, dogs, cows . . . Yes, cows! As we drove onto the main road there was a cow lying in the centre of the road! Welcome to India!

Incidentally, as I was a bit disorientated by all the external sensations, I said yes to the first taxi driver who approached me and was ushered into one of the small sturdy white cars that are famous all over India for their ability to go where even the bravest dare not go, on roads that shouldn't even be called roads! It didn't occur to me to question anything; I was completely dependent on the taxi driver. He must have been laughing at me all the way to town thinking of his commission. He's probably still grinning from ear to ear at his good marksmanship. Of course, he took me to one of those infamous tourist offices across from the train station, and in the dark helped to carry my bags up the crooked narrow stairway into a filthy, tiny office, where a second example of a supposedly honourable citizen proceeded to bamboozle me out of the first one hundred dollars of my precious one thousand.

Later that morning I was ruminating upon my folly in the day-car of a train to Lucknow with a ticket that should have cost 450 rupees (approximately 35 rupees to the dollar). I had given the tourist office guy 3500 rupees because that's what he said it would cost, since the train station was closed and tickets for the next day were very hard to get. I had believed him. Was I stupid or what?

"Satsang Bhavan, please. Papaji's satsang. Indira Nagar," I said hesitantly to the skinny rickshaw driver, as I awkwardly hoisted myself up onto the dilapidated seat, trying not to get the bottom of my dress dirty or caught in the wheels of the three-wheeled contraption that I was climbing into. No pavement! The roads were mucky, as the monsoon season hadn't yet finished. Holes in the road were full of muddy water that splashed up onto me as we rode along the bumpy streets of Lucknow towards Papaji's place.

I actually had no idea where I was, except that I was in Lucknow. The train trip had proven to be quite comfortable after getting over the shock of my misadventure at the tourist office. Gazing out the window, everything had looked so familiar, as if I had been there before, as if I were coming home. Astonishing and puzzling. I had expected to feel like a stranger in a strange land. Instead, I found myself fascinated by the familiarity of the passing view. Nothing seemed peculiar, not even the women in bare feet and saris carrying earthenware and metal jugs on their heads as they made their way over the chequered pathways of the countryside. Had I been here before? A past life, maybe? Questions I would never know the answers to.

Letting go into the chaos and unknowingness: wasn't that what Osho had suggested? Well, I was doing just that, trusting that all would evolve naturally and positively. Playing it by ear. I did have the address. The driver seemed to be innocuous enough, and very much in need of the fare, so I didn't think he would try anything on me. It seemed like rush hour but it was probably always like this. There were *so* many people. It was quite funny really to see all the cows loitering, lying and standing in the road, and the pigs feeding off the piles of garbage. Obviously, there were no garbage collectors from the look of all the piles of plastic bags and organic stuff rotting alongside the streets. Great for stinking up the place.

I assumed it was well over 35 degrees. I wasn't sure I would be able to bear the stench, but really had no choice; let alone the noise. It seemed as if we had been going for miles, and yet the rickshaw driver didn't look as if he were very tired pedalling my bags and me.

Oh! There! 'SRI H.W.L. POONJAJI-SATSANG BHAVAN'. I saw the sign, with other bicycles and rickshaws lined up in front. Four drivers were standing beside their rickshaws grinning at my arrival, and one was curled up on his seat sleeping. Satsang was on Monday, Tuesday, Thursday, and Friday from 7:30 a.m. to

10:00 a.m. It was 4:30 in the afternoon. Hopefully, there would be someone inside to help me find a place to stay.

"Twenty rupees, please," the driver said to me. I paid him, all the while trying to figure out in my mind the exact amount in Canadian currency. Seventy-five cents. It took forty-five minutes to get here. Hmm. He seemed quite happy as I handed him the two 10-rupee notes.

"Thank you so much. I really appreciate your help. Here's an extra three rupees." He grinned as I handed him the few extra coins and watched him climb up into the rickshaw. He seemed to sincerely appreciate my business. I continued to observe him riding off, going considerably faster than on the way up. I assumed it wouldn't be long before he picked up another passenger to take some place else. Interesting life, but not for me. I didn't even ride a bicycle.

As for the money experiences, the theory of relativity seemed to twist into a bit of a knot in my brain. Everything seemed a bit askew and I concluded that it wasn't due to jetlag, nor lack of sleep. Things definitely felt a bit warped and I was sure that it had nothing to do with time. The sense of oddness—a foggy disturbance—was lying close to the tip of my reasoning. I would have to think about it all later, when I was more rested and my mind more clear. This clearly was beginning to be an experience of contrasts and comparisons.

I stooped over to collect my things, turned, and entered the open door under a gold-plated sign that read JAI SATGURU DEVA.

The funniest home video couldn't have been more amusing than the picture that I was watching. The view in front of me? I was looking at well over a hundred devotees, all praying, meditating, crying, laughing, dancing, singing, and kissing the feet of a dead man covered in garlands of roses and marigolds lying on a block of melting ice! This florally blanketed corpse was considered one of India's most revered saints. (That was according to all the devotees that I had met within the last few days.) Papaji. Dead. Now what? Never in my wildest dreams could I have guessed that this would happen to me—someone who swore that she would NEVER kiss a man's feet, let alone those of a guru, was being encouraged to kiss the feet of both! It might sound a little sacrilegious or disrespectful, but coming from my corner of reality, this was too much! I didn't think so!

How had this happened? Such a predicament I found myself in. And not a very comfortable one at that! Only one of many, so far, since I had arrived. I had a feeling that this was the norm for India. I didn't know what to expect last Thursday afternoon, five days ago, when I entered Papaji's Satsang Bhavan. I walked through the open door and was met by an older man named Lee. He had a bald head, glasses, and looked rather harmless. He also had a nice smile.

"Papaji's not here," he said. "He's home in bed with monsoon fever. You know, he is eighty-eight and all of us are worried that he might die this time. He always gets it around this time of year, although the monsoons are almost over." Surprise to me. The skies were bright blue; it was sweltering, well over 30 degrees outside, no clouds in sight; it didn't look as if it had rained for weeks.

Of course, I was disappointed and a bit disorientated after hearing the bad news. I looked at the man, Lee, who was flashing his gleaming white teeth and clear, sparkling eyes. Noticing my consternation and confusion, he shrugged his shoulders and gave me a bemused look as if he were finding the situation rather humorous. My seriousness was always obvious by the deep double crevices in the shape of a V between my eyebrows. I thought they were permanently etched on my forehead by now. Life had been full of hard knocks that caused me to scowl or frown in concentrated effort to sort out the problem and get on with things the best way possible. A pessimistic optimist or optimistic pessimist I had always thought myself. Now, if self-fulfilling prophecy was true and my skepticism affirmed, I thought: "Wouldn't it be just my luck for the holy man to die, after my coming all the way around the world to ask him my question. Hopefully, his impending death won't point towards the answer as to how to find the truth. What now?" I had inadvertently been talking out loud.

"Well, you could come back to my place. I live not far from here in a rented apartment," Lee said. I couldn't think of anything better to do, so acknowledging the opportunity, I agreed to accompany him or rather follow him home, like a lost puppy in a foreign neighbourhood. Little did I know that as soon as we got there, he would strip off his clothes and bare his seventy-five-year-old body to my incredulous eyes.

"It's too hot to wear clothes. I always do this when I get home. I'll put the fan on. You can take off your clothes too, if you want to."

Nonchalantly, I responded with a "No, thanks." I asked him if I could take a shower and change; it was my third day of travelling in the same clothes. He nodded to the bathroom, and I quietly made my exit into it to decide what I should do. Should I go along with his nakedness as if it were the most natural thing in the world for complete strangers to strip and behave as if they were used to walking around without clothes? It wasn't as if I hadn't seen a nude man before. After all, I was a liberated woman and well into my forties! He was over seventy, seemed rather harmless, *and* American. (Over here, one tended only to be mistrustful of the natives!) Should I trust him? What he said makes sense; it was extremely hot; what need was there of clothes? They would just get clammy three minutes after my shower.

In the end, I showered and did as the Romans do while in Rome.

I just pretended to be a member of a nudist colony in Lucknow. After a few minutes together, it seemed rather natural, funnily enough. How did I get myself into these situations? Easily—by simply trusting everyone that I met, thinking we were all good people living in a good world.

It had all turned out to be quite harmless and rather humorous. Spiritual? Not sure about that, but by the next morning, we knew each other quite well without any sort of hanky-panky having gone on. We had shared a simple rice and curry dinner, then Lee had filled me in on all the details of devotee life and the happenings around Papaji. I slept under a sheet on a mattress on the floor. (The next morning, on our way back to the Satsang Bhavan, I was surprised to learn from Lee that it was not proper protocol for a man and woman to hold hands or touch in any way in public in India. Intimacy happened completely behind closed doors. No kissing or hugging in public on this side of the world.)

I later found myself situated in the Pink House run by an Australian man and a German woman, husband and wife, and long-time devotees of Papaji. Every door needed to be locked, including the kitchen and bathroom, because of the thieves. They gave me a lock for my room, as I hadn't brought one. It seemed most curious. I wondered how the thieves got in if people locked the outside doors? Lots of behind-the-scenes manipulation, I guessed. Maybe outsiders weren't supposed to know. I was woken up in the middle of the night by persistent whistle-blowing that seemed to go on for hours afterwards. In the morning I found out that the police go from street to street all night long, blowing their whistles to warn the thieves on the roofs of their whereabouts, so they won't get caught and can have time to move to the next street! Another Indian enigma!

Meanwhile, back at the Satsang Bhavan . . .

Sri H.W.L. Poonjaji, or Papaji as everyone knew him, died tonight, September 6. Actually, he stopped breathing two nights ago, on Sunday, the day of the birthday lunch given for one of his favourite devotees, but they put him on life support, desperately trying to keep him alive. I heard they even rushed in specialists from Delhi and Mumbai to help save him, but Papaji kept pulling the wires out every time he came to consciousness. Word had it that the last time he was lucid he shouted at everyone to just leave him alone and let him go, then yanked out the wires and went. From all telling, he seemed to have been quite a feisty fellow! I wasn't sure just how much of what was being said was true. Everyone seemed to be talking at once with all sorts of variations on the theme of Papaji's last breath. However, it appeared that he hadn't been too pleased that his closest devotees and family had been trying to hold him back from moving to the other side. I wondered for whose sake, theirs or his?

The energy in the room was intense. It had completely shifted since they brought Papaji back from the hospital. Before, people's emotions were the overriding reality, but now the room was permeated with a very strong sense of quiet, beauty, and bliss. Everyone had become very respectful and there was an aura of reverence and awe. Some women devotees had wrapped an Indian cotton cloth around Papaji from the chest down, over his habitual white Punjabi suit, draped garlands of yellow and orange marigold flowers about his body, and then had strewn pink and white rose petals all over him. On his heart lay a cluster of blossoms, including roses and some very fragrant white plumerias. Even though his face was pale and unshaven, he seemed very peaceful and composed as if he had just gone to sleep and was having pleasant dreams. No sign of any preceding distress or dispute. Papaji didn't seem dead, just asleep. If I were to touch him now, I would expect him to stir and open his eyes. Strange, his spirit still seemed to be lingering about him; he just wasn't breathing.

Papaji was lying on a huge block of ice covered by a large white piece of cotton cloth. The ice was melting all over the floor. There were Indian attendants standing by with towels to mop up the water, scurrying over every time the pools underneath the corpse started running. There was a sense of organization. Between the time that they had notified the satsang that he had died and the time he arrived, people had obviously been busy. The hall had been transformed. A shrine had been erected at the front of the room. Papaji's picture sat underneath a big photo of his teacher and predecessor, Ramana Maharshi, hanging on the wall. Camphor boat lamps were burning on each side, along with sticks of spiralling incense. The air was very pungent and a bit hazy, reinforcing a sacred atmosphere. There were piles of rose petals deliberately set on the floor and all over the shrine. Garlands of golden marigolds were strewn all about, hanging from the roof and along the walls. There was a sense of celebration as if they had prepared for a festival. I had been told that this was the beginning of Papaji's *Samadhi* (enlightenment upon leaving the body), which would last ten days, culminating in a Kriya puja and feast for his ascendance into higher realms.

I stood as an observer. Papaji was neither my teacher nor guru; I did not know this man. Aside from the Sunday lunch, I had never met him. He was a virtual stranger to me. I had no clue as to what all this was about, why everyone around him was experiencing such tremendous sorrow and grief, or so deeply lamenting. It was a very foreign play to me. People were all acting as if they were his real children. Some of them were talking about shaving their heads as the Indian sons did when their fathers died. Here, however, even the women were talking about doing it. From an outsider's point of view, it all seemed rather melodramatic, but I was in no position to pass judgment. I didn't feel anything, really, other than a deep respect. I felt honoured by the opportunity to be present at such an auspicious time. They had welcomed and accepted me as one of their own and were including me as if I were one of the community.

Remembering the past Sunday and the birthday party, how was I to revere a man who had completely ignored me when I was first introduced? At the time, it seemed rude of him, and my feelings were bruised. Others told me it was to test my ego to see if I went into rejection. Apparently, he acted like that with lots of people. I didn't know. I was not into head-trips or mind games. This was all unfamiliar territory. All I knew was that when I stepped up to Papaji sitting at the greeting table at the entrance to his home, presented him with the recommended gift of sweets, and was introduced to him as "the lady from Canada who had come all the way across the world to meet him", he looked right past me to the devotee behind, whom he recognized, and broke out into an incredible smile, dismissing me as he reached out his hands to embrace this person. Talk about invalidation and erasure. My very buttons! He never looked at me or said anything to me for the next hour while we were all in his presence, crammed into the small room where plates of *thali* (rice, dal, and vegetables) were passed about for everyone to eat. When he stood up to go back to his bedroom to lie down, we all left his house and that was the end of that. Later that night, he went into heart failure and died for the first time.

What I got out of that whole episode was that I really was not any of his business, nor he mine. Whether he consciously and deliberately ignored me to see how I would react, I would never know. I thought, possibly, that Papaji had nothing to do with me—nothing to do with a student/disciple relationship. This didn't mean that there was nothing for me to learn. Just being there put me in touch with myself, and that in itself was a teaching. I had my suspicions that India was just one gigantic mirror to reflect my limitations and beliefs. Whether or not I could maintain my centre of stillness and balance when all about appeared chaotic and unfamiliar was the question, and possibly the lesson.

That day, as we left Papaji's house with its large silver Om sign and meditating Shiva statue over the entrance, I remembered thinking that he was very close to dying. You could have almost put a hand through him; he was so close to spirit. I had a sense that it would not be too long before he went. I had worked with clients at hospice who felt and looked like him just before they slipped into death. For some, it seemed such a continuous and natural process of dissolving out of the material into the immaterial.

My present situation notwithstanding, there in the centre of the 'mourning' room, in the centre of all the commotion, I realized that I had never been to an Irish wake, let alone experienced an Indian samadhi. I advised myself to pay attention and see what there was for me to glean out of this most unusual situation. They said having darshan or audience with a holy person, or being in the presence of a realized being, whether alive or dead, would burn off hundreds of lifetimes of karma. Maybe I was there to do just that—to sear off some of my bad karma, promising me a better life in the future. Would it make any difference if I did or didn't kiss his feet? That, I guess, was the rhetorical million-dollar question.

I knew Dorothy wasn't a Disney character, but it sure seemed like I was in Disneyland. This was an incredibly fascinating trip and FUN! Believe it or not, I had just doused myself for the first time in the waters of the Ganges River! It was cold and rushing. I was holding on for dear life to the metal chain a few feet from the shore. I didn't want to be swept away with the current. Everyone else was doing the same and laughing. They said if you dipped yourself three times in the sacred waters of Mother Ganges you would be liberated.

"Well," I say, "Why not? I need all the help I can get!" A few dips and John 3:16. What more did I need?

Two more dips and a towel, although the heat would dry me pretty quickly. Because I was a woman, I had to leave my clothes on. I had taken off my new red *shalwar kameez* (long top and pants to match) that I'd found in the Lucknow market, leaving on the red nightgown that I'd been wearing as a slip and wrapping my black and white cotton scarf around me. Suitable? Not for Canada. For here though, I was properly attired and that's what counted. Follow the protocol: women covered. The men got to strip to their shorts. Some of the Indian men had just a small cloth covering their privates with a strip up the middle of their buttocks like a thong. The boys up to about twelve were swimming naked. Not so the girls and women. They were fully clothed from head to foot, the women in saris, the girls in shalwar kameez. Talk about unfair.

Haridwar. The sacred place of the Kumbha Mela that took place every twelve years, where millions of devoted Hindus came to bathe in the Ganges. We had brought Papaji's ashes here. We were waiting for his brother and other relatives to arrive to perform a puja at the water's edge. Then they would put his ashes into the Ganges River. We were all going to participate. But now we were patiently waiting as the family took a later train and who knew, it might have been late. Not unusual for the trains in India. When they announced over the train station loudspeakers that a train was late, everyone just sat down, took out their food, and enjoyed their meal. No big deal. No one knew when the train would arrive so they just continued on with life wherever they found themselves.

That was what we were doing. We had been gathered on the shore of the river since the train had arrived early this morning. There was cement along the edge, being in the middle of the city, with shops lining the entire embankment behind us. Blankets had been spread out. Everyone had collected little banana boats filled with petals and a camphor wick. These were symbols of purification, and before you put them in the water to be carried away on the current, you were supposed to light the wick. The flame represented the burning off of past refuse—people, events, feelings, etc., that were no longer needed or necessary to carry into the future. I had my boat and one of the devotees had taken a picture of me holding it. They cost around 10 rupees, which was about 30 cents. Just trying to blend in.

It was like a sixties hippie circus or sit-in. Some people had shaved their heads and put their hair in the banana boats ready to set sail! Children were everywhere. The Americans had taken the little ones' clothes off due to the heat. Naked on the blanket, they were pestering their parents to go swimming, but the water was too swift. The three-year-old beside me was very cute. Everything was so colourful. The devotees, mostly American and European (although there was a woman and baby from Korea), were all dressed in bright clothes found in the market. Some had on saris; others, suits like mine. Most of the guys were donning *lungis,* or cloths that they had wrapped around their waists like skirts. People had guitars and were sitting at the edge of the water. Everyone seemed to be singing *bhajans*, Indian songs that expressed love and yearning for God. I didn't know any, but the music was beautiful. Someone was playing a harmonium, a small instrument resembling a tiny organ that you pump at the back and play on keys in the front (just a couple of octaves). A European fellow accompanying them on his silver flute was quite an accomplished musician. The music was soothing and helped to pass the waiting time.

These were the same people that had made music around the funeral pyre at the burning ghats, where we went to burn Papaji's body. That was yesterday, the day after the wake. It was hard to believe that it had only been yesterday. So much had happened since then and since Tuesday night, the night before, when they announced Papaji's death.

Around 2:00 a.m. at the Satsang house, the night/morning of the wake, while everyone was gathered around the body doing what they had to do to pay their final respects, a couple came up to the front and spoke into a microphone addressing everyone. These people were Papaji's closest devotees and the ones responsible for organizing and managing the Satsang. I had seen them before but didn't know their names. They were Westerners from Europe. The fellow was tall and lanky with very long hair and dressed in a white Punjabi suit. The woman, very lithe and beautiful, was dressed in a white sari. They were both enwrapped in a very blessed aura that everyone noticed. Their appearance seemed unusually different, and from the story they subsequently told, it was understandable. They had just come from the hospital and were present when Papaji expired. They wanted to share with everyone the last few moments of their beloved teacher's life.

The man spoke, very gently and subdued: "May I please have your attention, everyone? I am sure that you all want to hear about Papaji's death. I want to assure you that he went very peacefully. Over the last few days, as you know, everything has been quite tense. We did everything possible to maintain Papaji's life, and at the end, it was his decision to go. We had him on life support but he kept coming to consciousness and trying to yank himself off. We thought he was delirious but, in hindsight, we now admit that he was quite aware and in control of his faculties. Just before 11 o'clock tonight, he woke up fully lucid, seemed irritated, and told us to just let him go. He pulled out all the tubes and lay back down on his pillow and sighed. Just before he closed his eyes, his face lit up as if he recognized a loved one, someone he hadn't seen for a long time. At that moment, he reached out his arms and with great pleasure and joy ecstatically whispered: 'Buddha!' Then he stopped breathing and we knew we had lost him."

The man started crying so the woman took the microphone out of his hand. "It was miraculous. Papaji's body seemed to light up and an energy field surrounded the room. There was something definitely special happening. We all believe that Buddha came into the room. We are still feeling this energy and presence. We believe that Buddha arrived to help Papaji make his transition, that Papaji met him before he left for the other side. Even though we can't see him, it is quite possible that Buddha is present here with us at this very moment! That may be why it feels so different in here this evening. Please feel free to spend the night if you wish. Do whatever you have to do and don't hesitate to touch or kiss Papaji if you feel inclined to do so. He has been a father to us and we are all going to miss him very much. In the morning, you are all invited to his house to pay your final respects and then we will take him by truck to the burning ghats. Please come and participate. We welcome your help."

We all did go to the house the next morning and then, after watching the family parade the body, covered in flowers and laid on a bamboo stretcher, down the street in front of his house so that all the neighbours could come out to say good-bye, we headed off in bicycle and auto rickshaws to the burning ghats. About fifty devotees climbed aboard the truck and accompanied Papaji's body in the back. They were all pretty jammed in, like sardines. It was, by then, well over 30 degrees, so it mustn't have been very comfortable; however, I didn't think too many noticed as they were feeling pretty privileged to ride with their master to his final resting place.

If you are ever in India, don't EVER feed the beggar children anything, particularly candy! I made a big mistake offering the orphans and other children candy at the ghats. At first, there were only a few little kids asking for money or food. A few minutes later, there were hundreds of kids swarming around me, clutching at me, desperately trying to grab the candy out of the bag even before I had a chance to reach in to give them some. What had I done? How would I ever get them to go away and leave me alone? I gave up any attempt to be decent or civilized and just threw them the bag, watching them fight over the remains. And I thought that was the end of that.

As it was, they pestered me non-stop throughout the afternoon. It wasn't until much later, when I sat down, closed my eyes, and pretended to meditate that they finally gave up and went away. It influenced my afternoon and my time with all the other people around Papaji. I decided to leave early, not waiting around to the end with the others, singing, dancing, sitting, and watching the body being cremated.

It might sound a bit morbid and horrendous to say that, in spite of the irritation of the beggar children, it was an incredibly exquisite time at the burning ghats watching Papaji's body burn to ashes. We all seemed to be swimming in a sea of beauty. Even though there were a couple of hundred people there, it was very quiet and sacred. When we arrived at the ghats, we were asked to form two lines, and wood was passed from one to the other of us until it arrived at the cement platform. Papaji was placed on the pile of wood and then a mixture of herbs and incense was sprinkled over him. Then we watched as his son took a burning thatch of grass or bamboo and lit the pyre. Everyone seemed stunned as they watched in silent awe. Once the pile started burning, people began to talk, sing, dance, laugh, weep . . . a stream of emotions were expressed in a myriad of ways as Papaji's beloved 'family' remained to see his body burn and his spirit released.

And no, it didn't stink of burning flesh. There was nothing repugnant about it at all. The smoke and air were filled with an enchanting and attractive fragrance that seemed to enhance the mystique and sacredness of the occasion. The whole experience had a purifying effect on us all.

The next morning we gathered on the dais, around the pile of ashes that was surrounded by a garland of marigolds and roses.

It was very beautiful and precious. There was a persistent hush on the platform regardless of all the chattering and singing. We watched as the brother performed a milk puja over the ashes. Then the family collected the bones and some of the bigger pieces putting them in a metal urn. After that, we were told we could collect some of the ashes, which I did. I wanted to carry them home with me. Hopefully, I would have no trouble getting them through customs.

The family had arrived in Haridwar. The puja should be starting in a few minutes. We were all being ushered over to the puja platforms, a ways down from where we had been waiting, just across from the clock tower. Tonight a fire puja would be held there, where thousands of people would gather at dusk and light their little banana boats, placing them on the river once it got dark. It should be quite spectacular seeing all the lights go sailing down the river. Profound and poignant. I hoped to attend.

I hadn't a clue what everyone was chanting, but the devotees seemed to know. The brother of Papaji was a priest, the one performing the ceremony. He was the one saying and singing prayers. He was in the water, along with the family and some of the devotees closest to Papaji, including the couple who spoke at the wake. Everyone seemed very reverent as the brother took the lid off the urn and began to pour the ashes into the river. He had passed some of the ashes around so other people could put some in. I didn't think I would participate. I was going to stay up on the edge behind the scenes and watch. It seemed like a family sort of thing and I didn't want to be intrusive. I would remain the bystander. Who knew, maybe in a past lifetime, Papaji and I had made an agreement that I would be present standing guard at his samadhi. I wondered if he would be present at my funeral? Invisible at any rate. Who would ever know but me? I was sure I would be there hovering about, just as I was pretty sure that Papaji was still around watching all this show. But then, how could anyone know what was really going on? One could merely surmise about things. *C'est tout.*

Apparently, the Indian people didn't believe that Papaji was a saint because he wanted his ashes put into the river along with the ordinary Indians. It was a very auspicious thing to take a father's ashes to the Ganges, for it purified his sins and liberated him. It also brought merit to the family and enhanced their chances of liberation, being the greatest thing a family could do for an honoured parent. However, a true saint didn't need purification. He or she was supposed to be pure already; hence, saints were placed directly on the river on bamboo rafts, left to float out to the ocean. Neither were they supposed to be cremated (that is if they were near the river) because burning was also a purification ritual.

While I was waiting on the blanket after I had had my little dip in the river, a woman named Jan, from Holland, told me the story. "We've brought Papaji here because he asked us to. We were supposed to ignore the regular tradition and put his ashes in the river because in the early seventies, at a Kumbha Mela here in Haridwar, Papaji had a miraculous experience. He agreed to offer his body to the river to help purify the water. Apparently, while he was in the crowd, a beautiful woman approached him, said that she was the Spirit Ganga, and that she needed a saint to help her. Her water had become so polluted with all the sins of the millions of people who came to bathe in her that she needed a saint to help cleanse her waters. She solicited Papaji's help and he agreed. After that, he watched her turn around, walk towards the river, and vanish into it!"

Now, if I were at home in Canada, I would probably deny the probability of the story. But now that I was in India, I felt that anything was possible. The reality of miracles was very close at hand. Who was I to query the miraculous? The Hindu people had many such stories. To them the extraordinary *was* the ordinary. Anyway, that explained why we were gathered in Haridwar involved in such a fantastic escapade.

Mid-afternoon, three days later. On a balcony of an Indian café/bar overlooking the Ganges River at Laxman Jhula (the second swinging bridge north of Rishikesh, the holy city, twenty kilometres or so up from Haridwar), I found myself fantasizing about my future and ruminating over the past, as I watched a fascinatingly attractive, unknown Indian saint walk out of my life and into his own.

Who was he? Every cell in my being was compelling me to get up and run after him, to follow him across the swinging bridge, up into the hills, and sit with him for the rest of my life. A call from a 'mystery master'? No matter that I had business at home, structure that had to be maintained—apartment, furniture . . . not to mention children. (At least I didn't have a relationship!) Just to let go of all that form and get lost in the spirituality of India, to truly seek my enlightenment—this was a call, an urge to follow a star. Why couldn't I just let go of everything, follow my destiny, surrender to the longing, and respond to the call? Was this a fork in my road, a choice to make?

I took the last sip of my banana *lassi* (yogurt drink) and sighed with resignation. I had to go home, back to the kids, to finish what I had started. Duty called. I had made my choice a long time ago—that motherhood would be the door to my spirituality. I could have come to India in my twenties. At that time I was travelling in Europe and had chatted with a young woman at the youth hostel in Barcelona, Spain, who had just returned by the overland route from India. I was fascinated, but too scared to follow her path. Besides, she had huge sores all over her body that she had contacted there. I didn't want to subject myself to the filthy conditions that she had described. India in the seventies. My journey still followed the lines of a philosophically intellectual quest. The word 'spiritual' hadn't entered my vocabulary yet. I hadn't been ready.

And now? Was there really any difference? Wasn't this a parallel reality, just a different picture? Like the story by Tagore about finally coming to God's door and then being too hesitant to knock for fear that life would drastically change, that it would involve letting everything familiar go? Jesus said that one had to let go of everyone to follow him, including parents and children. I did know some people in my apartment complex who had done just that when their kids were in their late teens. I wasn't ready, yet, to make that same commitment. How could my children bear to live without me, or I them? The risk seemed too high. Did my hesitancy signify that I was merely entertaining myself with the idea of Self-realization, that I didn't really want to go Home, and that I was just toying with the idea for something extraordinary to do?

This Indian man. There was something so alluring about him. It was *not* a sexual connection we had shared the other day when I had first met him . . . Papaji's devotees had just arrived in Haridwar. We were sitting on the blanket after I had bathed in the river. People were talking, singing, and waiting for Papaji's family to arrive. A man dressed in white, with long hair, beard, and exquisitely gentle eyes, stepped onto the cloth and sat down not far from me. His sensitive countenance and energy were auspiciously subdued and quietly ethereal. Everything seemed to be absorbed into him and stillness permeated the area, with him as the centre or nucleus. I felt such a profound peace enter my body. He sat silently with us until the puja started, then I lost track of him.

The next day he showed up at the ashram. We sat together on a wooden bench outside, on the veranda of the dining hall. I found my self mesmerized by his presence and didn't want to leave his side. I remember my conversation and the rest of the afternoon as if it were still happening.

"Who *are* you?" I had asked. "I saw you yesterday, sitting with the rest of us on the blanket down by the river. Actually, I noticed you just before that, walking over the Haridwar bridge and coming down the stairs. There was a tall, dark-haired, Western man walking behind you, but I don't see him around now. When you sat down in the middle of us all, I couldn't help notice because there is something extraordinary about you that is hard to pinpoint!"

I'd found myself swimming in the gaze of a long-haired Indian man with a salt-and-pepper beard, who looked very much like Maharishi Mahesh Yogi used to look when he was young and first came to America to start the Transcendental Meditation movement. It is hard to depict the age of most Indians because they look so young and their skin is so beautiful and smooth, but from my guess this guy was in his early forties. I thought him very intriguing; his presence was so alluring in a profoundly spiritual sort of way. Ever since he had quietly walked through the stucco archway into the compound, I hadn't been able to take my eyes off him.

Normally leery of starting up conversations with Indian men, I surprised myself as I flashed him a smile and waited for his response. We sat looking out over the courtyard of an ashram on the banks of the Ganges a few kilometres down the hill from Laxman Jhula. (The whole area is a pilgrimage site not far from the source of the Ganges, and known for the spattering of ashrams that attract enlightened sadhus, yogis, and teachers. The Ganges is very clean and peaceful here. This ashram is particularly auspicious as it was a favourite place of Papaji's where he came for retreats with his most beloved disciples.) We all felt privileged to be there. A feast had been organized and there were over a hundred people gathered for the occasion. Some of us were resting in the shade of the veranda while others were bathing in the river.

"I have a house in the hills in the forest, where I sit with people. I have about twelve disciples, mostly from Europe. We just spend time together," said the man all in white. He turned his head closer, looking me directly in the eyes. I felt my mind go completely quiet. Still. No thoughts. Then he turned his gaze to the disciples around us as I sat there vibrating at a frequency higher than my normal intention. It seemed as if my mind were inside his, united, noticing how the minds of all the other people were becoming increasingly agitated and frightened. Their spiritual father had died. What were they going to do without him? What would become of them? I sensed a panic beginning to seep into the collective conscious of the people in the group.

He looked back at me and smiled. "They haven't learned as much as they thought. Papaji hasn't really left. He is here now. He will always be here for them. No need to be afraid. He will continue to teach them if they open to it."

"How did you know Papaji?" I asked.

"A few years ago, I was in my meditation room with a few of my students when a man walked into the middle of it, sat down, and gave darshan. He entered as a stranger but immediately introduced himself as Poonjaji. Apparently, that morning, Papaji had gotten up, called a few of his students about him, and said: 'We're going for a ride.' They found their way to my place. He didn't know where he was going when he'd set out that morning. He just followed his intuition, just as I did when I left home yesterday at dawn," said the mystery man who hadn't as yet mentioned his name.

"Like Papaji, I had no idea why I had to come to Haridwar when I left. I just picked up my walking stick and called Jonathan to come with me."

"So, how did Papaji know who you were?"

"He didn't. He arrived, gave darshan, and then as he left, he came over to me, gave me his blessing, and told me to continue giving darshan. That was the last time I saw him. I had no idea who all you people were when I found myself sitting amid you on the blanket. It's amusing. I haven't seen Papaji since that day."

"So, you didn't know where you were going when you left your house?" I asked amazed at what I was hearing. He shook his head negatively.

People were returning from the river. An exceptionally stylish African woman with a turquoise silk turban and striking silver jewellery came over to tell us that the meal was being served and to come in to the dining area. She was at the Satsang house the night

Papaji died and, because she was a remarkable woman dressed so handsomely, I had noticed her and asked her name. She'd told me it was Jasmine.

The yogi's and my conversation had been interrupted. After the meal, he went across the courtyard to perform a cleansing puja in the room where Papaji usually slept. I went into the garden behind to rest and meditate. I sat down beside a little shrine that housed a small Shiva lingam (a cylindrical stone structure that Hindus worship as a symbol of the god Shiva) and a stone replica of the feet of the master who was the founder of this particular ashram. The little shrine had recently been attended and there were camphor flames burning and flowers strewn about the items. It was very precious, and I felt extremely blissful sitting beside it. Before I knew it, I slipped into a deep meditative state and didn't resurface until an hour and a half later!

I felt a strange impulse to go directly to the room where the amazing stranger was. I knocked on the door, went in, and sat down on the bed directly in front of him, listening to him talk to the Indian people who lived at the ashram. I sat there watching him intently and wondering if he were married. What would it be like to have a husband as spiritual as him? He then turned, looked directly into my eyes, and spoke in a gently personal tone: "The woman who was my partner recently left me to go back to Europe."

He seemed to leave a space for me to respond as if he were offering an invitation. Then, a moment of intimacy happened between us filled with a peculiar mutual understanding. I felt shy, and left the room. Later, just as he was about to go out through the gate and head up the hill back to town, he turned towards me. "Are you coming?"

I felt sadness as I shook my head. "No," I whispered, feeling my heart break open and tears come to my eyes. He turned and left. I was overwhelmed with a surprising sorrow. Everyone around seemed curious, wondering what was going on. I knew. An opportunity offered. An opportunity declined.

Two days later, sitting on that balcony, I again watched him walk away from me—this time across the Laxman Jhula bridge, past the monkeys swinging on the other side, off into the hills, and as far as I was concerned, out into the wild blue yonder. All the while, Jonathan, his true disciple, was trailing not far behind. I would never know what might have become of me, if I had followed him too. He never did tell me his name.

As for Jasmine, I had a conversation with her not long afterwards in which she related the most remarkable story. Apparently, the organizers had only expected about fifty people to come to the feast and had prepared food for that many. She was in the kitchen the entire time so served as a veritable witness. As they were serving and had come to the last of the rice and dal, the helpers were confused about how they were going to feed the rest of the people. They were conferring with the cooks about quickly making more food. When they turned around, the previously empty, large metal containers were once again filled with food! A miracle! Did Papaji have a hand in it, or maybe someone else . . .?

Don't ever believe any yogis who say that they are Tantric masters and have something to teach you. I had allowed myself to be misled, once again finding myself in a very precarious position. This time by an Indian who was the resident yoga teacher of an ashram in Laxman Jhula. He had asked me to come to his room, where he proceeded to show me photographs of himself in amazing yoga positions, photos that were to go into the book he was writing on hatha yoga. (Looking back, I now recognize this as a tactic similar to a 'Chinese etching' experience I had in France in my twenties!) He showed me his passport; it turned out that we had the same birthday. He was twenty years younger, but that didn't seem to deter his later advances. He gave me a rudraksha bead as a token of our birthday relationship, put it on a leather string and tied it around my neck.

At that time, I considered it a touching gesture. Rudraksha beads are precious and sacred in India and represent spirituality; they are said to display the many faces of Shiva, the Hindu god. I had been looking at them in the market places.

I had met the yogi or swami a few days before, in the small café across from the ashram, down the street from the big temple, and down the street from the hotel where I was staying with the German couple from the Pink House in Lucknow. I had just finished watching the mystery man cross the bridge and was writing about it in my journal. I was about to take a walk around the town when this young fellow with a shaved head, big smile, and orange robes approached me and asked if he could sit down. He introduced himself as Swami Ramananda.

He seemed quite fascinated by me. "Your energy is very light and strong . . . and very clean. You don't smoke, do you?" he asked.

What did he want? I was immediately suspicious. Indian men didn't usually start up conversations unless they wanted something, and what that was, was usually pretty obvious. Sexuality was suppressed between the sexes in India. With frustration and licentiousness running rampant in their glances and stares, they appeared eager to latch or pounce onto any innocent female who caught their gaze.

"No," I replied without appearing too friendly. You could never be too sure even if he was a swami practicing abstinence.

"You must teach meditation or something then," he continued.

I realized he was expecting me to continue to talk to him, and rather than be impolite, I put my journal into my bag and sat back ready to engage. Why not? A new person, a native, and one who shared my spiritual inclination. Let's see how committed he really was and if he walked his talk. Half the time, they were merely putting on a show for the Westerners. Maybe he wasn't even really a swami. One could never know for sure nowadays.

"May I buy you a tea or something?" he asked. I was surprised. Usually it was the other way around, with them expecting something for nothing.

"Chai, please," I answered. Hmm. This was a change. Maybe I was being too skeptical. I encouraged myself to relax and see where this went. "I teach Reiki. I'm a Reiki Master," I added, watching him order and receive the glasses of tea nearby at the cash counter.

"Where do you come from?" He tilted his shaved head as he queried me, lifting his eyebrows with interest, all the while setting the small, clear glasses of *masala chai* (spiced tea with cardamom, cloves, and cinnamon) on the rough wooden table, being careful to hold them at the tip so not to burn his fingers. The glasses always tended to be extremely hot because of the freshly boiled milk. His curiosity seemed very bold and genuine.

"Canada. I live in Victoria, Canada. I'm here for the samadhi of a holy man named Papaji." I couldn't help noticing that he had benevolent and trusting eyes, seemingly very open and eager to learn about me.

"We had some Indian Reiki Masters here for awhile, from Delhi. They are quite well known but they smoked and their aura was dirty and grey. They asked me if I wanted to learn but I said no. Didn't want them to touch me," Swami Ramananda admitted sincerely. "Maybe you could teach me. I've wanted to learn. We could do a trade and I could teach you some yoga."

I sat considering the offer, drinking my tea, and watching the Ganges pleasantly flowing past. We were perched over a cliff on the veranda looking down at the river. It was a very tranquil sight. I was beginning to open to the situation, letting my guard down a little and feeling more easeful. Maybe he was a nice guy after all.

We sat sharing silence for a while. After I finished my tea, he asked me if I wanted to come see his ashram across the street. Apparently, they rented rooms there as well. I thought maybe I should, since I might come back on my own sometime and it might be a good place to stay.

The ashram was built around a central courtyard just off the street. There were two floors composed of many rooms side by side, with a ledge and wall that overlooked the centre compound. The cement was painted pale yellow and pink with a bit of light green trim. It all looked a bit dilapidated, the paint peeling off in many places and mould growing on the walls in most of the corners. This was typical in India because of all the rain during the monsoon season. Laundry was hanging up on ropes strewn across the walls separating the veranda-like walkways, also a very typical sight, there being no electric washers and dryers to keep such domestic activity hidden.

Swami Ramananda did seem sincere about learning Reiki. He showed me around, being particularly proud of his yoga room. He took out a mat and proceeded to show me a few of his more complicated postures. There was no way in the world I would even know how to attempt such twisted manoeuvres! He tried to get me to do the tortoise, or frog, or something, and I thought for sure that I had pulled a muscle in my upper thigh. I surmised that he looked a bit disgusted at my lack of flexibility. (I'm a bit of a lost cause when it comes to exercise!)

As for the trade, I wasn't sure I wanted to learn yoga. If he wanted to learn Reiki, I could take two days to teach him. We were supposed to be staying another couple of days, so I'd have time. I knew he had no money, but he could always forward one of his books when he got it published. Money wasn't really the issue; moreover, my policy always was to be responsive to those who asked.

His room was very tiny and completely bare—just a small single bed with a sleeping bag. Everything in India seemed to be made of this boring cement. The walls were not even painted. It was a bit cold and musty; mould was all around the ceiling. Swami didn't seem to mind. After showing me the black and white pictures that he had just paid a photographer to take, of which he seemed extremely proud, he talked to me about his teacher over at the Sivananda ashram in Ram Jhula, over the other swinging bridge a few kilometres down river. Maharishi had had his ashram there on the other side. Anyways, although Sivananda was dead, his system was still extremely popular. Many teachers in the West had learned at his centres. Swami Radha, a student of his and a woman who brought yoga to the West in the fifties, had a very excellent centre in Victoria. I'd attended some courses there in the past. Again, the swami seemed quite boastful about his adeptness, and I thought that pride might be his downfall or a lesson that he might have to deal with this lifetime!

We made an arrangement for him to come to my room that evening, where I would give him the first initiation into Reiki and show him some hand positions for a self-treatment. I would need to meet with him four times. There was time, if we met twice the next day and once the day after that.

Looking back, I see that the mistake I made was in giving Swami Ramananda a full hands-on treatment. Reiki can be quite an intimate experience regardless of one being fully clothed, if the person isn't used to being touched, particularly by someone of the opposite sex. The problem and incident happened the last day when

I had just given him the final initiation and was treating him as he lay completely clothed on my bed.

I was leaving later that afternoon to go back to Rishikesh, to catch the train back to Lucknow. I was to meet the German couple around one o'clock. Swami came to my room at 9:00 a.m. for his last lesson. We needed to be finished by noon so that I could complete my packing. I didn't usually teach that early in the morning. Possibly, he was misled by the invitation to come to my room for the sessions, or else he was just taking advantage of it.

It's not difficult to imagine what happened. When I was in the middle of the treatment, he became quite amorous, overtly 'hitting on me'. As I resisted his advances, he got more persistent trying to coax me into having sex with him, bragging that he was a master of Tantra. Whether or not he was, I didn't take the time to find out. I became upset when he wouldn't take 'no' for an answer. I slipped out of his grasp and moved to the other side of the room. Luckily, he wasn't too aggressive. I told him that if he didn't leave immediately, I would march down to the ashram and tell the head swami about his antics. A monk was a monk, and there was something known as Right Action.

I refused to take responsibility for his indiscretion! I didn't regret teaching him. I was only sorry that it all took a rather twisted turn and that he used Reiki as his 'come on' while I, having let my guard down, fell for it and into his unworthy intentions. Tantra was Tantra. This was just plain opportunism. Thankfully, he departed without any further unpleasantness. I assured him that I would send his certificate in the mail, which I later did.

Oh, when the saints go marching in,
Oh, when the saints go marching in,
Oh Lord, I want to be in that number,
When the saints go marching in.

Papaji, Princess Diana, Mother Teresa, all within two weeks! Dear God, what was going on?

The 'Train to Glory' had been passing by and picking up the good ones. Maybe all three had been singing this favourite Gospel song from the deep American South, when someone 'up there' heard them and figured it might be a good time to pick up a few stragglers left down here on earth! Or maybe they'd earned enough points to warrant immediate departure tickets—Destination: Heaven!

Since coming to the Pink House, I had saved some newspaper clippings from the Lucknow Times about both Princess Diana's and Mother Teresa's deaths. Unfortunately, I wasn't able to find anything about Papaji in the paper when we returned. We had left for Haridwar the night after the milk puja at the burning ghats; newspaper articles were the last things on our minds at that time. After the fact, it was too late to find anything. There was no one here to save the papers while we were gone.

Recollecting that time, it seemed auspicious that the three events happened in such close proximity to each other. It seemed strange that three living saints (in my opinion) chose the same time to die. Made me wonder if it were all planned. Maybe in a previous lifetime (supposing that there were such things) they had made a pact to leave together. Then it would make sense. Just like my having been at Papaji's samadhi, while none of his other devotees from North America, not even Gangaji, showed up—again, quizzical musings that might never be satisfied with definite answers.

I did wonder, however, if all the blanks would be filled in once I died. Maybe once you leave your body, they take you to a room and you get to ask all the questions that you never found answers for. Wouldn't that be great? I have a long list ready, with all the coincidences and synchronistic events that have happened in my life that have rendered it so bizarre and curious. I am sure this tendency will only relinquish itself upon my demise. Until then, I suppose, I will just keep collecting the precious morsels for future telling.

Looking back, the German couple and I left Haridwar, again on the night train, taking a non-air-conditioned sleeper. Even though we paid for our seats, as we stopped at the various stations along the route, people kept getting into our car and occupying our berths, thinking they were entitled to take our space. It got rather annoying, particularly when I was trying to sleep and some vagabond would sit on my legs or try to budge me back into the wall. I kept having to shove the strangers off as they wouldn't take no for an answer. Like pesky swarms of flies onto a sweet slice of fruit, or something to that effect. I tried not to be too nasty, but after the first ten times or so, my patience ran out and I admit I wasn't too friendly.

It was also a bit scary because those guys were complete strangers, probably very poor and relatively desperate. They rode the rails for free! The situation was risky—my bag was underneath the bed, and anyone could have reached in and stolen it. I had been warned to always carry my money, passport, and other important documents close to my body under my clothes. I had a small cloth bag with a strap over my shoulder, underneath my pantsuit, to keep my treasured possessions hidden and out of reach, but all my clothes were in my bag along with my camera and journal. I spent a very uneasy night, regardless of the lulling of the rolling wheels over the track.

I loved trains. Ever since I was six years old and my mother first put me on a fourteen-hour train ride to Moose Jaw, Saskatchewan to visit my grandmother, I have loved travelling on them. I went every summer after that until I was twelve. I remember the big, black porter taking care of me like flight attendants do nowadays on planes. He left me relatively on my own. Incidents of throwing pennies down the toilet hole onto the tracks or sitting watching the country pass by through the window created fond memories. I still feel like a small girl in an enchanting world of my own when I travel on trains. Looking back, I was surprised that nothing seriously dangerous happened to me. Mom said that it was *different* in those days. I wondered. Maybe I was just protected by the angels and God's grace.

Our return to Lucknow was followed by preparations for the final puja, the Kriya puja, to commemorate the celebration of Papaji's release from the bounds of earthly existence and his entrance into the heavenly realms where his spirit could soar freely in the land of eternity. I wasn't too clear about all the particulars, only that a wonderful party and feast would follow the ceremony.

By that time I was beginning to realize my business with Papaji and his community was drawing to a close. I found myself disengaged from the proceedings. My mind took an unexpected turn and began to wrap itself around plans for the next leg of my Indian adventure. I would go to Dharamsala to see the Dalai Lama, the exiled spiritual and political leader of the Tibetans. I had heard that people could receive blessings from this special individual if they were willing to venture up into the foothills of the Himalayas to visit him. That's what I would do. After all, Buddha did appear to assist Papaji over the threshold of life into death. Maybe, he would consider accompanying me over a different threshold, as I personally ventured to step away from the familiar landscape of Christianity to explore the foreign and unknown territory of the Buddhist religion.

Regardless, this brief sojourn in the Hindu tradition had been extremely enlightening and colourful. I was looking forward to opening new vistas. I felt my learning curve stretching as I began to reach into the unfathomed heights of my imagination or the glossy pages of the old *National Geographic* magazines that my mother had subscribed to when I was growing up. From what I had previously read, Buddha was an Indian prince who was not satisfied with the doctrines or confines of his inherited Hindu tradition. He sought to transgress the bounds of his known reality in search of new ways to deal with the plights and sufferings of the worldly domain. Was his intention very different than mine?

Consequently, Buddhism had originated in India. Later, with the Mogul invasion, it travelled north to Tibet, China, and finally into the far reaches of Southeast Asia, where Buddhism took firm hold as the prominent religion of that area. It would be pertinent, then, to commence my pilgrimage into the landscape of Buddha by taking my first steps on the same earth that he had trodden 2500 years ago! And an apt beginning would be to receive a blessing from the most renowned and revered Buddhist on the planet today—His Holiness, the Dalai Lama.

I awoke to two Indian gentlemen peering at me with friendly, but concerned, looks on their faces.

"Lady, I think it's your stop," said the older one.

The train was slowing down and through the hazy window I could see people scurrying around on the platform, families rounding up their kids, gathering up their bags and boxes, edging up to get into the cars first, chattering excitedly as the whistle blew to announce the arrival of the train to Pathankot and beyond.

It couldn't be six o'clock yet, I thought, rubbing my eyes and panicking a little as I gathered my senses enough to locate my bag. Oh, yes, under the seat. There it was.

"Are you one of those Sisters of Mercy from the Mother Teresa hospital?" the other one asked as I hurriedly put on my sandals. Bending over to buckle them up, I nodded negatively.

"We thought you were because of your blue dress. So sorry. This is Pathankot now. Can we help you with your things?"

Again, I shook my head back and forth and quickly put the strap over my shoulder, turning to make my way out of the small sleeping compartment before the train started up again. I had noticed last evening that in these small towns trains didn't wait long in the station. One only had a few minutes to shove one's way out the aisle and down the steps without being thwarted by all the determined, pushy on-comers. I had spent the night tossing and turning on the thin plastic mattress of the lower bunk in the stuffy little compartment of a regular sleeper. It had been the only seat I could get when I had tried to get a ticket north at the last moment, yesterday in Lucknow.

As I stepped onto the concrete landing, barely missing a banana peel and left-over banana leaf dish from someone's breakfast samosa that they sell through the windows at the various stations, I secured my footing, turned, and I took one last look back at the first Indian train that I made my own way on to. I waved at the two men grinning their farewells out the window. Smiling back, I waved my free hand and mouthed:

"Thanks! Good-bye!"

"Pretty proud of yourself, aren't you?" I thought out loud and beamed at my accomplishment. "What a woman, making your own way alone in India!" I said to my alter ego, jiggling my shoulders and head as I had seen the Indians do when they were saying yes, when it looked like they were really saying no (cultural demeanours lending themselves to misinterpretation by the foreigners here, and vice versa at home).

"This is so much fun, and interesting!" I again chortled audibly as I took a look around. I was the only white person on the platform. The signs seemed mostly to be in Indian writing, probably Punjabi because Pathankot was in the Punjab. However, the EXIT sign was in English. It wasn't a very big station, so it wasn't difficult to make my way out into the street.

I was still thinking about the two university professors who had shared the compartment with me until Pathankot, and then were to travel on to attend a conference on forestry methods and implementation at a place farther up the line. They had been very considerate, sharing their dinner and waking me up this morning so I wouldn't miss my stop.

I had been delighted last evening as I had watched them undo their tied-up cloths, separating the stainless-steel dishes that were piled one on top of each other in what was known as a tiffin box. The stack was supported and carried by a handle, quite efficient really and helped to keep things warm. I had watched with curious fascination as they undid theirs and offered me some food on a stainless steel plate. No cutlery; we just used our fingers and pieces of *chapati* to scoop up the sloppy dal, rice, and curried vegetable mixture. Each food had appeared in separate containers and had been placed separately on my plate, but as I attempted to eat without cutlery, it all got mixed up somehow. I was trying to hold it all together so it didn't drip onto my new blue shalwar kameez.

I really was trying to behave like I was one of the people, to affirm that I did appreciate their ways. I didn't want them to think that I was critical or arrogant, thinking that Western ways were the *only* ways. Western ethnocentricity was an epidemic throughout the world, as far as I was concerned. It was comforting to feel one with the people by practicing the same cultural norms. I rather enjoyed scooping up the food onto bits and pieces of their round flat bread with my right hand and quickly getting it into my mouth before it spilt all over. The dal tended to be runny and if not careful, the turmeric they put in would stain one's clothes.

One must always use the right hand to eat. It is taboo to use the left. The left hand is used to wipe the behind after going to the bathroom! There are very few trees in India, so bathroom tissue is a precious commodity and, if it can be located in the stores, it is pretty expensive. Luckily, I had lined my bag with quite a few rolls, hoping that it would last until I returned home at the end of my sojourn in this foreign land.

As for using my fingers to eat, curiously enough, it made eating a much more sensual experience. There is something about feeling the food before one has a chance to taste it, like getting acquainted with someone by shaking hands first. Something is passed between the two that is sensory, yet the brain recognizes a *je ne sais quoi* from the first contact that enhances the reception—a tactile foretaste, preparing channels of trust and enjoyment.

Regardless, I had done well. Eating with the two men, sharing their meal and customs, brought us closer together so that when it came time to curl up on the bunk with them in the same little space, I felt quite comfortable and secure.

It was very unusual for a woman to be travelling on her own without being accompanied by a male family member, particularly at night. The men seemed rather protective of me, acting as brothers or husbands would do. I truly did appreciate their attention because admittedly, I was a bit scared when I first entered the compartment and saw I would be sharing it with two strange Indian men AND travelling in the dark!

I managed to make my way to the Pathankot bus station in a rickety rickshaw. Due to the monsoons, the yellow clay roads were ruddy and full of potholes. I was surprised that we didn't blow a tire on the way because the driver wasn't very successful at avoiding them. It was 7:00 a.m., already sweltering, and the sun was so bright. The blue sky had the white sheen of a heat haze. It was going to be a scorcher and I knew from hearsay that there would be no air-conditioning in the bus, if I ever managed to find it.

The bus depot was a teeming madhouse with *no one* speaking English and all the signs in a language I couldn't read. Oh, now what? Everyone seemed so serious. A few women with their heads covered by their saris were staring at me. Another woman in the corner, holding a large bundle wrapped with string on her head, seemed to be shaking her finger at me. I looked down at my clothes. No skin showing. I wondered what was wrong? Probably everything about me.

Trying not to feel too self-conscious and noticing that I was a bit hungry, I made my way over to the samosa cart and ordered three samosas with chutney. The owner handed me my little banana leaf dish as I handed him his 20 rupees. I then went to the chai counter and asked for some tea. Three rupees for a half of a plastic glass of steaming hot chai poured from a large metal container resembling the old farm milk containers I used to see in movies as a kid. Everything seemed so behind the times here, reminding me of the fifties most of the time.

"Miss? You speak English?"

I had been sitting on a wooden bench trying to decide how to find the bus to Dharamsala, where I intended to visit the Dalai Lama.

"Yes," I replied to the sixty-year-old man who was sporting a huge handlebar moustache. He was twisting one of its ends as he stood there smiling at me eagerly. An old army major in his ruffled, tattered khaki uniform. The brass buttons were gleaming in the morning sun. Oh, oh. Probably wanted to practice his English. Well, might as well use his expertise.

Turning towards the turbaned fellow, I again replied affirmatively. "Yes, I'm trying to find the bus to Dharamsala. I'm confused. Could you please tell me which one it is?"

He turned to his left and pointed to the old vehicle that looked like one of our large school buses but painted green. "Over there, number 376," he said. "You'd better get on soon, Miss, or you won't get a seat."

"Thanks." Grateful for direction, I quickly wiped the samosa crumbs and red chutney off my lips with my Kleenex and threw my dusty bag over my shoulder. It was amazing how things got *so* dirty here in India. Some families were ahead of me, but as I climbed the steps, the driver motioned for me to take the seat up front beside him. Well, at least I would get a panoramic view since I was surrounded by windows.

We didn't leave for another twenty-five minutes. I had time to get my bearings, make myself comfortable, and take a look around. The windshield was trimmed with a bright multi-coloured strip of cotton pompoms similar to the little cloth bobbles on the Mexican sombreros we saw in Westerns as children. In the centre, just under the roof was a gilded coloured picture of Rama and Sita. There were flower decals lining the window above the dashboard and in the middle of the dash was a little shrine with a small statue of Shiva. A fresh garland of marigolds and roses was draped around it. Lit incense wafted across the front seats while Indian singing blared out of the loudspeakers. The driver was blissfully chewing his betel nut and listening to the music with his eyes closed.

I found out later, on one of my subsequent trips, that all drivers perform a short prayer with the accoutrements of a puja—flowers and lit incense—every morning as a blessing for the safety and prosperity of their day's work.

By the time we left, at least two busloads' worth of passengers were crammed into the metal seats behind me. No animals, just families chattering, kids complaining, and babies crying. However, as we began the journey, they all seemed to settle in, pulling out their bags of food and containers of water, tea, or whatever, and babies were put to the breast. Relative quiet.

On our way. Too bad there were no shocks in these vehicles. At least, I wasn't in the back taking the brunt of the bumps. The motor sat beside me, between the driver and me. I began to feel the heat as the motor warmed up to prepare itself for the long climb into the hills ahead. Lush green scenery. The Punjab is regarded as the garden of India, where a considerable amount of the farming takes place. The Punjabi people are quite wealthy compared to most rural Indian people.

As we began the steep ascent, I started to feel a bit uneasy. The driver really seemed to be taking liberties with his speed. There were no real speed controls on the roads, let alone signs. The roads going up into the mountains were narrow and it was hard to believe that any oncoming trucks or buses would fit past each other. Things were getting pretty steep and at one point, when we had to pass a large van, our driver steered the bus up the side of the cliff so the other vehicle could get past! We sat leaning at what seemed a 40-degree angle or so for at least five minutes as the van edged itself past us. All accompanied by LOTS of horn blowing. I had heard of fatal bus accidents along these routes. I decided to close my eyes for a while and try to take a nap. After all, it was only supposed to be three hours until we reached our destination.

The trip up into the foothills of the Himalayan Mountains and to the old English hill-station of Dharamsala happened without mishap. I slept for about half an hour but it was quite gorgeous, actually. I didn't want to miss the beauty. We passed a few waterfalls and at one point could see the snowy peaks cushioned in behind the approaching hills. It was a pretty arduous climb. I worried about the sound of the gears grinding as the driver shifted down to make the steep inclines. It felt a bit precarious at times. I was afraid the clutch might slip or the gears strip, sending us sailing backwards or over the precipice that was looming threateningly beside us. Without incident, however, we arrived at last. Relief permeated the atmosphere as I, along with all the other passengers, descended the steps and inhaled our first breaths of Indian mountain air!

It wasn't even noon yet. The air was cooler and felt quite pleasant. I hoped it wouldn't be too cold at night, as it was nearing the end of September. I had heard that it snowed early up in the hills. Hope not.

I stood there momentarily, attempting to harness my exuberance long enough to get my bearings. The bus had parked on the hill just outside of McLeod Ganj, the actual town where the Dalai Lama's residence and monastery were located, a few kilometres up the road from Dharamsala. The air was so refreshing—such a change from the muggy heat of the flat lands below.

I took a look around before I began walking towards the town. The hills were heavily forested, and the road, cut roughly out the side of the small mountain, was very narrow and gravelled with large pieces of rock that were hard to walk on. Down below, I had noticed people working in the shallow edges of rivers pounding rocks and gathering them into piles. I wondered if these shards of stone under foot had once been shattered by the hard-working women and children of the lower valley. So much energy and manpower to accomplish things that were so quickly and easily done by machines at home!

I walked past an old Christian church, presumably Church of England, a stone remnant of the Raj (the time before India's Independence), up to the square at the beginning of the village where five streets converged. Facing me was a two-story building with its name 'McLlo Restaurant' on the awning. Everything else around seemed so makeshift: huts were perched on top of handmade stone walls, and huts made with sticks, with plastic or tin corrugated roofs, lined the streets.

I stopped in front of the restaurant deciding which way to turn. I pulled out my tattered Lonely Planet guide and stood perusing it intently. It was all relatively quiet, with only a few people walking the streets and a few scooters going past. I poked my nose into a few stalls and was astonished at the colourful collection of odds and ends: intricately knitted wool caps with tassels and ties, patterned wool socks, yak-haired shawls, beaded necklaces inter-mixed with rolls of prayer flags and incense—an interesting collection of cultural reflection.

I pondered the direction I should take to go find some lodging.

I decided to venture left; the book said there were some places, run by monks, on the path leading up that way. I hoped not too far up. My bag was a bit heavy, the sun was still bright and hot, *and* I was hungry. I hadn't eaten since those three samosas that morning!

As I ascended the narrow road, I was astonished that people seemed to be living alongside it in some of the very same little dwellings that were being used as shops in the centre of town. Poverty was evident everywhere. However, people seemed to be making the best of it. Sitting along the road were many elderly men and women, obviously Tibetan, counting and turning their wooden rosary beads between their thumbs and first fingers and mouthing barely audible chants in a soft reverberating hum. Praying in public! Wouldn't find that at home. All seemed happy as they nodded their heads at me as I went past.

Their shining eyes and open hearts, full of acknowledgement and acceptance, struck me. I was surprised by their intense looks of clarity and intelligence. Could it be the prayers? I wondered if all Tibetans had such pristine minds. I later learned that most people have their own personal mantras or prayers that they repeat and count as they pray. The ultimate goal to achieve 100,000 repetitions of a mantra in order to complete a teaching is probably their starting point. I was sure that these people did many more rounds than that.

"Do you have any rooms available?" I inquired. I had made my way up the street to a Tibetan guesthouse painted yellow and trimmed with maroon. Around the wooden doorway and windows were brightly coloured, painted traditional designs. I had found it very attractive, so I stopped there and I went in to see about a room.

The man behind the counter was a monk or lama. I recognized the shaved head and traditional maroon and golden garb of Tibetan Buddhist clergy. He nodded positively.

"How much?" I asked. Being on a bare-bones budget, this was always the next very important question.

"Seventy-five rupees. The shower is extra—ten rupees. The bathrooms are down the hall from your room. You can have number 14 on the second floor. Would you like to see it?" he asked as he reached around to take the key off a nail on the board situated on the wall behind him.

I followed the monk up the marble stairs, down the hall, and into the room. It was a bright corner room and out the window I could see the roofs of the surrounding buildings. Tattered red, green, yellow, blue, and white prayer flags strung from roof to roof were waving gently in the breeze, broadcasting their silent prayers into the air around and distributing blessings of peace and happiness for all life—very touching and picturesque, especially with the forest in the background. A lovely view and a clean room, all for $2.50!

"I'll take it!"

I woke up around 5:30 a.m. with a start. It was still dark. I heard the incessant drone of monks chanting outside. I had been dreaming that I was walking up a wide mountain path. The skies were bright blue and I was completely alone. I was heading towards a place, a dark room where there were two very old, evolved Buddhist lamas waiting for me. They were dressed in wine and saffron robes, sitting in lotus positions on mats made of colourful woven material of Tibetan design. There were butter lamps glowing and streams of incense swirling up into the musty air of the dimly lit room. Stooping, I crossed the threshold of the portal entrance and with hands in prayer position, bowed with reverence as I approached the two men. I seemed to recognize them. They nodded in unison, motioning for me to sit down on an empty cushion in front of them but over to the side. The wall of the hut felt cold and damp behind my back. I watched them intently, waiting to be enlightened about their intentions towards me. All was quiet and then the two ancients began to chant. Their eyes were closed. One of them was holding a metal bell in his left hand and a strange metal object in his right. He was ringing the bell and waving the metal piece around in strange movements in time with the chanting. This went on for quite a while. When they opened their eyes, their gazes were still distant as if they had just returned from some place far away. All of a sudden, the man with what I later came to learn was a *dorje* (Tibetan) or *vajra* (Sanskrit), meaning thunderbolt, cast a penetrating look directly at me and spoke:

"We want to instruct you in some very important teachings. We trust that you understand your mission and have done the necessary preparation to receive them. We are willing to initiate you . . ." Then I woke up; the dream had ended.

"Meaning what exactly? What am I doing here in Dharamsala?" I asked myself.

"You have to write a letter and take it to the Dalai Lama," a silent voice replied in my head. Where did that come from? Now what? What strange thing had I gotten myself into?

"You must inform His Holiness about the predicament you found yourself in at a local dharma centre last year. You must ask for his help. It must be made known, so it doesn't continue or happen in other places," the voice continued.

This was where following my instincts and intuition had led me? Why me, God?

I was feeling extremely reluctant to consider the past situation, let alone this mysterious directive. Last year, I had attended the birthday celebration of a local lama. I went to the dharma centre innocently and expectantly. I had always enjoyed my times there, despite the fact that the group held me at arm's length because I inevitably committed ignorant errors in standard Buddhist protocol.

In particular, a few years before, I had been privileged to attend the teachings and empowerments of the presiding lama's teacher, H.H. Sakya Trizin, the head of the Sakya lineage, visiting from India. The Sakya is one of the four lineages of the Tibetan Buddhist tradition. The other three are Nyingma, Kagyu, and Gelugpa, the latter being the Dalai Lama's lineage. One of the main things I remembered about that afternoon was that in the shrine room at the dharma centre, along with about thirty inner students of the *sangha* (community) there, I had asked what was considered a stupid question: I had asked Sakya Trizin if he was enlightened.

I was later reprimanded severely for asking my question. Apparently, it was taboo for a student to ask a great teacher such things, but I was sure everyone in that room wanted to know! I was free enough to ask because I had not as yet taken refuge (a ceremony like Christian baptism), and subsequently, was not considered an official member of the Buddhist group. I felt that there had to be room for my particular questions and that I had done nothing wrong.

Sakya Trizin, of course, denied his enlightenment and said that he was just like me, only a little farther along on the path. Another thing that he stressed was that, as initiates, it was very important to be aware and in control of our anger, as one angry thought or action could destroy lifetimes of merit and spiritual accomplishment. People like myself, who had not been initiated, would suffer less bad karma due to unmoderated anger. Innocence was sometimes a good quality. But due to my *faux pas* I wasn't exactly welcomed with open arms to the centre after that.

However, that particular afternoon of the party, a terrible thing happened. The sangha group and the lama were verbally attacking an older woman who was a prominent member of the group and also lived in the house. She suddenly fell over in a swoon, gasping and experiencing severe pains in her chest area. Whether or not she had a mild heart attack, I didn't know. I helped her up to her room on the second floor and spent the next six hours listening to her story and administering Reiki to calm and balance her system.

After she settled down, I left. I returned later to teach her Reiki so that she could treat herself and to support her further through this difficult time of conflict. As yet, things were unresolved and the situation at the centre was very tense and negative. I had the feeling that she was being used as a scapegoat for the others' anger. It was apparent that no one had listened to Sakya Trizin's advice.

The directive, then, pertained to this episode, and it was obvious that I was the 'chosen one' to take the news to the Dalai Lama informing him about this situation.

When I went outside later that morning, the streets were buzzing with excitement. The Dalai Lama was going to come out and greet the people for the second time that month because the 'government in exile' was in session. Many Tibetan refugee representatives had come from all over the world to meet, warranting an extra appearance from His Holiness. People were ecstatic. Faces were beaming. Another opportunity to cast their fervent eyes upon their cherished and most beloved leader! He was like a father to them. Many had left their parents and possessions behind to flee over the freezing, dangerous passes of the Himalayas in a desperate attempt to free themselves from Chinese oppression, arriving to settle in this haphazard Tibetan refugee community. Many died along the way or were shot by the Chinese guards at the border. The area had been donated as a safe zone by the Indian government after the Dalai Lama fled into exile in 1959. As I looked around, I caught their precious excitement and found my heart jumping with joy along with theirs!

I made my way along the street looking for a place to eat. Spotting a sign that said 'Tibetan Kitchen', I headed towards it, all the while trying to avoid getting my long skirt muddy; the monsoon rains still weren't quite over, even though it was the third week in September. I ordered some fried *momos,* a Tibetan dish of vegetable dumplings, which were delicious and certain to be one of my favourite things to eat here. Then I went exploring.

As I made my way down the hill towards the post office and Tibetan medicine centre, I spotted a familiar face. It was Lopsang Telong, or L.T. as everyone called him, a Tibetan who had lived in Victoria and who was married to a Canadian woman involved with the Friends of Tibet committee! I had never attended any of their meetings but had been to a few of the events. That was where I had met L.T. and heard him speak.

"Excuse me, I recognize you from Victoria, Canada. I met you at a Free Tibet event there." He smiled in acknowledgement and stopped. I introduced myself and we shook hands.

"Pardon me, I don't remember," he responded. "I've been here in the Dharamsala region for a few years, assigned to the post of International Relations Officer for the government in exile. I do a lot of travelling to visit the various Tibetan refugee communities around the world. I am here now because the government's in session."

I was impressed. He was a genuinely friendly man with such a lovely demeanour. He handed me his card and said that I should come to his office where we could talk further.

"If you need anything, let me know," he said.

Thinking of my decision to write the letter, I responded: "Actually, there is something I need to talk to you about. I'll come around later this afternoon. OK?"

He nodded, assenting. With that, we parted. He headed in the direction of the monastery while I went into the post office to inquire about sending some postcards home.

What a coincidence! Just when I needed some information as to how to go about getting a letter to the Dalai Lama, providence put the exact person on my path to further me along. Maybe there was indeed such a thing as Divine intervention.

Later that afternoon I sauntered down Temple Road towards the address that was on L.T.'s card. Even though I was on a mission, I couldn't help but get distracted by all the colourful market stalls! I found his office quite easily but his receptionist said that he was in a meeting. As soon as I gave her my name, she asked me to wait, exiting into the next room presumably to inform her boss of my arrival. I looked around. There was a magnificent picture of the Dalai Lama on the wall behind her desk. His Holiness had such beautiful eyes and lovely smile. No wonder everyone loved him so much.

L.T. came out of the meeting room. (He was probably conversing with some very important people, possibly the Dalai Lama himself . . . I wished!) He came out to attend me, leading me into a large room that had floors covered with beautiful Tibetan carpets. He held out his arm, pointing to some long benches with matching rugs and encouraging me to sit down and make myself comfortable. I had never truly looked at Tibetan weaving before. The designs were very particular to their tradition, the colours bold and earthy. I felt extremely honoured sitting there surrounded by the beauty of Tibetan art. On the walls were brightly painted cloth pictures of deities sitting on lotus blossoms. I learned that these were called *thangkas,* Tibetan scroll paintings used to enhance meditative practice.

We discussed my intention and I informed L.T. about the situation at home, what I knew about it, and why it was important to inform the Dalai Lama. He was very attentive, circumspect, and helpful, supplying me with the appropriate names and addresses. He advised me to write to Sakya Trizin as well. I felt assured that what I had imparted to him would be held in strictest confidence.

At last, the Dalai Lama was about to make his appearance! It was nearly two o'clock in the afternoon. I had first lined up outside his residence with letter in hand around 9:30 that morning. I had had no idea it would take so long to go through all the security. After all, he was a very important political figure. But all the police and army? I was beginning to realize that every time the Dalai Lama came out to greet the public, he risked his life. I mean, how often does the President of the United States come out without armed security? Never! I was more naïve than I had realized; it just never crossed my mind.

The process to this point had actually been quite an ordeal. When I went through the first security check, I told the security officer about my letter. He became quite excited and ran to get a few other guards. They stood huddled together looking at the letter I had handed to the first guy. All I had said was that it was very important that they took this letter to the Dalai Lama before he came out to greet the public. How presumptuous of me! Maybe they thought that there was a hidden threat in it. Or a bomb! I assured them that it was a friendly letter, with some information in it that needed his attention.

This seemed to satisfy them, and they then ushered me along with the rest of the people in the line-up. I noticed that one of the men scurried away towards the building across the way with my letter in hand. I had no idea that so many people would be coming to receive blessings. There were hundreds of people filing through the first passageway into the area leading up to the front of the monastery where His Holiness would be greeting us.

It was hours before we were able to start moving. I had been mistaken thinking that I would be granted a private interview! I was just one of the crowd. After a couple of hours waiting, I panicked a little and retraced my steps to the first of the three posts that we had had to pass through for security measures. At one of them, they had touch-searched us like they used to do in airports a few years ago.

There was a bit of kerfuffle when I asked the original guard if he had heard about my letter and if it had actually got to the Dalai Lama. He seemed rather annoyed, brusquely ushering me back in the direction that I had come from, assuring me that everything possible had been done to see that he got my letter. I wasn't quite as positive as he seemed to be, but made my way back to my place. Luckily, they didn't put me through all the previous security procedure!

They had told us that *no one* was allowed to speak to the Dalai Lama, yet here the guy in front of me was stopping and having a little chat! Well, if he could do it, then so could I.

I stepped forward to present my *kata* (white silk scarf). His Holiness took it from me and placed it around my neck. I smiled. I paused, ignoring the attendant monk directing me to move on. "Thank you," I said. "My name is Dorothy Margaret Skene. I come from Canada. I am the woman who wrote you the letter that they gave to you this morning," I quickly stated, much to the chagrin and scorn of the monk standing beside him, glaring at me.

"Pardon me?" the Dalai Lama asked, with a puzzled look on his face.

He spoke to me and wanted me to say it again! "My name is Dorothy Margaret Skene. I come from Victoria, Canada. I am the woman who wrote you the letter. I hope that they gave it to you this morning." I was nervous and the other guy was not happy with me. I could feel the people behind me in line getting impatient. The Dalai Lama gave me one of his precious, heartfelt smiles. His eyes looked into my eyes and a moment of light passed between us.

"Ah, yes," he said. "Thank you. I shall read it later." He lowered his head with his hands in prayer position at his heart, bowing slightly. I made the same gesture—a spiritual acknowledgement meaning 'I honour the light within you' or 'the Buddha in me greets the Buddha in you'.

I moved on to the monk, who handed me a single-knotted silk

thread that I was supposed to tie around my neck or wrist and leave on for three days, but not get wet. I received my auspicious Tibetan blessing (which would continue into the future for peace and happiness) with gratitude, receiving it for the well-being of my family as well as myself.

I had managed to put a face to my letter! What luck. Never one to follow instructions to the letter, I had jumped at the opportunity. Besides, the man in front of me had done the same. I was not the only rebel in the crowd.

My trip ended without any further memorable incidents. I boarded a plane at midnight a week later in Delhi. I had arrived in the dark and left in the dark. Hopefully though, my first trip to India had illumined my heart, mind, and spirit. I thought that I could fairly say I had at least moved a few steps further along the path towards enlightenment and truth. If not, I had most certainly had my fair share of remarkable experiences.

Not long after I returned home, I received an auspicious letter in the mail addressed from the OFFICE OF H.H. THE DALAI LAMA. Dated September 25, 1997, it read:

Dear Ms. Skene,

This is to acknowledge receipt of your letter dated September 22 addressed to His Holiness the Dalai Lama informing Him about dharma activity in your area.

I have been directed to thank you for your letter and the concern you have expressed in it. We think it is important that you inform this matter to His Holiness Sakya Trizin as you seemed to have done already.

With our best wishes.

Yours sincerely,
Tenzin N. Taklha
Deputy Secretary

I later heard through one of my Reiki students, a university professor who had been appointed by his faculty to lunch with the Dalai Lama, that His Holiness came to Victoria during his visit to Vancouver for the APEC conference. I wondered at the time if the university luncheon was the only reason he had come to the city.

I learned that the woman who had been targeted at the dharma centre had been made a lama for all her devotion, hard work, and commitment to the Buddhist teachings. Hopefully, the whole situation had been rectified. However, I did hear many years later that there had been a court case, the house had closed down, and the woman concerned had given up the Buddhist religion and was exploring other avenues of spirituality. The lama has since passed over and is presumably living in another Buddha realm awaiting rebirth. That is, if he hasn't already been reborn. The center continues to offer the dharma to those interested in Tibetan Buddhism, albeit under the auspices of another Tibetan lama.

I never returned to the centre after that, as my path took me in a completely different direction for a while. Curiously, life did seem to take its own course despite any help from human sources. And what did I learn from it all? That no matter how far along teachers may be, they are all still in process, subject to the same karmic laws as all the rest of us.

As for that peculiar dream I had had the first morning in McLeod Ganj, I couldn't help wonder if the high lamas were Sakya Trizin and the Dalai Lama. The initiation? Possibly the empowerment gained when one speaks and acts in a truthful manner, standing up for rightness and justness. I tend to believe that that is the meaning of Right Speech and Right Action—two of Buddhism's most important premises.

Author standing beside the Ganges River at Haridwar, holding banana boat flower offering.

Rajasthani women at the river in Haridwar.

Pictures and flowers on the shrine in the Satsang Bhavan the first night of Papaji's samadhi.

Statue of Buddha in the shrine room at Gyuto Monastery.

Papaji's ashes at the burning pyre.

2003
Enlightenment

Asatoma sadgamaya
Tamasoma jyotirgamaya
Mrityorma amrtamgamaya
Om santih santih santih

Om, lead us from untruth to truth
From darkness to light,
And from death to immortality
Om, peace, peace, peace.

—Brihadaranyaka Upanishad (1: 3: 28)

When I went to check-in at the Singapore Airlines ticket counter, I was told that there was a change in plans. We would have two stop-overs instead of the single one in Singapore, the ticket agent informed me.

"There is a typhoon in the area, so you are being re-routed to Hong Kong for a six-hour stop-over, until it passes. Then you'll be flown to Singapore and on to Trivandrum, India as designated on your original ticket. Don't worry, you will be provided with a meal ticket when you arrive at the Hong Kong airport."

She handed me my boarding pass and I looked at the seat number. At least I had an aisle seat to stretch out in. It would give me time to rest and think about the last six years, to put everything into perspective. I wasn't distressed by the change like some of the other passengers seemed to be. On the road once again! And going back to my beloved INDIA!

This time I was travelling with a new name, Veda Mata, truly committed to my journey towards enlightenment! Actually, Veda Mata was now my official name, having changed it in 1998 after meeting Amma, or Sri Mata Amritanandamayi, for the second time. That in itself was quite an adventure and a remarkable story. It had been six years since I had returned from India and since then, I had been longing to go back. I had known I would but didn't know when.

The years between had been very fruitful. I had been travelling in another way, taking an inner route, all the while with my feet firmly planted on the ground at home. I had seen myself through the transitions of menopause and empty nest syndrome. I had undergone intensive and extensive gestalt and primal scream therapy to relieve myself of the traumas of single parenthood, attempting to understand my subconscious tendencies to thwart efforts to achieve freedom and success. My patterns of self-sabotage had become clear. Consequently, I had set myself the task of making a list of my dreams and setting them in motion. I had closed down my family home, sold all my possessions, given my treasures away to my sisters, bought my ticket, and packed my bags. My grown children being settled into their individual lives without any pressing concerns, I gave myself permission to fly the coop and get on with 'getting a life'!

After motherhood commitments had been fulfilled, I was free to wander into the lands of my stored hopes and dreams. It felt reasonable and I was doing it. "I'm entitled to my own life, aren't I?" I whispered out loud as I stood there in the centre of the airport before I went through security.

Of course, the first thing on my list had been to return to India to sit at the feet of enlightened beings, continuing my pilgrimage into both the Hindu and Buddhist holy lands—to continue where I had left off. My meetings with Amma had confirmed that there truly were people on earth who had realized God-consciousness and who lived from the place of Absolute Awareness, such as that which I had touched upon during my time with Gangaji so many years ago. In fact, I was on my way to celebrate the Golden Anniversary of this very beloved Indian guru, considered the embodiment of the Divine Mother or God incarnate in female form, who hailed from the backwaters of Kerala, Southern India. I wanted to sit at her feet and bask in her radiance.

I had had many experiences of Amma's bliss when she had come for her regular summer tours to North America. I wanted to appreciate and experience her in her home setting, amid her own people. I wanted to visit Amma's birthplace. Surprisingly, I had seen it on the Lonely Planet channel one day last year when I had turned on the TV. I wanted to have hugs from her in her own shrine room.

After all, she was known as 'the Hugging Saint'. I could attest to the fact that her hugs were delicious and went well beyond the scope of an ordinary mother hugging her children. Amma had hugged over 20 million people and had been honoured for her humanitarian efforts by the United Nations. She was not a hoax or a scam! She was solely committed to the happiness and well-being of everyone. I had witnessed her hugging people, not moving from her decorated chair for hours on end. Sitting for unusually extended periods, welcoming people into her lovingly maternal arms and attending to their questions and concerns confirmed that she truly was a 'living saint'. I was on my way towards her divine embrace.

I was looking forward to a very auspicious next three weeks at Amma's ashram, participating in the preparations for and consequent celebration of her fiftieth birthday in Cochin, a bit further north.

Millions of people were expected to attend, including some of the most celebrated citizens of India—the President and possibly the Prime Minister, and other state officials—and many humanitarian activists. I had heard that Martin Luther King's daughter would be there to host the Women's Conference to be held on one of the five days.

Then I planned to board a train taking myself up to the furthest reaches of the northeastern corner of India to visit Darjeeling, the famous tea area. For some reason, I had always dreamt of going there when I was a child. After that, I would be travelling by bus and train to various holy cities, hopefully returning to Laxman and Ram Jhula to sleep beside the enchanting and lulling river waters of the Ganges.

"I might as well have a short meditation as we take off, to settle me down," I encouraged myself, talking softly out loud. I opened a long-distance Reiki treatment for a successful flight and began silently repeating my Amma meditation mantra.

Always nervous during take-off, that's me! Sometimes my mind would dart into the dark shadowy corners of trepidation, skipping from one frightening thought to the next, imagining the worst possible scenarios and dwelling on all the most negative things that could happen during a plane trip. Reiki and meditation usually worked to curb my paranoia . . .

The ding of the seatbelt sign went off, and I realized that we were OK. Take-off had been successful. We were well above the clouds and could relax and enjoy the flight. The pilot was giving his 'spiel', welcoming the passengers and informing us of the details of altitude, times, etc. I usually didn't pay much attention. Nowadays, you could watch it on the screen on the back of the seat in front. I didn't feel like reading the book that was packed in my carry-on. What to do? Might as well just close my eyes again and take a trip down memory lane. I had wanted to take this time to sort out the last few years and put everything into perspective, to set my life's course by reviewing my past intentions and actions since my last trip.

Not long after I had returned from India, a friend phoned to let me know about a 'happening' at the Truth Centre on Fort Street in Victoria. I had attended some of the group's positive living sessions many years ago but hadn't been there since. It was a beautiful venue with gardens all around. My friend knew people from a different group who were hosting an afternoon presentation by a Swami from India. I agreed to accompany her.

The following Sunday afternoon I was introduced to Swami Krishnananda, a close disciple of Amma, the famous guru. She was considered an *avatar*, a person who has no further karma on earth other than to serve, helping living beings achieve the Ultimate

Truth, Self-realization, God-consciousness or Enlightenment—all meaning the same thing. The Buddhists would call her an incarnate *bodhisattva,* a divine being who has pledged to remain on earth to help sentient beings achieve nirvana or Buddhist heaven. Swami sang songs of praise to God and the Divine Mother and then told his story, mentioning that Amma was considered an embodiment of the Divine Mother. People in the Western world seem very unfamiliar with, and skeptical about, the concept of God being female. Personally, I found myself quite excited about meeting this incredible woman. I heard she would be coming to North America on tour the following summer. I made a vow to attend the retreat in the Seattle area at that time.

What was supposed to be a few hugs from Amma the following June turned out to be an entire summer of Divine embraces! How had that happened? How had the 'best laid plans' turned into something altogether different? Life had a way of creating itself. Or, possibly, this woman known as Amma had had a hand in it! That was what everyone told me at the time.

I was extremely excited about my itinerary. I had planned to attend a one-night event at Fort Flagler, Washington, a celebration of *Devi Bhava,* the final evening of an Amma weekend retreat. (On this night she dresses up in a colourful sari and becomes the Divine Mother.) Then I had registered for two retreats, one in Los Angeles and the other in Santa Fe, New Mexico. I was combining the retreats with an extra week of holidays where I hoped to travel around soaking in hot springs on the Rio Grande and visiting the Four Corners area famous for the Hopi and Navajo Indians. I had read about this in the Lonely Planet guidebook.

My teenage children were used to managing on their own, and I thought I could trust them to keep things together for a couple of weeks. My oldest daughter was in university, competent enough to manage things at home while I was away.

I crossed the Juan de Fuca Strait by ferry to Port Angeles, where my friend Penny and I managed to catch a lift with some people who were also going to Devi Bhava. We were quite fortunate because the bus that we had planned to take didn't head in that direction!

The most touching thing I remember about the evening was that as soon as I entered the hall and sat down, I burst into tears and cried for a full ten minutes from the bottom of my heart. As if all the years of sorrow had stored themselves in a lake deep within my being. The high vibrations of the room activated some sort of switch, causing an inner dam to break, leaving me swimming in rivers of tears spilling out of my eyes and dropping onto the beautiful silk clothes that I had purchased especially for the evening.

Amma was of course, her usual beautiful self. I recognized her exactly as I had seen her in pictures. The evening went without further incident. My hug was very comforting and precious. She held me to the breast of her extraordinarily beautiful teal-blue sari, whispered sweet nothings in the form of "my darling daughter, my darling daughter" into my ear, and released me into a sea of bliss which continued to pervade my being throughout the entire evening while I sat watching all the others going up to receive their hugs.

Around 1:00 a.m. Penny and I went back to our tent. She was tired and didn't want to cross the field alone in the dark or stay by herself in the tent. I was reluctant to go. I hadn't had enough of this marvellous woman. Because I didn't want my friend to feel uncomfortable, I accompanied her. I was, as yet, uninformed that the best part of the night happens after everyone has been hugged and all the weddings have taken place. In the early hours of the morning dynamic music is played by Amma's musicians and all the participants circle the hall, passing the stage in front of Amma, who showers blessed flower petals on everyone. I, however, went to bed and fell asleep quickly, only to be roused by loud singing and shouting around 5:00 a.m. coming from the communal area. I later realized that I had missed Amma's glorious farewell to her northwestern devotees.

I took the ferry back to Victoria and waited another week before I headed off to Seattle and then on down to Los Angeles on Southwest Air to participate in my first Amma retreat.

The Los Angeles Retreat . . .

I slipped the plastic key into the door slot, turned the handle, and opened the door to the hotel room. I entered, set down my bag and sighed. At last I had arrived. First I would get settled, then showered and dressed before going down to take a look at the hall where Amma would be appearing for the first night of the Los Angeles retreat. My first full retreat! I was so glad to be there, free, leaving ALL my familial and community responsibilities behind!

I turned on the light and noticed a woman crumpled in a chair in the corner of the room. Must be my allocated roommate. What was she doing sitting in the dark, I wondered? I looked more closely at her—short, ruffled, bleach-blonde hair, pudgy and not very healthy looking. She was dressed in the white Amma apparel that many people wore to these retreats. I, too, had brought a bag full of 'whites' to wear for the weekend. The woman looked up at me beseechingly; she had been crying.

"Would you please sit with me? I am feeling really confused and frightened. I tried to commit suicide last weekend. Rather than go to the hospital, I told my doctor that I wanted to come to Amma's retreat. I am sure that Amma can help me."

I nodded, assenting, and pulled a chair up beside her while thinking how fortune keeps me the mother and babysitter, regardless of any effort on my part to shirk my humanitarian responsibilities. When I leave this body, I am surely going to check in at a different counter to get my ticket for next lifetime. I want another job!

Luckily the woman couldn't hear my thoughts. "Is there anything else that I can do for you?" I asked.

She pointed to her water bottle. As I handed it to her, she continued: "Actually if you wouldn't mind, I would appreciate it if you would stay with me for the night. I am afraid that I may try to hurt myself if I am alone."

Despite my underlying need to be alone, to completely grasp the reality of actually being in the presence of a Self-realized woman and to bask in her glory without interruption, I resigned myself to my fate. Maybe service rather than retreat was my true calling in life. Maybe I would never escape this seemingly urgent request to attend to other people's needs. Maybe my happiness was solely dependent upon the happiness of others. (I mean that in a functional not a dysfunctional way.) In other words, maybe it was impossible to be free of responsibility as long as there were people around who were suffering. Maybe I was just an unacknowledged bodhisattva after all!

Questions to ask Amma, if an occasion arose. Regardless, I already had other more immediate concerns and requests to lay at Amma's feet, if the opportunity arose to speak to her. My son, for example. His situation at the moment was well beyond my ability or capability. I had brought photographs of my children which I wanted her to bless. There were many things on my mind that I wanted to relinquish in her presence. I wanted her blissful intention to wash my slate clean. Now I was being confronted with a situation that was more urgent and present. A dilemma. A sacrifice or a compromise? It didn't really seem like there was much choice considering my benevolent personality . . .

"Of course," I replied.

Anna and I went down to dinner together and sat beside each other until she received her hug from Amma. I was also up most of the night listening to her tragic story. What a way to spend my first night in the luxurious Orange County Hilton Hotel! I considered this extra *seva* (service), so when asked if I wanted any further jobs to do on site other than the two assigned to me upon registration, I declined, figuring that I already had my hands full for the weekend.

The Swami in orange perused the letter I had handed to him, leaned over Amma's right shoulder from behind, and spoke into her ear. She nodded, speaking in an animated and fully engrossed fashion, responding in her native Malayalam tongue. I didn't understand a word of it. All the while, Amma had a woman in her arms hugging her to her breast. She looked at me for a few moments then turned to whisper something in the woman's ear. She rubbed her back, released her and handed her a rose petal and Hershey candy kiss.

I knew the routine. I had already received two hugs from Amma, the second being last night, the first night of the retreat. She had blessed the pictures of my family and given me a hug that penetrated my being completely. I had spent most of last evening crying, releasing my tears into Amma's ocean of compassion, back to the Source.

Amma had asked my roommate, Anna, to lie on the stage directly behind her for the better part of the evening. I trusted that being closer to Amma had an amazing healing effect because I was finding, after having been in the question line for the past hour waiting my turn, that the vibrations of Amma's energy were much stronger up close. I wanted to try sitting nearer to her in the future. The seat that I had chosen earlier this morning was halfway back in the room.

"I can see that your son has many obstacles in his path. No problem. He is MY son now. I will do a *sankalpa* (mental intention) for him." From Swami's translation, that was what Amma had said. I started crying; I was so relieved. What more could a mother desire than confirmation of God's loving blessing for her children, particularly from someone who was a Divine emissary?

"Anything more?" Swami asked me. I nodded, ready to show him my second question. I looked directly at Amma, with tears in my eyes.

"Are you my satguru?" I asked trustingly. Swami translated my question. Amma again turned towards me, casting her knowing glance completely on me, enveloping my openness and vulnerability and shedding light into my entire being.

"Yes," she said.

"Then, may I have a name and a mantra?" Amma nodded affirmatively. I left the question line overwhelmed with joy, spending the rest of the morning darshan in a bubble of Amma's bliss.

Later, that Saturday afternoon, we sat listening to Amma respond to our questions. At supper we enjoyed eating her *prasad* (food blessed by her), which she personally handed to each and every one of us. The dinner was Indian food, bringing back memories of the time I had spent in India years before. Now I was eating food blessed by the Divine Mother herself!

The next morning, during darshan, after I had received my hug, Amma had me stand up in the front of the hall away from her chair, in front of over a thousand people. As she was hugging each person from the darshan line, she would look across at me and then go back to her task. This happened many times while she was pondering a suitable name for me. Then all of a sudden, she threw her arms up in the air and shouted: "Vedamata! Vedamata! Vedamata!" The atmosphere was sliced by her joyous definition!

Swami called me closer and handed me a piece of paper where he had written down my new name in Sanskrit, as well as English: VEDAMATA. Simply translated as 'mother of truth' or 'source of true knowledge', in actuality Vedamata relates to the 'Mother of the Vedas', referring to the Gayatri mantra, a verse from the Rigveda that is highly revered in Hinduism. Its English translation declares, roughly: *We contemplate the supreme glory of the Divine Light that permeates the Universe, and ask that it illumine our intelligence.* This mantra, this calling upon God, has been chanted to this day, throughout the streets of India as the sun rises. I felt extremely privileged to be granted such a sacred and auspicious name. I had asked for a name that would take me to the Truth and Amma blessed me with a name that invoked the Truth itself! I could never thank her enough. Thank you, God!

That night, over four thousand people came to the Devi Bhava. I was sure the crowd included many famous people, possibly even movie stars. The clothing people wore was spectacular, Amma included. She wore a magnificent purple silk sari with silver threads that matched her Devi Bhava crown. I had never experienced anything so colourful or exquisite. Of course, being in the presence of the Divine, everyone wanted to show their very best.

My name wasn't the only gift that I took away from that weekend. I left Los Angeles equipped with a sacred mantra (Sanskrit divine name or phrase) as a means to stay connected to Amma and to further my progress towards my most cherished intention—the Truth. Whether or not I would achieve my goal seemed to depend upon my commitment to use my mantra in meditation, and to continue my practice involving both spiritual study and selfless service. This was Amma's way.

I couldn't help wondering, though, how my new name was going to affect my life. Would it alter my persona? How would people respond to it? Would I lose my friends? What would my mother say to THIS?

As for the rest of my holiday? It took a surprising turn after the retreat in Santa Fe. Instead of attending just one more retreat, I was offered the opportunity to continue along for the entire tour, embarking upon a new relationship with a man, a long-time devotee of Amma, to travel across the breadth of the United States in a motor home looking after his four-year-old son and to attend every single program and retreat offered by Amma that summer. This miraculous time ended with seeing Amma off at the airport as she embarked on her European tour. Never has such an opportunity been offered to me since. Of course, with pleasure, I accepted. My incredulous children remained at home, shaking their heads with dismay each time I phoned them from a different American city. What WAS their mother doing now?

Everything turned out fine in the end. The children survived my absence; the house remained intact. I experienced Amma's personal attention many times throughout the summer, as she often stopped in front of me, holding my hands and repeating: "Vedamata, Vedamata, Vedamata!" She so intensely attempted to get her point across, trying to get me to realize that I *was* my name, that the truth lay *within* my being not without. The same with God, for wasn't God the Truth, the whole Truth and nothing but?

I still hadn't got it. Or maybe I just hadn't finished occupying myself with knocking on doors.

Meanwhile, up, up, and away, soaring the highest heights over the Pacific in my comfortable seat on the fancy Singapore Airlines plane, I continued to contemplate my past, which seemed at the time a little more constructive and discreet than contemplating my navel. Something to pass away the long hours other than viewing videos on the mini TV set.

The years had passed. Dorothy had slipped away. Where were her dreams now? She hadn't found that place "where troubles melt like lemon drops, away above the chimney tops . . ." However, that's where Veda Mata was situated now, up in the clouds riding her way to that place somewhere over the rainbow. The mystery and mystique of India were still drawing me. Why did I find it so alluring? What was I seeking that I couldn't find at home?

My family and friends were accusing me of running away from my life and my responsibilities. I was still seeking the extraordinary because the ordinary bored me to tears. And God knew how many of those I had cried over the years. I was tired of being unhappy. I wanted to master this life, find a way to achieve happiness despite the overwhelming and never ending onslaught of 'trouble' that came my way.

I had found my motherhood job extended by the birth of a granddaughter a year and a half before. I had always told my children that when the youngest was nineteen I was going to sign off and take to the hills. I wanted to travel the world, see the sights, meet the people. THERE WAS A WORLD OUT THERE and I wanted to see it. However, the month before my youngest turned nineteen, she told me that she was pregnant. She needed me. Some mothers might have turned their backs and carried on their merry old way. Not me. Duty called. So, I signed on for another stint. How many years more? Was there no mercy for this wretched soul?

When my daughter told me that she was expecting and would be a single mother like myself, I thought I had died and gone to hell. I saw the future stretching out in unending horror in front of us. (And I thought that my mother was negative when she found herself in the same boat with me so many years ago!) I tried to keep my thoughts in my own private corner. Throughout my daughter's pregnancy, I had many dreams where I saw myself as an elephant tethered to a stick in the ground or myself behind bars. Particularly in my daydreams! I saw no way out of motherhood. And I so very much wanted out. I wanted to be free as a bird—free to test my wings, fly to the highest heights, and to perch on whatever branch I chose, particularly one with no nests in sight.

Consequently, I was astounded when my first granddaughter was born and my hell turned into heaven. It was love at first sight. Since then, I hadn't been able to keep my loving hands or mind off her. We were the best of friends, spending almost every weekend together since she was six months old. I thanked my daughter and her boyfriend for being so generous and liberal with me, sharing their precious daughter so trustingly. I hadn't acquired a new babysitting job; I had acquired a new lease on life. It was wonderful to hold a new baby in my arms, a being so close to the heavenly side. I felt renewed and reborn as I opened to every new experience that she had. We were in it together, and I no longer felt so alone.

For a while at least. I had a continual, underlying, gnawing sensation in my psyche. A hint, a whisper in my inner ear prodding me to acknowledge the fact that sooner or later I had to relinquish my 'distraction', no matter now precious, and get on with my search. I began to have dreams about doors, doors, and more doors.

Then, when I attended the Seattle retreat in June and discovered that Amma was celebrating her fiftieth birthday, wanting as many Western devotees as possible to come, I found myself telling people that I was going! Surprise to me.

I entered the pink stucco gates of Amma's ashram in Kerala after getting off the bus sent to pick me up at the airport. Not that I could tell the colour of her ashram at the time of arrival. It was still dark, around three in the morning.

Once again, I had arrived in India around midnight. I felt the most endearing feeling as I exited the doors outside of Arrivals and was hit by that wall of heat and pungent air, filled with the aromatic fragrance of Indian potpourri. I had forgotten how much I loved this place. The organic-ness of it all came back to me.

Welcome back, Dorothy/Veda! One name walked out, another entered! What would happen to me this time round? What cracker box tricks would I find up Destiny's sleeve this trip? I chuckled to myself as I looked around for a sign with my name on it.

I had been informed that there would be someone waiting for me when I arrived. There were other passengers like myself going to Amma's birthday party. I noticed some bedraggled people in white standing together beside a pile of suitcases. I walked over to them and joined in with their chatter. I was correct. It was pretty obvious. Amma radar! An old yellow bus had been sent along with a driver. We left not long after, making our way up the mainland and over onto the peninsula separated by the backwaters of Kerala.

We were all pretty tired. Upon arrival, an attendant who had stayed up to greet us assigned us our rooms. It was very dark and hard to find the way up the elevator of the tall building to the twelfth floor where my room was located. I had been told to bring a flashlight. Without it, I'm not sure I would have been able to read the numbers on the door.

There seemed to already be a few people sleeping on the floor. I found a space over by the wall and climbed over a stack of clothes and baggage to set my things down. I was trying not to make too much noise. One of the women turned over and grumbled, asking if I needed any help. By then I had grown accustomed to the dark. There was a beam of light shining in through the window of the far wall, which cast some light into the room. I said no, then settled myself down on the spare mat, covered myself with a thin bed-sheet that I had brought from home and went to sleep.

I opened my eyes to watch a petite blonde woman tidy her bed. "Hello," I said. "My name is Veda."

"I'm Michelle," she whispered, careful not to wake up the other two women still asleep. "No need to get up yet. It is only six o'clock. I'm going to the shrine room to chant the thousand names of the Divine Mother. Unless you want to come?" she asked.

"No. It's OK. I'll go back to sleep for a while. I'm still very tired. I got in very early this morning and have been travelling for a couple of days."

Michelle left quietly. I sank back into my reverie quite easily. I remember wondering if she came from France. She seemed to have a French accent.

Later that morning, she told me about herself. "I was not happy in France. I was a very successful businesswoman. I also had inherited a large chateau and fortune from my family. After seeing Amma a few times in Paris, I decided to commit myself to the spiritual path. I asked Amma last year if I could come to her ashram in India and become a *sannyasin,* a person who gives up the worldly life and dedicates herself solely to the pursuit of spiritual things. Amma said yes. I came here last April and gave Amma everything that I owned. I hope to live here for the rest of my life and to live a life of service with my beloved Amma."

A bit too much information for me to take in at that moment. Just how much had she given up? Heavens, how could anyone do such a thing? I couldn't. I wondered what would happen if she changed her mind. Would Amma give everything back to her?

Later, I was to perform the first duty of my seva by sweeping the pink steps underneath the overriding statue at the entrance to Amma's shrine. It was a statue of Arjuna driving the chariot with Krishna, directing him towards the battle outlined in the

Bhagavad Gita. The very same steps that I had seen on TV! Amma was to appear around eleven as she did almost every day. I hoped to receive a darshan hug from her. Each evening, she appeared in the large auditorium for bhajans. Afterwards, she led a procession into the compound where she enchanted everyone by feeding her pet elephant, Rama. I was sure to be there to witness that precious scene!

It didn't take long to get into the rhythm and routine of the ashram. Many Indian devotees lived with her; it looked as if the ashram was able to house thousands of people. I wondered how many people lived here year round. I was one of the first of the Westerners to arrive who were coming especially for her birthday celebration.

Onam. At Amma's ashram this holiday celebrated the elephant-god Ganesh, responsible for removing obstacles. I could do with a god like that. Even my own personal trunk-aided genie! Particularly a trunk full of jewels or money! Or a personal pachyderm taxi to drive me around, keeping me out of harm's way!

Not meaning to be sacrilegious; I was letting my imagination and humour run away with me. I was watching Amma feeding her baby elephant special food for the occasion. Onam was a universally observed festival in Kerala, celebrating the annual return of the legendary King Mahabali. All over the state, people of all religions had closed shop and were out in the streets, decked in new clothes, celebrating what is like a New Year's Day for them—food, dance, music, all particular to this day. A man in the elevator told me the story:

Many long centuries ago, a famous and kindly king ruled a very peaceful and prosperous nation. Everyone had all that they needed and there was no need for amorality. There was no theft, nor violence; everyone was happy and well taken care of. They loved their neighbours because they had a loving king who could refuse no one's needs. Everyone followed his example and all was shared amongst the people.

One day, the god Vishnu decided to come down to earth disguised as a mortal and test the king by making a request. He asked the king for three steps of land and of course the king could not refuse him, being the generous king that he was. Suddenly, Vishnu grew long legs. His first step covered all the earth and his second the heavens. Some people say his third step encompassed all the hells. Others say that the king offered his forehead, which Vishnu stepped on, and the king died. He went to the underworld, asking only that he might return one day a year to visit his beloved people, who loved him very much. That day is Onam.

Today, everyone would be out in the streets dressed in their finery, to celebrate the return of their beloved king. There were to be many festivities. The streets were all decorated with hanging palms in the shape of blossoms, as well as many hanging strings of flowers.

Amma was sitting on the stage in the large auditorium of her ashram, speaking to a sea of faces. She was dressed in white, in contrast to the many Indian women in splendid multi-coloured silk saris, looking like emanations of the divine rainbow, many of whom were sitting cross-legged on the cement floor, perfectly comfortable, with their faces beaming up at her. Like thousands of small children waiting expectantly in front of their beloved parent, the faces of the men and women were filled with innocent, open trust and obedience. It was impossible to describe the delightful effect. One could never view anything like this at home.

The attention of the crowd was undivided—all eyes and ears fixated on the words of their beloved guru delivering a New Year's message equivalent to that of the Pope for the Catholics or the Dalai Lama for the Buddhists. She was a great saint for millions of people here, far away from her meagre beginnings. Then she had lived in the streets, as an outcast by both her parents and the people of her village, fed by the animals and attended by only a handful of devotees who believed that she was a living incarnation of the Divine Mother.

Now millions flocked to receive her sacred hugs and to witness the showering of love and healing that are derivatives of her Divine presence. Her darshan left one touched to tears and humbled by the experience of her generosity and compassion. A touch from her has the power to change a life forever—for the good. She has the power to awaken us to our own Divinity. Jesus said that he and his Father were one. I am able to understand his words and experience the possibility of that within myself every time I find myself in Amma's presence.

After chanting *Aum* three times along with Amma, the crowd entered into a transcendent bhajan. Imagine thousands of hearts and minds merged into solitary attention and song, a unifying resonance matching Amma's omniscient attention—heart, body, mind and voice. Such exquisite beauty is incomprehensible to the secular, linear mind of the West. This most certainly was an incredible experience, unparalleled by anything I had been exposed to at home. People don't gather together in such large crowds unless they are attending sports events!

It is very common in India to see people flocking to see their 'living saints'. It is said that one solitary darshan with a holy saint purifies the karma of thousands of lifetimes, accelerating one's process towards enlightenment—the merging back to Oneness. Seeking and achieving ultimate happiness, joy and union with the almighty One is a common goal for the Hindus, verified and exemplified by the presence of such great souls as Amma.

Amma was continuing to communicate with her enchanted audience. Even the Westerners who couldn't understand her Malayalam were giving her their rapt attention, absorbing her every word on a vibrational level. The crowd had begun to move, clapping and singing along with their rejoicing leader, soliciting God's loving attention and guidance. Having once heard her voice, one never forgets its throaty resonance filled with a magnificent vibration that affects every cell of the body, permeating one's essential being-ness. Amma relished these times with her children. She was completely absorbed as she clapped and sang: *"Jai, jai, jai, Gopala!"* She masterfully worked with the vibration of everyone, bringing the energy of every single participant into harmony with her own.

It was impossible to capture the mood of the crowd in words. It was extremely charismatic. I joined in as everyone gathered around Amma. Waving my arms in the air to the rhythm of her clinking hand chimes, I realized that together we were all experiencing the ecstasy of Divine energy. As it rose to a frenzy, Amma danced around in front of us as if in a trance. What better way to spend time on earth than to mark the universal time and rhythm with a saint's dancing, or should I say, with the dancing of the Divine Mother?

Once the dance was finished, Mother sank onto the floor and went into a deep meditative state. The juxtaposition of the heightened energy against the notable silence was awe-inspiring. Thousands watched as Mother sat communing with energies and elements far beyond our lowly human dimension and understanding.

I did not consider myself gullible or deluded. I was experiencing something very tangible. All the aches and pains that I had started the day with (which were considerable, considering I was sleeping on an almost bare floor with only an inch of padding between my body and the cement!) seemed to have vanished. My mind was extremely clear and spirits bright. Whatever was happening was having a good effect upon this middle-aging body.

A few minutes later I noticed many people scurrying towards the stage. Just by happenstance, being nearby, I joined the parade towards the ramp that led onto it. I found myself caught in the steady stream of bodies rushing up to receive a hug from Amma. I did not possess a darshan ticket. Consequently, I was ushered into a space on the floor no more than an arm's length away from Amma. I was delightfully surprised at my luck and remained, fortunately, close to Mother for the duration of the three-quarter hour darshan.

I tried to push my luck by asking to have my new sandalwood *mala* blessed, but the attendants encouraged me to wait until another day when there would be more time. Amma was like a queen, having arrived to remind us of another time, Utopian-like, when all was love, peace and harmony in the world. I replaced the mala around my neck, feeling the radiance of her blessings just by being so close to her. This truly was a blessed and memorable day for me.

The day ended with a procession of young men carrying a *papier-mâché* statue of Ganesh, the Hindu deity responsible for removing obstacles, out of the ashram and down the road to the ocean. The men led the procession, with everyone following out towards the sea just on the other side of the village. People came out of their huts to watch the parade go by and some of them even joined in the fun. The men carried the statue a fair distance out into the ocean. The waves appeared quite strong and high. At some point, the statue fell off and everyone let out a hoot and started clapping and jumping up and down.

The men stayed in the water to have a good swim since they were already wet. The current was extremely dangerous. I felt uneasy and worried about them. As I watched the guys thrash around in the waves, I remembered a Reiki student of mine who had come to visit Amma, who had died in the ocean not far from her ashram. He was a lovely young man—a Polish fellow with dark hair and vibrant blue eyes—who had inquired about going to visit Amma a few years back. I was very fond of him and appreciated his ardent and eager attention to spiritual things. I encouraged him to go visit her when he went to India. A few months later I heard the tragic story of his drowning. I felt reasonably responsible. However, I guess that it was his time to go. What better way to depart than within close proximity of such a Divine presence?

Thousands upon thousands of Indian people had been sitting and lying about on the stadium grounds for days. They had come to witness and participate in the Amritavarsham 50, the Golden Jubilee Birthday Celebrations of Sri Mata Amritanandamayi Devi. Organizers were expecting more than a million people over the next five days. The papers were full of articles proclaiming the event. It was probably the most significant thing that had happened in the Cochin area since the arrival of the spice traders from Europe hundreds of years ago!

Most of the daily events excluded the crowds. Important meetings and programs had been set up involving selected representatives from around India and beyond. Every evening Amma appeared on stage to witness the various cultural events, followed by darshan. The Westerners were told that there would be NO hugs for them during the celebration. We had already had our fair share of hugs beforehand at her ashram.

I found myself floundering in the sea of people and sought retreat in my hotel room, feeling at cross-purposes with my being there in the first place. Although it was fascinating to see how Indians congregated so peacefully and co-operatively in masses, the whole situation proved too overwhelming for me. I had a tendency to disengage in large crowds.

I had never experienced anything of this magnitude. Family upon family set up camps on the grounds remaining there as if 'at home' for the duration of the event. The organization required to accommodate so many people was amazing. Just thinking about the water and food facilities needed to take care of everyone was mind-boggling. Amma's people did a remarkable job, everything going without a hitch. The police worked gently and agreeably with the crowds, making their presence felt in case of any emergency or terrorist activity. 9/11 was only two years in the past and still in the forefront of everyone's minds. There was always a possibility of disruption, but it seemed that Amma's protective intention surrounded the site with peace and harmony. The event happened miraculously without serious incident.

The Westerners, having registered by Internet at home, were placed in various hotels around the city not far from the stadium grounds. After living in the cramped quarters of the ashram having only one roommate and a double mattress bed was a luxury. There had been six of us in one tiny room the two weeks before the event. One of the women in my room was a psychiatrist from New York who assumed a privileged position, taking most of the space and regulating the breeze through the windows. She had undertaken a *panchakarma* program, a series of healing and detoxifying oil massages, whereby she couldn't be exposed to any drafts. Consequently, the heat and smell of the room became quite intolerable. I felt suffocated under the heat of a pressure cooker, waiting for tempers to flare. However, Amma's energy quelled the undercurrent flames amongst us.

Space at the ashram had become minimal. Hundreds of Western devotees arrived day after day. Amma must have been very pleased at our response to her call for a strong Western contingency. However, the delicious quiet that I had first experienced upon arrival soon vanished as the chatter, excitement and flurry of activity grew around me.

Unnerved, I moved across the backwater channel to a small village for some respite a few days before the celebration. It was quite a novelty being transported back and forth by the ferry-boatmen and native villagers with their dug-out palm canoes driven by long poles that were stuck into the bottom mud to move the boats along. I was later informed that there were poisonous snakes in the waters! So glad I didn't fall in.

There were two sides to the story. I found my mind waffling between the two, not sure how much responsibility I should take for the fact that I did not enjoy Amma's fiftieth birthday party. Near the end of the five days, while thousands were absorbing her Divine radiance, I found myself hightailing out of the area and her presence as fast as I could, making my way up to Darjeeling

I had read somewhere, I think Osho said it, that "Knowing

happens to those eyes which are absolutely without the dust of knowledge . . ." and "The prejudiced eye is blind; the heart full of conclusions dead." Maybe I had come with a head full of expectations. Amma had dangled a carrot in front of us, offering a new meditation technique if we came. I had been practicing her mantra, but for the last year had been feeling at a stalemate regarding my spiritual development. I was craving a certain unidentifiable something. My dissatisfaction prompted me to seek more stimulation and engagement. I had been feeling pressure to 'move along' in my process.

I had thought maybe her I AM technique would suit the bill. I was extremely disappointed when I went through the rather lengthy and arduous two-day class to find myself already very familiar with the visualizations. Possibly, the combination held Mother's energy that would activate a deeper response within me. I had expected a new mantra and felt 'gypped' when none was offered. I encouraged myself to be patient, to give the meditation a fair chance to take hold.

My heart felt resistance and my mind craved something less informational. A long time ago, my father wrote me in his last and only letter: "The heart has reason which reason can't understand." I had always trusted my intuitive heart intelligence. In this case, my reason was also in accord and the strong dialogue between the two encouraged me to let go of Amma for a while.

Besides the severe disappointment in both the meditation technique and the event, my body felt extremely uncomfortable around the hordes of people circulating around Amma. The energetic attraction, magnetic perhaps, no longer held. I gave way to the release and gave myself permission to 'let go and let God'. I bought myself a train ticket north in hopes of exploring, once again, my Buddhist connection.

The little toy train sat waiting expectantly for its eager passengers to board—like "The Little Train That Could" in the children's book, I thought, grinning with amusement, imagining a broad smile stretched across the face of the blue steam engine in front of me. I stepped up into the miniature passenger car and found my seat with pleasure. Plunking down my bag underneath the worn burgundy velvet seat, I figured that this train had well surpassed the original intentions of its designers a hundred years ago. The toy train to Darjeeling was one of a few such remaining steam-powered trains left in India from the colonial days of the Raj. How many aristocratic families had climbed the same steps and entered into the same carriage, heading up to the popular 'king' of hill stations to escape the unrelenting heat? I was boarding the train in Siliguri, a town at the foot of the mountains. I was informed that it would take around eight or nine hours to make its way to the top.

I discovered myself sitting with a charming family from the Punjab who were holidaying in Darjeeling for the Durga festival, a nine-day celebration of the goddess Durga and her many emanations. The festival would commence with the celebration of Lakshmi, the Goddess of Abundance, and would include a re-enactment of destruction by the wrathful goddess Kali in her war against the negative forces. The square in the centre of town would hold a token sacrifice of a goat in commemoration of the blood spilt in the war, followed by the Day of the Tika, when everyone would receive a spot of vermilion powder in the centre of their forehead to signify the victory of Good over Evil. I felt overjoyed to be arriving along with all the other holidaymakers. There was a very festive mood within the coach. I looked forward to being a spectator at this festival, anticipating learning more about the Indian culture first hand.

I sat back in my heritage compartment and relaxed. It had been a long and tiresome journey. Closing my eyes, resting, thankful that I had made my way safely so far, I reviewed the last three days. I had spent the entire time in a 2AC, or two-tiered, air-conditioned sleeper compartment on the Howrah Express from Trivandrum, Kerala, to Calcutta in West Bengal. It actually continued on through Siliguri (where I descended to catch the toy train) into the eastern province of Assam, but I believe its name changed after leaving Calcutta.

I had occupied myself fairly well doing my Buddhist Ngondro meditation practices and simple yoga exercises I had recently learned. The people in the seats opposite marvelled at the contortions I accomplished on the bottom berth, despite the limited space! I only did a few simple postures but the people were quite unfamiliar with hatha yoga. (Or the yoga system for that matter. Apparently, to my surprise, not all Indians were versed in traditional spiritual practices or religious texts such as the *Upanishads*, wherein the means for attaining Self-realization are expounded. Sadly, I recognized that modern Indians seem to be leaving their roots behind in much the same way that other cultures have done.) Such exercise was necessary because I didn't get out of the train to walk around except at a couple of stations, nervous that the train would leave without me.

Regardless, I was becoming quite an acclimatized and adept train passenger! I had purchased 'Trains on the Go', a schedule of departures and arrivals of all the trains throughout India. I had used the last few days to become familiar with it and study its map. I loved maps, so this was a pleasure I indulged in quite often over the long hours aboard. I was tremendously proud of myself, having come a long way (in more ways than one) since my last trip to this intriguing country.

The Howrah Express was extremely different than the miniature passenger train I presently found myself in. The express train had many types of coaches, from first- and second-class air-conditioned to the regular cattle-car type of passenger coach, all ranging in price. I had discovered that the 2AC was very clean and convenient. Freshly laundered sheets and blankets were provided, along with meals that you could purchase at a very cheap price. I only ordered the evening thali, eating usually once a day when travelling, if at all. (To avoid 'loose running', better known as dysentery, it was better to decline food *en route* since bathroom conditions were often horrendous. On bus trips one usually had to hitch up one's skirt and pee, etc., in the ditch! As a white woman travelling, this provided unending mirth and amusement to the Indian passengers who watched, entranced, through the dirty or open bus windows.) On trains, however, hawkers came around regularly with containers of coffee or chai, which I enjoyed and which had no adverse side effects.

I had also discovered that educated Indian people rode in the 2AC; consequently I participated in a variety of interesting conversations along the way. Very few people, it seemed, undertook the lengthy trip from bottom to top like myself. Three days on an Indian train was no one's idea of a good time! Except, possibly, mine.

My train of thought had been shattered by the screeching of the locomotive's brakes. The train stopped. We sat. For how long, or for what, we knew not!

It was hot. We still were not far up the hill towards Darjeeling. We had been chugging slowly along for about two-and-a-half hours. A conductor dressed in a traditional English conductor's uniform, black suit with a black and gold striped pill-box hat, entered the coach. "Ladies and gentlemen, we are unfortunately delayed because of a break in the tracks that will need repair. Please descend the train and wait for a return engine to take you back to the Siliguri station." With that, he went on to the second and last car.

Everyone started chattering; the Indians descended and congregated in groups trying to sort out who would join whom in the four-wheel-drive vehicles parked outside the station. There seemed to be some sort of organized system people adhered to on such occasions. I, unfortunately, was out of the loop and left to wait for an unknown amount of time until the return locomotive arrived.

Breaking my habit, I approached a vendor selling strips of cucumber with salt and bought a few slices. It was juicy and would quench my thirst as well as satisfy my appetite. Hopefully, that would be all. There appeared to be no available public washrooms in this remote station. Rural villages in India do not compare to country towns in Canada. I didn't relish going over to ask the occupants in the neighbouring mud houses (huts?) if I could use the facilities. My guess was that they would direct me to the road to take care of my business.

We chugged our way down the hill with much less anticipation than on the upward climb. My enthusiasm seemed to wane as the sun rose higher in the mid-day sky and the temperature in the coach mounted. I mused upon a poem I had once read ("The Stage Coach and the Steam Carriage" by Victorian poet Charles Mackay), raving about the glory of railway travel:

> O luxury of travel! joy refined!
> To fly steam-harnessed, in the ponderous train,
> And feel the victory of mighty Mind
> O'er space and time, for uses not in vain!
> Yet ever in this world must loss and pain
> Balance each other. Is it speed we prize?

It was all relative (and so innocent back then). Mackay measured progress from the turning of the wheel of the horse and cart to the glorious steam engine. What about the Concord, Space Travel, computer technology, or nuclear missiles? It seemed that I was going backwards in more ways than one as I retraced the rails back to Siliguri. There was no hurrying progress here!

I found myself drifting with the rhythm of the wheels on the tracks, as the Wheel of Life churned its way around in my psyche. Was there really any such thing as progress? Was I heading in a particular direction or not? Was I deluding myself that there was such a thing as enlightenment? Maybe I was just involved in a make-work project to keep myself occupied, since I really hadn't come up with anything more interesting to do. What was I supposed to do with this body in time until the end of this lifetime? Did it really matter?

The Wheel of Dharma. What did Buddha say? His first teaching after he got up from the Bodhi tree, walked to Varanasi, sat down, and touched the earth as his witness was that life was an endless wheel of suffering. We could either stay whirling around within its incessant grasp or we could use our will and set our intention to step off the Wheel of Karma to determine our own course. He spent the next forty-five years of his life refining his teachings as to how a person could go about doing that.

Amma's path was devotional. She elicited our heart's surrender as a course to the Divine. By practising selfless service and letting God in to play out Him/Her/Itself through us, our ego would step aside for the greater soul to act out its true purpose. LOVE on earth. She also asked us to come to her through meditation and feed upon her delicious love as often as we could remember her name. Such was Amma's intention. I had heard it before. Very much like Jesus's covenant to 'love each other as ourselves' and 'come to Him' as often as we were able, through the sacrament of communion.

My hunger for mental sustenance continued to gnaw me to the bone. This 'heart path' was valid but I couldn't ignore my resistance. Maybe I was what the Buddhist called a 'hungry ghost', greedy for knowledge, with an insatiability for mental nourishment that could possibly never be fulfilled. I, however, trusted my intuition and wanted to *understand* the spiritual process. I longed for a mentor to sit with, like my father in my adolescence. I also had a craving for efficiency, feeling that I had wasted too much time already in distraction. Maybe I did need to go through all those years of motherhood, its delights as well as its agonies. It was hard to see the forest though the trees, or the growth through all that chaos. I really did want a definite 'line' to follow that engaged the mind. I valued the mind for its strength and clarity—an invaluable instrument to gauge the course. I refused to think of it as a detriment rather than an asset. I wanted to exercise its muscles and develop its strength. I didn't want my mental capacity to atrophy in case I needed it in the future. I loved Amma but devotion and surrender weren't enough to satisfy this soul. The male aspect, which I equated with mental intention, needed recognition and validation. Then again, I might have been underestimating Amma's scope. I had heard that she was omniscient and omnipotent. For all I knew,

Amma might have been orchestrating this part of my journey. I chose to believe so.

The next segment of the journey to Darjeeling became very much a comedy of errors. I disembarked from the little toy train rather disoriented. I had no plan B in place. The rickshaw I solicited was in tatters, the cloth stripped off the weathered wooden skeleton of a hood, the bicycle itself in not much better condition. A tire did go flat heading over to the area allocated as the bus station. Because I had no idea where that was, I hesitated to trudge over on foot. Besides, it must have been 40 degrees Centigrade. It was hot. I didn't want to disappoint the driver; he had fought so hard to beat the other drivers to my feet. From the looks of him and his contraption, he hadn't succeeded in convincing too many people lately to pay for his services. I wondered if they had success seminars for rickshaw drivers.

The bus station turned out to be only two blocks away. For all the time it took, I could have walked and saved myself half an hour of waiting. It was well past mid-day by then. I began to worry about getting up the mountain before dark, not liking to arrive anywhere after the sun went down. Just taking precautions. Shirley MacLaine coined the phrase 'Don't Fall Off The Mountain'. Well, I surely didn't want to do that. The road looked as if it were going to be pretty steep. I also was aware of the reckless tactics of Indian drivers.

Unfortunately, I was unsuccessful locating a bus going to Darjeeling. Everything was in Hindi and people were not very helpful. After about an hour of going around in circles lugging my baggage, I sat down on a bench. Noticing over the way that there was a bustle of people around a few Land Rovers filled with passengers, all with luggage stacked and tied on their hoods, I made my way in that direction quite hopeful that I would find one going north.

It was 2:30 p.m. Nine hundred rupees ($30) later I found myself scrunched between the driver on the right and an army

Captain in his late thirties on my left. There were a couple of families—children, parents, and grandparents—squished in the back. No seat belts. The driver seemed pressed for time, already going well over an acceptable speed limit.

For a while we were on a paved road heading along with the buses and cars. Then, suddenly the driver had an idea, muttered something out loud, and swerved off to the left, onto a dirt road. I turned and frowned at the Captain. "What is he doing?" I asked.

"I'm not sure."

He started speaking very fast to the young driver, who couldn't have been more than eighteen years old. I had a premonition that I had trustingly gotten myself into something that I couldn't get out of—the same feeling I had when I entered labour with my first child. The Captain spoke again. His voice was deep and resonant. I found that reassuring when he said: "He wants to get to Darjeeling quickly because he has to get back down to Siliguri before nightfall. He is concerned about driving down in the dark."

"Oh. So where is he going?" I was feeling less than confident.

"He knows a shortcut. We are heading over to it," said the Captain curtly, as if it were unnecessary to talk about it any further.

I was holding on to the edge of the seat, too afraid to keep my eyes open and too afraid to close them. I never even went on rides at the fair as a kid. What was I doing here? If it weren't for the Captain beside me, I was sure I would be having a heart attack. We were going the wrong way on a one-way gravel road, heading straight up! The distance down the cliff on the left was increasing with every spinning of the wheels and shooting of the gravel stones behind us. The dust in the vehicle was making it hard to breathe and the windshield was getting cloudy. The driver was speeding along as if he were having a 'whale of a time', like my son used to ride on his bicycle when he was ten. Why do the incorrigible youth think they are so invincible?

Hopefully, he had an angel on his shoulder because I didn't know what we would do on one of the switchback curves if we met any oncoming vehicles, particularly trucks. We did. I thought I was going to die of heart failure—the same terror I felt in Disneyland when my kids coerced me to go on the 'Splash Mountain' ride against my better judgment. I left my body out of sheer terror the last descent of the ride. I swore NEVER to get myself in a similar predicament. Ha! Served me right for swearing!

Every cell in my body was terrified. I rode on the strength exuding from the Captain, sure that he was used to orchestrating his troops through precarious manoeuvres such as the one we found ourselves in. He gave the driver directions as we inched our way past the brightly painted truck on our right, which had the privilege of the mountain face, while we had the company of the side cliff taunting our nerves with its invitation to carry us down thousands of feet to the bottom.

Not again, I thought. This day was becoming a live reproduction of the childhood game 'Snakes and Ladders'.

"Please, dear God, get us through this," I pleaded. "Today really isn't a good day to die!"

"Ever heard of the Rainbow Light teaching?" I timidly asked the lama who was running the hotel where I was staying.

Last evening when we had arrived in Darjeeling, I had found myself led up a steep path behind a Nepali woman porter who had my bag hitched to a piece of leather strapped across her forehead, over her shoulders, and down her back. Not unlike the Sherpas of the Himalayan hill region near the borders of Tibet that I had once seen in the *National Geographic* magazine. She had set my things down on the cement stairs of a yellow building mentioned as low budget accommodation in my dear friend the Lonely Planet guide, a friendly place run by an honest Tibetan man.

The lama was more concerned about looking in the guidebook to see if he was still in it. I had purchased the latest edition before I left Canada. With a relieved look on his face, after having found a favourable description of his hotel, he shrugged his shoulders.

"I'm not a real lama, although my father was. I'm not a practicing Buddhist. I just manage this hotel for the Tibetan woman upstairs." He glanced up the steep flight of narrow, red-painted cement steps to the floor above. "Maybe she can help you. She knows a Rinpoche with a *gompa* (monastery) near by. I'll ask her," he added, tilting his head to one side and smiling broadly at me.

I thought that he was sizing me up, for what particular reason I knew not but could probably guess. His train of thought didn't look particularly spiritual. I got the feeling he was attracted to me (or possibly attracted to thoughts of possibilities . . .).

I had asked him the question because it was one of the things that had top priority on my list regarding Buddhist inquiries. I had spent the better part of the long train journey from South India doing my Ngondro practice, the preliminary text for the Dzogchen teaching, the highest teaching of the Tibetan Buddhist tradition, known as the Lightning Path. I had high hopes that I would be able to find a teacher to instruct me in it. I'd recently read a book by a fellow doing his doctoral research who had met some incredible Dzogchen masters living in the hills around Darjeeling. I hoped to do the same.

I had met a young Bhutanese lama at home who was overseeing students there in the preliminary practice, but not able to initiate people into the Dzogchen teachings. His teacher, Ganteng Tulku Rinpoche, lived in Bhutan, a small country perched between Nepal, India, and China, just north of Darjeeling and Sikkim. Bhutan was, as yet, relatively inaccessible to foreigners, protecting itself from Western influence. It would be hard and expensive for me to visit the Rinpoche. As I sought individual attention, it seemed impractical to continue on with the people in Victoria.

Was I still the girl chasing rainbows, looking for her La-La Land? You bet! Why wouldn't a person be fascinated by the possibility of dissolving into rainbow light when she died, leaving only fingernails and toenails behind?

In fact, it had been a standing joke in my family that I would make things easy for my children when I passed—something that would save on funeral costs or funerary preparations. Nor were they to expect any grand inheritance, just a pile of toenails and fingernails! However, if they were present when I expired, they would be party to a spectacular light show comparable to the one I treated them to in Disneyland on my forty-fifth birthday, when we all stood eyes gazing upwards to the incredible firework display in the night sky as we left Fantasyland, where we had spent the day. I only asked that they didn't fight over my nails and that they distribute these relics evenly and fairly amongst themselves and any children that they might have!

Of course, each of my children had doubts about my sanity, all three mutually coming to the conclusion that their mother was just plain 'weird'! They put thoughts of me in some hide-away drawer in their minds and got on with their lives. I, needless to say, had left them behind.

The Rainbow Light teaching was not a fantasy. It had been described in a book by Namkhai Norbu Rinpoche, a notable Tibetan scholar and teacher situated at the University of Milan in Italy. He had written a book that someone had placed into my hands when I first became a Reiki Master. The synchronicity of the two events had not gone unnoticed. I had been interested in pursuing the search for the Dzogchen teaching since then.

I had asked around in Dharamsala while I was in India last time, but all the monks seemed very secretive and told me that the Dalai Lama didn't teach it. They told me to go to the Namdroling Monastery in South India. I didn't have time, so had promised myself to continue the search the next time I came to India. I hoped to go to the southern monastery when I returned for my flight home; however, no harm asking around in Darjeeling.

I had been practicing the Ngondro religiously and was now at 7,000 mantra repetitions of the Vajrasattva, the purifying section of the preliminary exercise. Ganteng Rinpoche was asking Westerners to finish only 10,000 each of the five sections of the practice, rather than the usual 100,000, before he gave the empowerment and practice to the first part of the Dzogchen teaching. I was in a very clear and strong space, anticipating finishing the whole practice before I went south. Maybe Penor Rinpoche could help me, being the presiding Rinpoche at the same monastery the monks from Dharamsala had spoken about.

"Do you recognize this Ngondro Practice?"

I handed the booklet to a short, maroon-clad lama in the parlour of the Tibetan hotel owner. He was standing beside me while she was sitting on a blue-and-gold-carpeted seat across from me. I held my breath, quite excited that I may, at long last, have a lead on a Dzogchen master.

He looked at it intently, turning it over a couple of times, browsing through its pages. It was obviously well worn, being already three years old and used almost daily since I had been given it. He was silent for a few minutes, then looked up and stared blankly at me. "These are just ordinary prayers. Not special. Not Dzogchen," he said, quietly and precisely.

What? How could he say that? Not after the hours and hours I had spent practicing them. "Are you sure?"

"Yes," he replied. He sat down, and another woman, a friend of the hostess, handed the lama a cup of tea. I already had mine.

My eager bubble of enthusiasm was instantly deflated. Whatever connection I had had to the practice immediately vanished. I experienced a jolt of anger. Had I been fooled? Were Westerners being tricked into practices that were being extolled as incredibly important, when all the while these Tibetan teachers were laughing all the way to the bank with their handfuls of Western money that would pay for the restoration of their ancient monasteries, promising us the limitless skies while tethering us instead to our gullibility and naïveté? How would we ever know?

"My Rinpoche will be coming here in the near future. If you would like to meet him, we could arrange it. He works with a group of women, including these two women, hoping to build a gompa in Darjeeling. If you stay, you could join them with their studies. If you would be so kind as to help us when you go back to America, we would appreciate it. If you would be our sponsor, we would be so happy!"

See? Here we go again. Were they all just opportunists? Maybe they were just very smart, recognizing the value of their knowledge and unwilling to impart it freely. Maybe it was the Westerner who was the opportunist? Myself?

I left all three sipping their tea and eating Indian biscuits as I made my exit downstairs. I bowed politely with my hands in prayer position at my heart.

"Thank you," I said before I turned, stooped to avoid knocking my head, and thoughtfully made my way back down the red steps to my room. What to do now?

After that, I found myself completely unable to do my Ngondro prayers and at a bit of a loss as to which direction I should take with my inquiry while still in the hill city.

The next morning, I got up very early to climb to the top of the hill behind the hotel to watch the sunrise. Situated near the equator, Indian sunrises and sunsets occurred around six o'clock. I proceeded up past the youth hostel, resting at the top, perched on a stone listening to the morning song of the birds. How peaceful it was; so good to feel this close to the earth. At home I was always walking on concrete and the sounds of the birds were drowned out by the noise of all the motors, cars, buses, boats, etc. How I longed to live in the country away from all the sonorous commotion of the city.

As the sun came up over the hills across the way, I turned to see the morning sun hit the snowy peak of the third highest mountain in the world, Mount Khangchendzonga (formerly Kanchenjunga). Its 8,598-metre towering peak dominated the skyline. Then I headed into town towards a lovely remnant of the Raj, Glenary's tearoom and bakery, overlooking the valley and mountain range. I would nestle into a white wicker armchair, order toast and fine Darjeeling tea served in a century-old silver tea set, and write in my journal. After that, I would revisit the Kashmiri shop to purchase two jackets emblazoned with colourful Kashmiri-silk embroidery, exquisite and unique.

My plan seemed a lovely way to spend a morning, avoiding the hordes of Indian tourists celebrating the Durga festival. I had hoped to participate in some of the festivities, but had missed the public events. During the day, the rituals seemed to be happening behind closed doors, and in the afternoons, the crowds came out to congregate in the square, eating and taking their children on pony rides. Wanting to consider myself a seasoned traveller rather than a tourist, I found that mulling amid the holiday masses threatened my freshly cultivated traveller's identity.

Also, for some reason, I was beginning to feel disengaged and restless. Everything seemed to be happening at an arm's length from me. The encroachment of a pervasive fear was scratching at my inner comfort. There was a growing sense of unease. I realized that without a pre-planned agenda, the tentativeness of what I would do next was becoming disturbing. I didn't want to settle in Darjeeling, although it was tempting to stay and join the ladies under the direction of the Rinpoche. The need to keep on the move was strong.

My restlessness was double-edged. It wasn't until I got home and went to my doctor that I learned about the psychotic side effects of the antimalarial drugs I was taking.

No, I couldn't look out the open window one minute more at all the piles of feces lined up along the sides of the road, or see one more Indian squatting with 'loose running' pouring out of his bottom. This was absolutely the most disgusting thing that I had ever witnessed. Even when I closed my eyes, I was revolted. This was worse than any horror show I'd ever heard about. Even the women in the distance were squatting with their skirts hoisted up. "What horrible fertilizer for their crops," I admonished under my breath from my Western ethnocentric bandstand seat! People back home were not going to believe it when I told them about this.

On the road again! What would I see next in this multi-faced panoramic mirror of India? The worst of the worst. Where was the best of the best? I was on the road to Bodhgaya from Patna, where I had arrived by train in the rain from Siliguri. I thought I'd been shafted by a cab driver who had taken me to a tourist office (re-run!) and then over to a bus, all the while wading through mucky, muddy clay up to our ankles. I was sure that I had paid too much. It cost far more than the train ticket down here; the distance was only about a quarter of the way. My sandals were completely covered in an inch of dried mud. I was not a happy camper nor a satisfied customer. Just a cantankerous, cranky passenger.

I was shoved against the bus window, regretting my persistence, having argued with the man beside me over who would get the window seat. I had thought that I needed the air because I knew that as the day wore on it would get very hot, regardless of the rain. I'd thought the breeze would be cool and refreshing. Mistake. It stank. And the guy beside me kept trying to cop a feel. Every time he inched his fingers onto my thigh, I glared at him and brushed them off. Would this ride never be over?

And then, the next morning, I encountered a crippled young man who laid a bouquet of long-stemmed lotus blossoms at my feet while I was sitting at the outside tea stall, taking my morning cup of sweet chai. He approached me from a distance, where there was a wooden cart laden with purple and white flowers piled high, attached to half a bicycle which I presumed he rode. He limped towards me grinning from ear to ear, shyly carrying a bouquet of pristine white lotus flowers tied up with a string. Just as he stood in front of me, he stooped over and laid the bunch neatly on the dusty ground in front of my chair. I stared at him trying to figure out what I was supposed to do. Other people around me were watching, some of them chuckling, bemused. I reached into my bag to get a few rupee notes for him, but he had already turned and limped hurriedly off, dragging his bad leg behind him. Didn't even turn around. Just lifted his arm and waved his hand in a backwards fashion to say good-bye as he went off back towards the cart. What was I supposed to make of that?

Bodhgaya touched me. In a precious way. It appeared as the pearl in the centre of a dung heap. Quite literally. Bihar was the poorest state in India. I had experienced India's poverty, but this region seemed emphatically barren. I did not know how people survived. Nothing looked fertile. Just flat, colourless, and scorched.

I was staying in the Nepalese Tibetan Monastery Guesthouse. It was unusually clean and quiet. The rooms were vacant except for one, occupied by an American doctor who had just arrived from Kathmandu. Otherwise, the corridors were empty. The doctor was there to set up a free infirmary for the people of Bodhgaya. India provided no medical insurance system as at home in Canada; people were far too poor to pay for medical care or hospitalization. As per custom, religious institutions and spiritual teachers set up free medical facilities for the people here.

The doctor's Rinpoche, or root guru, would be arriving later in the season, closer to December. Many teachers from Tibet, who lived in the Himalayan regions of northern India and Nepal, escaped the mountain cold by coming to the flatlands during the winter months. I had been marvelling at the beautifully painted murals along the walls of the shrine room when I met the doctor on the steps, and had learned this information as we exchanged a few pleasantries, but it was apparent he was particularly busy and didn't have time to talk. He was the first Westerner I had met since I got on the train two weeks ago in Kerala. Much to my chagrin, at the time of our meeting, he wasn't interested in chatting; I would have liked to have learned more about Bodhgaya from him.

As it was, there were only the pesky guides to resort to for information. They only wanted money, even though they fronted with friendliness. I was becoming wary and overwhelmed by their need.

I had my tour of Gautama Buddha's territory: I stood on the edge of the river and viewed the hill where Buddha had fasted and the forest where he had lived; I saw the banks of the Falgu river where the maid approached and offered him his first meal of milk; I surveyed this river he walked across and circumambulated the temple stupa harbouring a golden Buddha, stopping to marvel at the Bodhi tree under which he sat for forty days and meditated—there he became enlightened. I joined many pilgrims sitting under the granddaughter tree of the original one (the mother being in Sri Lanka) and collected some Bodhi leaves which I have to this day. Finally, I walked around the area visiting all the monasteries and temples constructed by the various Buddhist countries and stood gazing at the incredible 80-foot, marble seated statue of Buddha, attributed to the Japanese contingent, which the Dalai Lama had unveiled in 1989.

I did my rounds impressed by the sacred energy that seemed to permeate the area. Feeling blessed, I slept soundly at night regardless of the stifling heat. Each morning on rising, I was genuinely glad that I had survived the unpleasant journey from Patna to experience this recollection of Buddha's beginnings.

SUFFERING. Somewhere between poverty, sickness, old age, death and man's inhumanity to man, people dream of glory. Ever hopeful of clawing their way out of the muck and mire of human existence, humans search for meaning and method. The compassionate self extends itself to others for relief. We share each other's burdens to make the load lighter. Happiness looms on the horizon of the psyche as an ever-present carrot dangling in the wind or a flag of redemption hoisted on the masts of our consciousness, blowing with divine grace for those who surrender to its call.

We believe in happiness and know it is possible. Everyone strives to keep the baby laughing. As parents, we seek the best for our children, trying to keep them out of harm's way. We do not want them to suffer, or rather, we try to extend the grace-filled period of innocence for them by sheltering the young from the storm until they have developed the skills and means to deal with the responsibilities and choices of the adult world. We try to steer them in the right direction by giving them a set of values so that their choices will not bring harm to themselves or others.

Religions are filled with laws and doctrines to control the chaos and to maintain a relative order, keeping the lid on suffering. Are they healing aids, slings, crutches, to assuage and remedy the woundedness, or glasses, binoculars, telescopes and microscopes to bring clarity to the vision of our divinity and the gap between its presence and the relative reality of our humanity? An age-old question deliberated upon by many an intelligent mind.

Enter Buddha. Born in the fifth century in Northern India, Siddhartha, son of a king, was confined to his father's palace where he wouldn't be exposed to the suffering and ills of mankind. He was an extraordinary youth, excelling in all the pursuits of his time. It was clear from the beginning that he would become a remarkable person later on. He was destined to become Gautama Buddha. Although he became a husband and father, he felt dissatisfied with the luxury of palatial life; he began to doubt the validity of his own.

He left his family and home, seeking a way out of suffering. Despite years of strenuous ascetic practice, he failed to find a way beyond the limits of conditioned existence. Leaving practices behind, he went to Bodhgaya, sat under a Bodhi tree and meditated. There he became enlightened. His discoveries were so profound that at first he was hesitant to share them for fear they wouldn't be understood. He later felt compelled to teach for the relief and benefit of others. Buddha's impulse towards compassionate action established him as one of the greatest teachers of all time.

He went to Deer Park (Sarnath), just outside of Varanasi, and gave what was to be the first of thousands of teachings adjusted to the diverse temperaments of those he taught. His first teaching was known as the great Turning of the Wheel of the Law. He afterwards developed three sets of teachings that have since been collected in the Pali Canon. The First Turning consisted of the Hinayana text stressing morality and discipline, the achievement of enlightenment for oneself only; its foundation being the Four Noble Truths explaining suffering, the cause of suffering, the way out of suffering, and the Path. Gautama Buddha taught this for twenty-six years. The Second Turning, the Mahayana or Great Vehicle, stressed compassion and concern for others, with enlightenment being for the benefit of all sentient beings. He taught this part for eighteen years. The tantric or esoteric teachings of the Vajrayana vehicle provided the foundation for the Third Turning of the Wheel, which also included the Dzogchen or Rainbow Light teachings. It is believed that Buddha taught this for two years before his passing. He predicted that those who came after him would teach this in future times. The Vajrayana comprises most of the present teachings circling around the globe today, transmitted by Tibetan Rinpoches (reincarnated masters) who are planting the seeds for the spread of Buddhism in the West,

Enter Veda. My first introduction to Buddhism, particularly Tibetan Buddhism, came from an exiled Tibetan lama residing in Victoria. I could still remember my first meeting so many years ago. My friend David invited me to go to a 'dharma centre', a house not far from mine, where people meditated and learned about Buddhism. Apparently, there was an older man there who came from Tibet, who was a renowned scholar and practitioner. He was the residing lama and teacher, giving empowerments and teachings to those who asked.

Trusting David's judgment and driven by a need to understand more about the nature of initiation and empowerment, such as that which I had experienced with my Reiki attunements, I consented. We made a plan to go for tea with the lama the following week.

I remember my first conversation with the lama. I was sitting comfortably on an oak chair at his kitchen table. The room was bright and cheery with lots of windows and two yellow canaries singing in a cage in the corner. The lama, who was already a senior at the time, took my hand in his, looked smilingly into my eyes, and spoke in very broken English with an accent that was extremely hard to understand: "Come upstairs to my room; I would like to show you something."

His eyes twinkled with mischief and I thought how often I had heard that line before. What did he mean? "What do you mean Lama?" I asked.

"You know. Come up to my room and find out." He squeezed my hand a little and continued to gaze directly at me, encouragingly. I couldn't believe what I was hearing.

"I don't think so. You are a lama, Lama. You're not allowed!" I laughed uncomfortably.

Amazed at his offer (in front of David!), I tried to be polite. I turned to my friend and told him I thought it was time to go. I couldn't figure it out. I thought monks were supposed to be celibate. Was that what he really meant? The language barrier was prone to misinterpretation. But facts were facts. A man doesn't invite a woman to his room for nothing.

I later learned that lamas are allowed to have wives as long as they haven't taken vows of celibacy. I didn't think that I had misunderstood Lama's intentions, and I was pretty sure that he had taken monk's vows. Afterwards, I noticed the lama around town. Often, I rode with him on the bus. He always asked me if I had a boyfriend yet; he always wanted to give me a kiss. When I asked him about becoming enlightened or receiving teachings, he usually told me that I needed a husband first and invited me back to his house. I wondered if it were my destiny to be continually accosted by men, including Buddhist clergymen.

Regardless, I went to the centre from time to time over the years, feeling the need to seek the company of others who were drawn to the dharmic path. The Buddhist practitioners who sought Lama's teachings upheld his integrity and in his defence thought that he was just testing mine.

Over the next twenty years or so, I had many opportunities to learn about Tibetan Buddhism, sitting in the presence of many great Masters, including His Holiness the Dalai Lama and His Holiness Sakya Trizin. I received many teachings and empowerments and was introduced to the preliminary practice of the Dzogchen teaching, the Ngondro, which I was at the time struggling with. My history revealed that there was no fast track along this path that didn't include many obstacles, as well as arduous and deliberate practice. Every turn of the way challenged my commitment to my own enlightenment. However, every time my face was set against the wall of my resistance, either my own suffering or the suffering of my loved ones, I was inspired to take up the teachings and continue. I had tried to drop my interest in Buddhism and simply pursue the regular joys of living entertainment, but found that that created stagnation and depression. I had an inkling that I was merely seeking distraction to feed my tendencies toward laziness and cowardliness.

I had enjoyed my first visit to Bodhgaya, establishing in my mind the veritable history of Buddha and placing him within the context of his country, and Buddhism within the context of the present time. I was looking forward with anticipatory curiosity and excitement to my visit to Varanasi, the oldest and most sacred city in India, both to the Hindus and the Buddhists.

Between flight and contemplation, the journey is full of the expectation of sensations whose purest form is always that of a gaze full of complicity and serenity. Is it because every dazzling sight seems to make time stand still for the traveller? Here gestures have a sensuality that seems to be rooted in tradition. Move by move, the actors in this great theatre, this town where life never stops, play their parts in the chaos of merging crowds, traffic, noise and smells. Their wisdom arouses respect and plunges the traveller into the divine motor of Benares, its spirituality.

—Simon Allix & Benoît de Vilmorin

Varanasi, aka Benares. I had entered the city from a Buddhist perspective; now I was faced with Hinduism in its most ascetic form.

I was standing face to face with a real live wandering sadhu—a veritable religious mendicant; a beggar-like person who lived mostly on alms, completely free of personal or communal possessions. All that he owned walked with him. A yogi in its purest meaning, he was considered dead to this world. Whatever family he might have had, had already buried him, so to speak, by preparing and carrying out funeral rites for him. His sole aim in life was to achieve deliverance from earthly attachments by practicing complete renunciation in order to develop an inner strength called the *kundalini*, or 'fire-snake', that would help him to attain supreme detachment. Hopefully, he would eventually realize enlightenment or the ultimate release from the ego self. What if he didn't? Would he then consider all his practice a waste?

I had heard that nowadays beggars were posing as sadhus to make money! Should I ask him if he was real? Should I ask for his autograph? I pondered the questions and came to the conclusion that as an outsider, it would be very impolite. Instead, I asked him for his picture. I mean, how often does one meet such a person?

I felt confronted as he glared at me. Looking through the lens, I gladly took my picturesque photo. The sadhu was standing very easefully in front of a stand that sold plastic water bottles for the collection of holy water from the Ganges. Large banana boat containers held flower blossoms and garlands for the river offerings. He sported a costume very versatile for both the weather and the occasion. He wore an orange piece of cloth (dhoti) wrapped around his waist, held up by a colourfully decorated woven belt that he had probably made himself. The same with the pale striped woven vest. He had nonchalantly slung a peach silk scarf and tan pashmina shawl over his shoulder. His chest was hairless and bare while his head hair was conveniently dread-locked, presumably due to his homeless circumstances. Washing didn't look as if it were written down as a priority on his 'to do' list. His greying beard wasn't that long, considering the fact that it probably wasn't trimmed all that often. He wore a metal tube on a string around his neck. Containing prayers? He was without the usual trident, symbolizing triumph over materiality. I suspected that he wore the same costume to every occasion including weddings and funerals. For some reason, he didn't sport an alms cup. I offered him some rupees regardless. He declined.

I had arrived in Varanasi last night around ten, by train of course. I wasn't too pleased about the dark. Fortunately, I paired up with a young German couple who were also feeling vulnerable. We took an auto rickshaw to Assi Ghat, the last bathing place on the Ganges River and to the Yogi Guesthouse where they had previously made a reservation. I piggy-backed their reservation and was found a room on the top floor across from the roof top restaurant. Not a bad view. Facing south over the Ganges, it would be a great place to watch both the sunrise and sunset. The bed was pretty hard, the mattress made of cotton. At least it wasn't straw! The sheets were laundered; I didn't notice any bed bugs. The shared bathroom (hole in floor and shower spout on wall) was painted red, covering up any stains. It was kept reasonably clean.

The outstanding feature of this budget hotel, according to my famous guidebook, was the resident 'yogi' owner who offered yoga lessons on site. I had scrutinized him pretty carefully this morning. I didn't think he was as spiritually advanced as he professed to be. However, there seemed to be lots of gullible young travellers staying over who seemed to be innocently impressed with his presentation. Looked a bit put on to me. Sometimes my age spoils the show. I tried to be as invisible as possible, watching and listening to him socialize and 'show off' with the guests at breakfast. I thought that I was becoming rather skeptical.

Tired of the scams maybe. They seemed to dwell around every corner. Varanasi was renowned for them. I was told to be wary of the silk merchants particularly. However, I got drawn into a situation once again charted in a little 'side box' in the Lonely Planet guide. Earlier in the day, I took a bicycle rickshaw into the oldest part of town, to the labyrinth of market stalls by the Main Ghat. I found myself wandering in and out of narrow streets, encountering sites that could have existed hundreds of years ago—particularly the cows that I had to dance around, avoiding drooling mouths and piles of dung heaped underfoot. Luckily, I didn't step in any.

I eventually located a rather famous old hotel where the 'hippies' used to stay in the sixties. I had my first close-up view of the Ganges River from the restaurant on the roof. I was chatted up by a clean-cut young man who invited me on a tour of the burning ghats just over the way. I jumped at the opportunity because I had lost my bearings and was hoping that he would accompany me back to the main street. He treated me to a tour of a hospice building next to the ghat where many dying people were lying about. Donations were solicited; these people were very poor and didn't have enough money to pay for the wood required for their cremation next door. He introduced me to another man who led me to a balcony that overlooked the ghats.

I appreciated the second fellow's explanation of the details of the final Indian death rite, the cremation ceremony. He pointed to the ever-burning flame of Shiva (the destroyer aspect of their tri-deity, the others being Brahma, the creator, and Vishnu, the sustainer), situated on a slab of concrete under the balustrade of the ghat. Apparently, there was a perpetual stream of attendants throughout the day and night so that the flame would never go out; it had been burning continuously for hundreds of years. Everyone on site was a Dalit, or Untouchable, the lowest caste on the Indian caste totem pole.

I watched and listened intently as he deciphered the proceedings going on across the way, four stories below. A young man having his head shaved was left with only a little string of hair on the top back of his skull, signifying him as the eldest son, the one responsible for performing the funeral rites over the next twenty-four hours. I watched as the dead father was laid on a pile of chopped wood. Various herbs and spices were sprinkled over him. Then the young man took a thatch of bamboo over to the flame, lit it, and walked the burning brush over to the funeral pyre to set the wood on fire. To my surprise, the flame caught quite quickly. The young man proceeded to walk around and around the pyre chanting some sort of text. We left not long after that. The son would stay throughout the night and in the morning a milk puja would be performed over the ashes. The bones would be collected and put into the river for purification. I asked what all the boys were doing swimming underneath the water in the river. I was told they were looking for gold and jewellery from the deceased, put in the river along with the ashes. (Extra benefits listed in the Dalit's funerary job description?!)

The proceedings were familiar, very similar to the funeral

ceremony of Papaji. This time, however, I had a native Indian explain it all to me. I quit the site shortly after that, leaving a donation for the poor in the old wooden locked box by the door.

As I went out the doorway and down the steps, I encountered the friendly young man from the restaurant. He told me that he had an acquaintance he wanted me to meet who sold silks. I responded that I didn't want to go to a silk emporium like the ones I had read about in the guidebook. I was being cautious, thinking that I was on top of the precautionary directions for the old city. I accepted his assurance and followed him down the cobbled lane, twisting and turning the corners behind him. I had no idea where I was. It was early afternoon; there was no danger of impending darkness. I sighed with relief when we arrived at a shop that looked quite respectable. He led me up some stairs and into a room where two men sat on an exquisite Indian carpet. There were pieces of folded silk lining the walls from floor to ceiling in row upon row. It was wonderfully colourful. Enchanting.

I was introduced to the gentlemen. Then to my surprise, the young man excused himself and departed. I was stunned and felt uneasy. Here I was once again in a dubious situation. Were these men trustworthy? They seemed quite congenial, offering to show me some silk. With no intention of buying anything but curious and possessing a passion for beautiful fabric, I told myself to relax and enjoy.

When I noticed the men glance at each other before they offered me some tea, I panicked. The guidebook had warned against accepting drinks from silk vendors. The hair on the back of my neck stood up. I felt shivers down my spine. Drinks with drugs! The notorious story went that silk merchants drugged buyers, particularly women, by offering them drinks that the women innocently drank. Then the women were robbed and raped, sometimes violently. There had been some killings of female tourists recently. I immediately jumped up and raced out of the room, down the stairs, out into the street, and without looking which way, ran and ran.

Whether or not I escaped a close call will never be known. I didn't really care to know. The main thing was that I was safe. These unforeseen circumstances happened so quickly and unexpectedly. One inevitably had to be on guard, prejudging the Indians (especially the men) as dangerous adversaries. I resented having to always watch my back, wanting to trust the people and travel freely and easefully. I learned quickly that that was an unreasonable wish. A traveller must always be wary, walking with eyes and ears open, attentive, and ready to take immediate action if necessary. One's life was always at risk. (No wonder my mother worried about me.) I decided to keep this to myself and not inform her. She was getting too old for all the various shaky details of my escapades and 'near death' adventures. Was I?

All in a day's entertainment. Five-thirty the next morning, a boatman arrived to take us to the river for a sunrise boat trip down the Ganges. Last evening the yogi manager arranged for a man to show us the bathing ghats where people performed their morning bathing rituals. Varanasi was famous for its ghats. The idea seemed attractive at the time; I enthusiastically agreed to join in when the invitation was extended my way.

We left the guesthouse in the dark, trailing behind the young navigator towards the river, where we arrived as the first light of dawn tinted itself over the horizon. The boat sat complacently awaiting its sleepy passengers. Stepping into it was tenuous—the old wooden boat rocked with the tempo of the rippling waters, moving unpredictably upon each entry. I questioned the waterproofing of the vessel! I didn't store much confidence in what I saw, there already being an inch of water in the bottom. The boatman assured us we would be safe, even without lifejackets. He took his long pole, shoved the craft away from the bank, and steered us off on our first seafaring voyage along India's greatest waterway.

Although the river appeared quite wide with sandy banks on the other shore, we crept tortoise-like along the city side not far from the ghat steps that stretched many kilometres ahead. The tour was to last an hour. People were leisurely beginning to appear out of the woodwork of the city, slowly making their way down the steps to their favourite bathing spot. Farther along, we saw intended bathers stripping down—the men to their short and the boys to their birthday suits. The women of course, just rearranged their saris so as not to get caught in their veils.

The ghats strung along one after the other, some being more populated than others. It was obvious which were the favourites, they being the most crowded. It was all very colourful. Some people, taking the opportunity to wash their clothes as well, laid the multi-coloured pieces of cloth along the steps, making a brightly chequered design against the grey concrete. Many lime-green parakeets flew about, perching on the walls and steps, sprinkling the arrangement with their delightful presence.

The morning bathing ritual was actually a very sacred event. I felt an intruder as I observed the morning prayers and dipping process. Most stood, hands in prayer position, eyes closed, chanting to the rising sun. The Gayatri mantra? The boatman was reluctant to offer the information. "Just prayers," he replied adamantly when we asked him what they were singing.

We continued along, passing the Main Ghat where a popular puja was performed each evening. The fire ritual was supposed to be very spectacular in the dark. I would have to take a rain check because I was leaving later that day. We went past the burning ghats, where I recognized the building in which I had stood the day before, spectator to the death ritual. I had a better view of the ghat and could put it all into a clearer perspective from the boat. I was shown the mansion of the owner of the burning ghats and told that he was one of the wealthiest men in Varanasi. Death was a certainty and cremation an expensive necessity in this overcrowded and religious country. He was obviously a good businessman. I wondered if he had inherited the business and if he had, how long it had been in the family. Probably for many generations.

I was glad that I had participated in the ride, yet felt an impostor. I questioned the moral ethics of turning a sacred ritual into a tourist attraction, wondering if the people felt outrage—like being in a zoo with strangers staring at them, clicking their cameras in an attempt to capture their curious daily ablutions. I would. Privacy was sacred. I wondered if they resented relinquishing it in order to fill the government coffers or the tourist managers' bank accounts. I suspected they certainly did.

The ride was full of wonder as I surveyed the situation to the lull of the boat-stick swishing the waters. The captain rhythmically lifted the pole in and out of the river, making his way gently along to the accompanying sighs of his captivated and mesmerized passengers.

After the burning ghats, the boatman expertly manoeuvred the boat around with his stick, without bumping into any oncoming boats, returning the same way we came. Back at Assi Ghat, we each hopped out onto shore, shaking our rubbery legs, and made our way back to the guesthouse for breakfast. The sun had already risen quite high in the sky. Removing my shawl and carrying it over my arm, I pondered the moral dilemma of a tourist in India, trespassing upon the sacred territory of these spiritually devoted people. Would the progress of tourism once again destroy a precious culture, removing it from the divine roots that it was so deeply embedded in?

As for the Ganges being filthy, filled with dead human bodies and carcasses of animals . . . Well, I did see a couple of bloated bodies floating on the surface of the water, along with the streams of dead garlands. I was told that the only human bodies that are put on the water on bamboo stretchers are the ones that do not need purification, such as the saints and children who have not lived long enough to acquire sins, and the people who have been bitten by snakes, as it takes three days for their spirits to leave their bodies; the spirits may be retrieved by the sacred prayers chanted by holy men to bring them back to life. I did see a few bloated dead cows, rats, cats, and a pig. Other than that, it wasn't too bad.

Later, in the heat of the afternoon, 'me and my suitcase' started down the side street from the guesthouse, out onto the main drag, where I would solicit an auto rickshaw to take us to the train station. It was, sadly enough, time to go. I had less than a week before I had to make my way back down south to catch the plane home. I was standing in the middle of the road gazing with amusement at the most hilarious site yet.

A ragged old man, head wrapped in a tattered scarf, was driving three black oxen down the street amid the flurry of vehicles, vendors, pedestrians, cows, dogs, pigs . . . you name it. I had been walking down the centre of the road because there were less potholes for the wheels of my heavy suitcase to fall into.

Hearing some yelling and commotion behind me, I turned to witness a comedy worth its weight in gold. One of the oxen had decided to break away from the group, venturing towards a laden banana stall. The ox charged towards the bananas in an inspired fashion, sending the fruit tumbling onto the road. The vendor was yelling at him furiously, eliciting little response from the animal. The owner was rushing towards the scene waving his stick and shouting at the top of his lungs at the recalcitrant ox, who eyed him sideways without remorse. The vendor then turned towards the owner hurling threats of some sort or other. I wasn't party to the exact nature of them, as I didn't understand the language.

Meanwhile, the other two oxen, seizing the unexpected opportunity of liberation, took off at full speed towards the main street, where the traffic had escalated due to the noon hour rush. Imagining unending 'freedom of the road' without master, their momentum increased as they approached the intersection. In the meantime, the owner suddenly remembered his other charges. He abruptly turned away from the angry vendor, flabbergasted that the oxen were no longer behind him. He then took off as fast as his short legs could carry him onwards towards the madding crowd.

I stood there wondering whether or not traffic lights would have made any difference.

My crazy sense of humour had been sparked for the occasion. My tendency towards surrealism was rewarded. As the impending disaster approached fruition, time slowed down so that I could capture the imprint of the hilarity forever in my brain. Indelibly memorable.

The owner found himself stretched between two uncontrollable situations. The truant first ox refused to follow him and headed straight towards me and my suitcase. The owner, chasing behind the other two to try to thwart their progress towards the inevitable disaster, was thrashing his stick aggressively in the air shouting Hindi obscenities at them. Fortunately for all concerned, he caught up with the oxen before the crossroads and was able to ward off any further accident, saving his precocious animals.

As for myself, I stood spellbound, watching the banana ox march calculatingly towards me, eyes fixated upon my vulnerable valise. His head was down and his horns aimed directly at my navy blue suitcase. Luckily, some of the other bystanders, whose activities had also been arrested by the melodrama, noticed and began hollering in the direction of the ox. One man jumped between the ox and me, waving a short stick at the beast. I remained transfixed. There was major difficulty for me to get moving anyway—my luggage was awkward and the road 'hole-y' uncooperative. Caught between a rock and a hard place, horror and fascination, I continued to stay put.

The arrival of the puffing owner brought me to my senses. However, it was rather anti-climactic. The drama was over. Everyone started up their previous business as if nothing had occurred. No one minded. The old man and his oxen merged into the distant crowd. The street stage rearranged itself, adjusting to the continuation of life. Merely another incident in the flow of daily happenings. I felt dazed. I felt included. I was just another factor in a kaleidoscope of intentions swirling within the apparent chaos of modern India.

Would you like a toke?" offered Geoffrey, the lanky Englishman with long curly brown hair.

I looked into the clear intelligent eyes of a pleasant-looking young man and wished that I were thirty years younger.

"It might make you feel better," he added reassuringly, reaching the joint out in my direction. "You look a bit rough around the edges. You OK? I think you could use a bit of this."

My angst had been mounting beyond my ability to cope with it. I was experiencing higher than normal levels of anxiety and disassociation, and I was puzzled because there really was nothing for me to be afraid of. No apparent danger, although at times I did unsuspectingly get myself into situations I quickly had to get out of but usually found a way. I was a curiously cautious traveller accustomed to the duress of travelling in India. I had no idea what was wrong with me.

I looked awkwardly at him and nodded, shaking my head back and forth, feeling as awful as I obviously looked.

"I got this from a friend who took me up into the hills where they were growing fields of the stuff. It's pretty strong. You ever smoked before?" As if having second thoughts, he hesitated a moment before reaching over to pass the stubby hand-rolled cigarette of Indian marijuana to me.

I nodded again, affirmatively this time, and took the stubby cigarette carefully out of his fingers, not wanting to drop it into the pool of water we were sitting in at the base of a lovely waterfall. We were about four kilometres downhill from Laxman Jhula and not far up the road from the ashram I had once gone to, the time Papaji took his definitive leave from the world. "I used to smoke this stuff a little in my twenties, with my oldest daughter's father. That was a long time ago," I replied.

Looking back it seemed eons ago, another lifetime for that matter. Could have been. My life had changed so much since those early idealistic days of young adulthood. I had thought I would accomplish so much that nothing would get in the way of my dreams. I wondered if this young man was as hopeful. He looked as if he were in his mid- or late twenties.

I took the joint and nervously put it to my lips. I could do it, I thought to myself. Anything to make this feeling of disengagement vanish. Not wanting to show my lack of experience, I nonchalantly took a drag, wondering if I came across as confident. I unfortunately inhaled too quickly AND too deeply. God, my lungs were burning! I pressed my lips together and held my breath, trying not to cough. I did anyway.

After a few moments, I felt more settled and could feel a quiet calm permeating my body. "I'll try almost anything at the moment to calm me down. I've been feeling so terrible lately. I don't know why. I feel like a free balloon or kite lost to the wind, getting farther and farther away from the earth—so disconnected and frightened. I've never felt this way before," I plaintively added.

Maybe I was experiencing a spiritual purification process, releasing something unknown from deep within my subconscious mind—something that I wasn't aware of. Maybe I was being forced to face my inner dragons like Carlos Castaneda did in the Don Juan books. Regardless, I wanted reprieve and if it came in the form of drugs, so be it. Marijuana wasn't too bad.

"Here, let me take that," Geoffrey said, reaching over to take back the joint, brushing the back of my hand with his fingertips as he did so.

Was he coming onto me? I smiled at the thought! It had been a *long* time since I had had an affair and *never* with a young man. Always a first time. I was beginning to feel relaxed enough to contemplate the possibility.

"A couple of puffs won't do you any harm," he added, possibly misinterpreting my thoughtful look as worry. He looked me directly in the eyes and for a few moments, we were both caught sinking into the depths of each other's gaze.

Stunned and feeling a bit numb, I smiled shyly and looked away to the waterfall. Lovely. Such a romantic place. Was I letting myself get into something here?

"That should settle you down. It's a pretty smooth ride. Enjoy. I'm here if you need me," he said as he moved away to the other side of the pool to enjoy his privacy and to leave me to my own.

I looked around, a bit astonished to find myself in such a beautiful place with such a sensitive person. I felt quite attracted to him and whenever I could, snatched glances at him without his notice, wanting to study the man.

I waded over to a large rock in the middle of the stream. A good vantage point to inconspicuously keep my eye on Geoffrey. I wanted some time out to ponder the situation. He had very subtly offered me an invitation. Would I accept?

The paranoia subsided, leaving me feeling deeply calm and quiet. The cool mist of the splashing waterfall making its way downstream felt refreshing on my skin. I was sitting on a huge rock with lots of room to stretch out. Putting my hands behind me, I leaned back and stuck my feet in the rushing water. I closed my eyes to simply enjoy, noticing that I felt somewhat stoned! Opening my eyes again to take another look, I assured myself that it was all very real and I would remember everything exactly as I was experiencing it, regardless of the little bit of 'help from my friend'. Then, I sank back into the tempting reverie.

The walk uphill through the dense deciduous forest and brush had left me hot and sweaty. I had been amazed at the number of butterflies that flew across my path. The climb had been enchanting even though I wasn't in the best of shape. My blue rubber thongs kept slipping sideways underneath my feet on the jagged rocks and knotty tree roots sticking out of the hard dried dirt. I had had to pay extra attention to each step, not wanting to appear a fool. Nor did I want to fall and hurt myself. When I did have a chance to look up away from my feet, the elegant beauty of the little creatures flitting back and forth from one bush to another surprised me. Everything was very green, creating a verdant backdrop for their enchanting wings. So many sizes and colours! Thousands of insects everywhere;

my first butterfly experience. I had never taken the time to visit Butterfly World at home. Here, they were *papillons au naturel*!

A lovely one landing on the rock beside me mesmerized me. Lavender wings with about a two-inch wingspan. All of the sudden, it came to life and I entered the reality of a butterfly making its way to the edge of the stone . . .

Such an idyllic picture. Quite a while later, I looked across the pool at Geoffrey dousing his head under the waterfall. He looked ecstatic and completely free. I indulged in a long gaze at his tanned bare chest. Oh, to be in my twenties again! How I longed to swim over to join him and run my hands over those smooth muscles. My God, the marijuana was having an effect! The sensations aroused by my meandering imagination startled me. He looked over, catching my gaze and smiled. For moments' lengths we shared an understanding. I could almost fall in love!

I quickly glanced back down to the butterfly fluttering around and landing beside my hand—a tiny guest to keep me company in the middle of an Indian stream. A welcome diversion. I wasn't quite ready to acquiesce to the inevitable. I didn't know how long my fascination lasted, resting enchanted and gloriously suspended in time.

I'd never viewed the mechanisms of a butterfly up close before. I watched, for what seemed like ages, as a yellow beauty tested its feelers along the rock, exploring the rough slippery surface. It seemed oblivious to the moist mist coming from the water. A moment captured in a bubble of time. I remembered a poem I had written years ago when I was a bit younger than Geoffrey:

The butterfly flees its destiny;
In two days it shall die.
Preserve it in a plate of glass
Or on a block of wood
To prove that beauty can be caught,
Just as we want to love.

Love needs to remain free. I identified with the precious insect. I hadn't yet allowed myself to be caught for any length of time, even a quarter century later. Maybe I was a butterfly last lifetime!

Could I allow myself to contemplate a brief encounter with such a young man? I thought of the moment that had passed between us when we had first arrived, and the shared look that we had just experienced. Something was happening between us that felt so delicious and free. Should I abandon myself to the flow? Who cared but me? Who did the censuring voice belong to? My mother? My Victorian grandmother, or her mother? And on and on it went. Would it ever leave me in peace?

Who was he? Just a traveller like myself, lonely and eager for comforting association and intimacy. However, unlike myself, he was just beginning his journey. It would be refreshing to reconnect with that energy and intention. I could remember myself at that age, so open to encounter regardless of age differences. I wanted to shed the tainted glasses of middle age and reclaim the rose-tinted lenses of my youth. Even for a brief interlude. What harm would there be in it? More pleasure and benefit than anything.

Considering my lack of endorphins lately, accepting the invitation might be medicinal. Anything to dispel the fear for a few days. Like a fool, possibly, I gave myself permission to allow my intuition to lead. I had already fallen over a cliff, into the gentle recesses of a stirring heart. I had experienced Geoffrey's caring attention earlier, convinced that he was regarding me with consideration. He had respected my privacy most of the afternoon, not intruding upon it, honouring my space, yet keeping an eye on me from a distance. Now I could feel his eyes on my bare shoulders.

I stepped into the water and swam over to him. He held out his hands, catching me as I approached. I hadn't felt this free and happy for ages. He manoeuvred us over to the waterfall where we stood laughing, the water plunging onto our heads and spilling down over our bodies. It felt wonderful. We were *so* in the present. Nothing else mattered. Moments of togetherness—communion.

Harboured under the tumbling waterfall splashing all over our faces and bodies and enveloped in tumultuous laughter, we embraced.

The kiss became a seal, binding us together in mutual acceptance. Presented with an opportunity to enter into time without judgment, and space where two intentions, regardless of age, could merge together in sensitive and care-full interaction, we shared sacred intimacy. We made love beside the waterfall under the mid-afternoon Indian sun. For a few hours, we were swept away by the enchantment of the emerald forest of the Himalayan foothills cushioning us from the chaos of the outside world, with only the butterflies as our witness. Its memory remains scented with the delicious fragrance of cardamom and cinnamon, the aroma of the chai that we shared at the small tea stall at the bottom of the path, after we had made our way lazily, hand in hand, down the hill.

The reprieve lasted two more days. Together, we explored the unique sights of the two swinging bridges and the twin towns Laxman and Ram Jhula, ensconced along both sides of the river. We shopped in the intriguing shops and stalls along the narrow roads of each of the towns and languished over hot café latté in the various cafés, favouring the German bakery located on the opposite side of the swinging bridge from the temple at Laxman Jhula. I managed to find a copy of Swami Ramananda's yoga book there. On the back cover, it mentioned how he had learned Reiki from a Canadian Reiki Master (although he didn't mention my name) and that he was presently residing in Switzerland. No wonder we couldn't locate him when we had asked at the ashram.

We tried to avoid the monkeys on the bridge, desperately holding on to our possessions as the annoying beasts grabbed at our bags hoping to find food, their favourite occupation as far as I could tell. It was a novelty to watch them swinging from wire to wire keeping their grip. It appeared dangerous, since the water rushed far below and I doubt that they knew how to swim. We sidestepped some different monkeys with black faces that darted in and out of the bushes and bracken, along with all the cows and dogs we encountered on the dusty road. The walk between the towns took about half an hour, providing an opportunity to view the rural life along the Ganges River.

Our time seemed out of a storybook; everything that children loved to see and hear. I felt like a child again as we were captured in fascinated enchantment, watching the snakes dance out of their little woven baskets to the tune of the snake charmer's horn. Its penetrating and audacious sound grated on the nerves as a sweet and sour candy felt on the tongue. I had never before heard such peculiar resonance. On one of the afternoons we watched a small band of Indian men practicing music in the courtyard of a hotel, bellowing out of tune on their tubas, trumpets, trombones and drums. It was hilarious and awful at the same time. Covering our ears, both Geoffrey and I shook with laughter wondering which one of them was the bandmaster and what his credentials were! They were a sight, dressed in their old Raj band uniforms. At least, their design was a remnant from those olden days—red turbans and military-looking gold and blue uniforms with brass buttons gleaming in the glaring sun.

The idyllic interlude seemed out of time yet in harmony with it. Carried along with the current of River Time, we swam in the clean milky waters on the banks below the tall temple. We rang bells as we raced to the top of its thirteen floors to watch the setting sun through the portals of the open window spaces. One evening we attended the fire puja on the steps of the Swarg Ashram (Maharishi's old haunt) and hummed along with the hundreds of orange-clad young pundits chanting their prayers in unison with the falling of the setting sun, in front of the Shiva statue that sat meditating in the middle of the river. The last evening, we rested on the river bank listening to the taped music of a woman chanting the Gayatri mantra, watching the sun drop over the hills and twilight pervade the sky. At night, we lay on the balcony under the reflection of the Indian harvest moon, tracing each other's bodies with the delicate fingertips of friendship and falling asleep folded within each other's arms, soothed by the lullaby of the gentle Ganges making its way down from Gangotri, its source, to the wide expanse of the Indian Ocean.

I have never regretted abandoning my will to the leisure and bliss of that most innocent and intimate experience. The sense of balance and ease we felt in the centre of our life and time together along the banks of the glorious Ganges was sacred, worth every bit of the guilt and astonishment that filled the vacant spaces of my mind after we parted ways. Whoever said that freedom came without a price? That price was the courage required to purchase the ticket needed to take the risk.

"Truth is a naked lady, and if by accident she is drawn up from the bottom of the sea, it behoves a gentleman either to give her a print petticoat or to turn his face to the wall and vow that he did not see," said Rudyard Kipling not quite a century ago.

I was sure that I had laid my feet on some of the same 'dirt' that he found underneath his feet and in front of his eyes. However, my eyes were of a gentle woman with a heart of gold and a spirit of iron. I didn't shirk to offer kindness and trust where others might have turned away or seen through the glossy pages of the same old story: *Man Seduces Woman into Thinking He is Honourable When All He Wants is the Same Old Thing.*

I will bare this part of my tale trusting that I will not be judged through my grandmother's Victorian eyes. Remember that I crossed the threshold of adulthood in the late sixties about the time when members of the 'Women's Liberation Movement' were storming down the doors of the 'Old Boys' Club', claiming the right to roam the world and traverse upon men's territory demanding equality, liberty, respect, and safety.

Fifty years later, I can attest to the fact that some things haven't changed. Women are still viewed as 'sex objects' rather than human beings deserving honesty and consideration, in Asia anyway. The Women's Movement has made little ground in the consciousness of the average Indian man. I will continue along in Kipling's vein with lines from his "The Fabulists":

> When all the world would keep a matter hid,
> Since Truth is seldom friend to any crowd,
> Men write in fable, as old Aesop did
> Jesting at that which none will name aloud.
> And this they needs must do, or it will fall
> Unless they please they are not heard at all.

Reviewing—in an effort to disengage the nuts, bolts, and chains of the medieval chastity belt of consciousness that I have struggled so hard to refuse wearing, but which has bound itself around my psyche regardless (may it be forever dismantled so that my daughters and their daughters may never know the nagging voice of shame and condemnation that has accompanied the mindset of most women of my generation or those preceding) —I proceed. I shall offer my side of the story. (And Mother, if you don't like this part, cover your eyes and ears. That will spare you your horror and disappointment that I have failed to learn THE lesson of womanhood—Subjection, Containment, Compliance—or the need to say "I told you so!" in hope that I will change my ways.)

I have no regrets, only disappointments. And, yes, the censuring voice taunts me with its evaluation that I needlessly set myself up for them—over and over again. The flipside to that coin would be covered in bitterness and jaded withdrawal.

The *chakras* (energy centres) of humanity still need some work. Here in India, reality is survival of the fittest, in a land where tradition views sex as something that is permitted solely within the bounds of marriage—even if the marriage is between a four-year-old girl and a forty-year-old man. The horrendous implications of this situation are, I am sure, happening this very moment upon matrimonial beds in remote villages in India.

However, my story is that of a fifty-two-year-old divorcée treading upon unknown territory, with a distorted nostalgic vision of the exotic India portrayed by the Modern writers of the early 20th century whom she had studied in her university literature classes. Men in India are starving for sexual encounter. A starving man doesn't salt and pepper his meal with politeness or temper it with the spices of honesty and respect; hence, the error of her reasoning. Far too polite and far to 'good' of a girl to say No, all the while hanging onto the fantasy of Prince Charming, thinking that possibly this one is THE ONE, she gave herself permission to enter into an invitation to find out . . .

After the lovely encounter with Geoffrey I surprised myself, opening doors and cupboards of my heart and mind that had been tightly closed a long time ago. Would I ever find my *dream come true*? Was there really a man made just for me, as my mother always assured me? I allowed myself to re-awaken that dream. Our intimacy, was it a jester or a fortune-teller? I revered its memory as a poetic vision of future possibility.

This journey so far had not been beset with men trying to accost me around every corner. Or at least, I hadn't noticed. I was entirely focused upon seeing India from a spiritual and cultural perspective. I hadn't been conversing with many Indian men. I learned last trip that Indian men had a tendency to view single Western women as free for the asking, or taking, depending upon how polite one wanted to be. It was extremely unusual for Indian women to enter into conversation. If I were to talk with people to ward off my loneliness and exercise my vocal chords, I had to talk to men—usually vendors of some sort, depending where I was shopping at the time. However, I resented constantly being channelled into the 'material girl' program, although I often caught myself singing or humming Madonna's theme song as musical accompaniment to the spree.

I reluctantly left my favourite spot along the Ganges early in the morning while the air was still fresh and cool. Geoffrey and I had amicably and tenderly parted ways, never to see each other again unless destiny called for it. We mutually understood.

It took about half an hour to get from Ram Jhula to Haridwar by auto rickshaw, costing around 150 rupees ($4.50). I wanted to enjoy the road before the rush of vehicles and the trailing exhaust of all the diesel fumes. Riding in an auto rickshaw was always a challenge and exercise of tolerance. The three-wheeler possessed no shocks and had open windows, resulting in a very bumpy, noisy, and smelly ride. The irritation was balanced by the cheap price. Taxis were considerably more expensive, albeit more comfortable. By the end of an auto rickshaw ride, one was usually covered in a layer of grey soot, feeling grimy and stinky.

This was how I arrived at the Haridwar train station. I managed to find the tourist office and purchase a ticket for the same day, most unusual for India. I was scheduled to catch a night train to Agra around nine o'clock that evening.

I decided to head over to the clock tower. I wanted to revisit precious times—waiting on the banks of the river with all the devotees, my first dip in the Ganges, putting Papaji's ashes in the river . . . It was easy to find my way. The clock pillar towered above all the other buildings in Haridwar. It was becoming hot with the sun beginning to climb rapidly in the sky. I sought a place to leave all my bags, which I should have left in the cloakroom at the train station. I found a very old hotel where I took a room for about two dollars for the day and left them there. Then I continued to walk about a mile down the dusty road amid the morning traffic.

It took longer than I thought, being farther than it looked. I decided to stop at a restaurant to have breakfast or at least tea and toast. I laugh now remembering the moment I looked up from writing in my journal to see a man riding an elephant down the street in the middle of all the vehicles. "Only in India!" I chuckled out loud. The waiter arrived at the same time looking quizzically at me, wondering what I was laughing at.

How many times had I repeated that same phrase?

Arriving at the river, I got some great photos of Rajastani women crossing the bridge; their purple, green, gold, scarlet, orange, yellow, indigo saris presented rainbows of colour. A group of women laughed at my photo endeavour and one older one shook her finger at me, all the while laughing and chattering with her friends and relatives. I was the odd one out. I didn't feel strange, just in the moment with their humour and jest.

The river, however, was *not* there! How could a river disappear? There was just the riverbed *sans eau sacré*. Apparently, the river had been diverted for some reason. Cleaning? How could all those stones be cleaned or the water for that matter? The place looked bare and not at all like before. Deserted. What had happened to all the pilgrims?

There were all sorts of little shrines with orange-clad swamis presumably soliciting people for pujas. I curiously went over to inquire and unwittingly agreed to a puja (unbeknownst to me, for marriage!). Before I knew it, the two fellows were chanting, lighting camphor lamps, and praying in front of a Lakshmi statue. I thought it was for prosperity. They later said that as I was a woman alone, they thought it appropriate to do a puja for a husband for me! When it was finished, they asked me for an equivalent of $50! I gave them 50 rupees, much to their disappointment and chagrin. Had they thought me a sucker or that I would put much store in their prayers to find me the man of my dreams?

While I was walking towards the tower, I had noticed a cable car going up the little mountain across the road from the river. I returned to inquire about its destination. What lay at the top of the mountain? There was a shrine to Durga, the powerful goddess that rode the tiger. I thought going up to pay my respects might be an adventure to affirm the goddess power within myself, to be blessed by her, or to establish my relationship to the goddess in me. I wasn't sure; it would be fun and something to occupy the day.

I elected to walk up the mountain path; after all it didn't look that high. There were steps going all the way up, so it wouldn't be too hard a climb. Very civilized. I noticed all the stalls at the bottom of the slate path laden with packages of offerings for Durga. I bought a red plastic net filled with packages of puffed rice, incense, candies, coconut, and flowers. I later regretted my hasty action.

Just around the first turn about thirty steps up, a HUGE monkey jumped out at me and grabbed at my bag of goodies. He snatched it out of my hand, ripped it apart, and tore open the bag of rice, throwing the rest down on the walkway and jumping back onto the stone fence overhead to eat his fill, awaiting another ignorant and innocent pilgrim. A rascal who had scared the wits out of me! I had tried to resist him but was afraid that he would attack. The people in some stalls a few steps up the way were laughing hysterically; presumably, they were rooting for the nasty monkey. Certainly, they had seen it many times before. Oh, how the ignorant Western tourist deserved what she got!

It was a lot farther up hill than I had anticipated. By the time I reached the top, I was covered in dirt. Perspiration trickled down my face, my neck, the centre of my breasts, under my arms, and down my legs! It was just past mid-day. The discomfort of the pounding sun and its scorching heat magnified the temperature of my menopausal 'hot flashes' aggravated by the climb. It was almost unbearable. I finally reached the top, to be quickly ushered around the shrine.

My newly purchased offering seemed quite small and insufficient compared to the opulent packages unwrapped by the priests, which had been taken from the Indian families in the procession in front of me. I felt rather ignorant and foolish. They were probably wondering what a Western Christian woman was doing making offerings to one of their Hindu deities.

I didn't care. I wanted to cultivate my own relationship with Durga. I later realized just how she wanted to manifest her presence in my life. Maybe it had been Durga herself who had summoned me up the mountain. Was it my imagination or were men now very conscious of my presence? From the moment I exited the shrine room, I caught men of all ages looking at me as if I were the most fascinating woman on earth. I even caught a few fellows pointing towards me and talking amongst themselves, all the while regarding me with obvious attraction and interest. It wasn't the usual licentiousness either, and more than just curiosity.

Maybe I was wearing Durga's face? I didn't have a mirror to look into to check my appearance. It was all rather odd. I hurriedly bought a ticket for the cable car, feeling it necessary to leave before the men came over to me. A necessary risk. I wanted to leave quickly and not be followed, yet I was wary of the rustic look of the machine I was about to enter. The car itself looked sturdy enough. The cable and the pulley system were rather questionable, rather elementary. I wasn't sure about the precautions they had in place. Would the cable slip, sending me spiralling down the mountain? I had never been in a cable car before, let alone an Indian contraption.

In spite of my fear, I enjoyed the ride. Inside it felt quite safe, progressing very evenly and slowly down the mountainside. In the end, I was glad to reach the bottom but sad that the ride was so short—a bit contradictory, yet in accord with my Gemini personality.

It was around three o'clock when I ventured back towards the hotel where I had left my belongings. I was feeling hesitant to return remembering how dirty and dingy it had seemed. After all, I had only paid sixty rupees for it. I could afford to find another place to rest and return to pick up my bag later, before I headed over to the station to catch my train. I contemplated the solution and veered to the left, walking up a side street past some more respectable-looking hotels.

There was a handsome and kindly man standing out front of one of them. He gave me a genuine smile, and I thought that he looked trustworthy and sincere. We chatted for a while and I found myself liking him. He invited me in, introducing himself and the other people in the hotel vestibule. It was a traditional Indian hotel. The marble floors were covered by tastefully luxurious Indian carpets. There were traditional paintings in gilded frames on the white stucco walls, mostly of people riding elephants.

The fellow seemed a gentleman of means, his behaviour reflecting class. He graciously introduced himself and offered to show me a room. I was curious to see the inside of one. The place looked expensive, considerably out of my range. However, I wanted to see. I had time to spare. It was the middle of the week and there seemed to be few people staying there. Maybe he would offer me a deal for the afternoon since I needed a place to wash and clean up before I left. I could always ask how much he would charge for a few hours, telling him I would be out by seven.

Raj seemed extremely friendly, genuinely interested in my story, offering me a room at a very low rate. The hotel where I had left my things was not far away, making it easy to retrieve my belongings. Returning within ten minutes, I proceeded to get cleaned up.

Afterwards, Raj offered to serve me dinner in his restaurant. I hadn't eaten since the tea and toast early in the morning. Accepting with pleasure, we continued our conversation throughout the meal, our actions reflected in the thousands of pieces of mirrors in mosaic design that covered the walls according to the Rajastani artistic tradition. I found his voice enchanting and could hardly taste the thali with rice, curried vegetables, dal, cucumber yogurt and very tasty dessert with tapioca, raisins, cardamom, and cloves, I was so carried away by his attention. I was extremely thankful for his generosity and not a bit suspicious.

He chatted cheerfully about his life in Delhi, where he went regularly and where his friends were. He was excited about our meeting and offered to put me up in Delhi for as long as I wanted to stay. He wanted to introduce me around. Oddly, for his age, he wasn't married. He seemed about forty, a bit portly for the average middle-aged Indian man, but quite attractive. I was glad for his company and appreciated the entertainment. As we had established a friendship of sorts, I agreed to look him up in the capital after my visit to Agra.

He accompanied me to my room after dinner, offering to watch TV with me until it was time to go. We still had an hour or so to spare before I had to make my way to the station. There was only the bed to sit on. What the heck, a cuddle and a few kisses from an intelligent respectable Indian would be a gift. You never knew; maybe he was the man I had been waiting for all my life?

One thing led to another . . .

Later, settled into the bottom berth, snugly tucked into the freshly laundered sheets of the 2AC train compartment, I reminisced upon the events of the afternoon.

Was it the comfort of a stranger, the grief of never seeing Geoffrey again, the need of an antidote for the re-appearing anxiety beginning to encroach once again on my peacefulness, the whimsical dream of living in India as the mistress of a successful businessman, a desperate attempt to escape from the overwhelming needs and responsibilities of adult children, a simple response to an invitation to love, or *the call of the goddess Durga, using me as a means to satisfy her longing?*

More than likely, I hadn't had enough loving and I just wanted more.

"More, please," said Oliver Twist, the starving English boy, to the shrewish matron, Widow Corney. (I played her once in our elementary school play.) Did it really matter who the man was? The female wanted to mate. As long as there was loving kindness exchanged did it matter who the partner was? A man. A woman. In time. Exchanging love the way men and women do. How my reticence to open had been exchanged for new, re-found woman-ness.

Who was I, anyway? The Madonna, the Whore, or the Goddess? What was sexuality all about? Men could express it freely without condemnation. Women? It was 2003. What did I care about what others thought? Two adults consenting. I questioned the appropriateness of sexuality after the procreative years. I was excited that it still existed. But two men in less than a week, after months of drought?

My own sexuality wanted freedom of expression. Did I want a husband and all that that would entail? No. I demanded freedom to make my own choices without accountability to anyone other than myself. I no longer wanted my mother taking up residence in my head.

Maybe I was just enjoying my fortunate circumstances. It wasn't every day that I had had such attractive offers. If I were a man, my mates would slap me on the back and regard me with envy. My girlfriends at home would probably immediately ask if I had used protection and then, after hearing the affirmative response, would just giggle and say: "Give me Five!" Most of them were considering applying for early pensions. We weren't getting any younger. I could hear them saying: "Take it before your luck runs out or the well runs dry!" Meaning it quite literally.

I wouldn't want to simply justify my actions by surmising that possibly Durga had a hand in it all that afternoon, but I will. Did she simply want to use me to experience her *shakti* and absorb the energy of Shiva through me? After all, I was in India and stranger things had happened. The Goddess worked in mysterious ways. And I trusted her.

Incidentally, we could leave it at that and that would be all. But that was not the end of Durga's call.

Henceforth, let the inhabitants of the world be divided into two classes—them as has seen the Taj Mahal; and them as hasn't.
—Edward Lear

Someone was knocking on my door. It was still dark outside. I wondered what time it was.

"Good morning, ma'am. It's 5:30. You asked me to wake you," a male voice said on the other side of the door.

"Oh, yeah." I rubbed my eyes. "OK, thank you," I replied.

"Don't be long or you'll miss the sunrise. I'll wait for you on the rooftop," he quietly added. I heard him shuffle away, remembering our conversation the night before.

I had mentioned to the fellow who worked in the hotel restaurant that I would like to watch the sun rise over the Taj Mahal. The view was supposed to be 'out of this world', the sun shining pink through the early morning mist, touching the domes of the Taj with a mystical morning light—a bit of rose-tinted heaven. At least, that's what I'd heard!

I had chosen this particular budget hotel, Hotel Kriya, over all the others because of the rooftop view of the Taj. It was located in the south quarter of Agra, not far from the front gates of the attraction. I mean, why would anyone come to this city if it weren't for the famous Taj Mahal, the magnificent symbol of India? I was anxious to see this masterpiece in the morning light.

I didn't think anyone could get enough of the beauty of the impeccable Taj. I thought maybe it would be a bit anticlimactic since I had seen it on TV and in books so many times. NOT the case. I could hardly keep my eyes away from it, couldn't wait to get dressed and get up there before the sun began to rise, not wanting to miss a single moment of perfection.

I had arrived in Agra mid-afternoon the day before. I had a few days before my train south to Trivandrum, where I would be catching my plane home to Canada a week after that. My time in India was drawing to a close. I couldn't leave this country for the second time without seeing this remarkable monument.

I expectantly climbed the narrow stairs onto the rooftop to the cadence of the droning call of the taped Islamic voice summoning people to the mosque for morning prayers. The air was cool, moist, and misty. I held on to the banister for support as the cement stairs were uneven and the light minimal. I made my way into the first chair and sat facing north, anticipating the emergence of the mighty Taj Mahal through the mist, as the brilliant orb rose over the horizon.

Yesterday afternoon upon arrival in Agra, after I had descended the steps of the train station, I was accosted by a horde of taxi and auto rickshaw drivers. Electing for a change, I hoisted my things onto the nearest bicycle rickshaw, which seemed to be in much better condition than the ones standing outside the train station in Siliguri. There must be more affluence here with the excessive tourist trade for the Taj.

The driver offered to take me for a sunset view of the Taj Mahal on the other side of the Jumna River. I agreed to meet him after I had a chance to get cleaned up at the hotel, but wasn't prepared for the effect that the experience would have on me. I stood transfixed on the sandy banks of the flats that stretched along the riverbed. The sun sank into the sky, a huge red ball falling in slow motion over the edge of the earth. Its effect upon the white marble domes and pillars was poignant and breathtaking. I stood spellbound at the awesome beauty and magnificence of such an architectural wonder. A miracle. A thing of perfection. A thing of Truth. I was reminded of the poet Keats when he wrote:

"Beauty is truth, truth beauty"—that is all Ye know on earth, and all ye need to know.

No truer words had been spoken as far as I was concerned. I wasn't sure I wanted to get any closer to the object of beauty, too overpowering, comfortable from a distance. I was inspired to keep it at arm's length—to preserve it in my memory as untouchable so as not to mar it with my tainted limitedness, my imperfect humanness. Little did I know that this would be the case.

I graciously and gratefully sat on the roof, sipping steaming lemon tea, watching the monkeys scurry from roof edge to roof edge, jumping and skirting around each other as dawn broke through the morning mist. The silver moon disc faded with the brilliance of the morning light while the white doves danced their matinal flight across the sky. The sun rose orange-red over the horizon, dazzling the dark with its exhilarating appearance. How could one measure the value of such beauty or hold it in the palm of one's hand? The beauty of dawn rested ever-presently within the treasures of a heart filled with appreciation.

I whispered: "Thank you, God, for your glorious creation!"

Again, I was not disappointed as the outline of the Taj Mahal gradually took shape. I retraced the lines of its story, a tragic love story. The 17th-century emperor of India, Shah Jahan, built the Taj as a mausoleum for his beloved second wife, Mumtaz Mahal, who died in 1631 while birthing their fourteenth child. He loved her so much that his hair was said to have turned grey over night. He commissioned the construction of what has been described in the Lonely Planet guidebook as "one of the most extravagant monuments built for love."

I have since learned that a Mughal mausoleum is a combination of a circle and a square that, in Islamic symbolism, represents the marriage of heaven and earth. This explains the poignant rapture that inevitably enthrals everyone who lays eyes upon this magnificent *chef d'oeuvre.* It most definitely should be included as one of the Seven Wonders of the World. I watched with reverence as the day rose, and with it emerged awareness that my appreciative presence was an act of prayer, in gratitude to Life itself.

Beauty has a way of opening the heart to the romance and divinity of life, airbrushing the horrors of the human condition. Regardless of the poverty around the city, the inhabitants of Agra wore a countenance of knowingness; all was not as it seemed on the surface. One only had to look over to the perfection of the Taj to be reminded of the divine nature of human consciousness. After all, what we saw on the outside was a manifestation of inner potential, a product of the simple equation that thought + energy = manifestation:

"Ta da! The Taj Mahal; therefore God exists!" so my thinking went.

My time in Agra was not totally consumed with introspection, pondering the profound nature of relative reality as much as I was able to decipher it at the time. I happened to trip once again into the ongoing predicament of my femaleness. I went shopping.

Anyone familiar with Agra would recognize the symptoms of what is known as Agra-phobia—its many and varied scams and persistent touts and rickshaw wallahs. They were inescapable. I was taken by surprise, this being my first encounter with this disease. No offer of assistance or opportunity came without shoestrings attached in the form of money or side trips to souvenir, carpet, or gem shops. The varied attractions did not escape my fancy. In the end, I suffered from mild hysteria and fatigue. The time I spent warding off the hounding approaches of all the taxi, auto rickshaw, and bicycle rickshaw drivers wore my nerves and patience thin. The flipside to the duress of the next couple of days was that I departed laden with beautiful purchases of traditional art, my suitcase stuffed with embroidered clothes and a luscious scarlet Indian carpet.

Nor did romance slip out of the equation. Another trip.

I toppled into a daze the moment my eyes met the violet blue gaze of the handsome Kashmiri emporium owner. Looking back, I am inclined to admit that he must have seen me as a veritable 'mark' on his score sheet. At the time, I was completely innocent of his ulterior intentions. Why was I so blind? So gullible? So trusting?

Whatever. The fact was that I fell under his enchanting spell and oh, how those men from Kashmir could be so captivating.

They used the words and poetry that Rumi used to weave rapture into the hearts and souls of his readers, seducing them towards the Divine. So smooth were the tones and intonations of the emporium master's talk that I fell on my face with honour and appreciation for this undivided attention. He wove a spell around me as I was paraded around his emporium. The enchanter artfully strung beautiful ruby, sapphire, and emerald jewellery around my neck and marvelled at my beauty as if I were the gems themselves, leaving me dazzled and powerless against his advances.

I trailed after him as he tastefully and professionally showed me his most beautiful wares, encouraging me to try them on or consider their effects in my home. I fell in love with the absolute, remarkable excellence of the embroidered rugs and clothes. I offered to purchase a jacket, a robe, and a rug all of exquisite quality. I had never in my life experienced such beauty in material things. I made a commitment to return with traveller's cheques the following day. To this day I have no regrets—about the purchases, that is.

He graciously offered to show me around Agra the next day and to take me to dinner the evening before my departure. A perfect host, Mansour acted as though he were struck by MY remarkable beauty. He commented on that fact and I inclined myself to believe him. By then, I was apt to believe anything, so smitten was I! Bound in a spell of romance, I caught myself thinking about my mother's penchant for Harlequin Romances, concocting a story that I could write around the experience I was having. Of course, I was the heroine of it. You would think that I had had enough of men by then, but from my point of reference, how could one ever have enough romance? Maybe I was just a cat chasing the tail of my own desires or fantasies, believing they were real.

Putting myself in context, I needed to consider a few factors. I was feeling extremely disturbed by the mounting anxiety and distress caused by the antimalarial drugs, although at the time the cause was unknown to me. The need for comfort and escape was paramount. Secondly, my body and heart had been opened by the intimate encounter with Geoffrey at Laxman Jhula. The comfort and diversion had been extremely sweet, and I was reluctant to let them go. Thirdly, the two pujas experienced in Haridwar were playing havoc with my body and psyche, manifesting their effects. I had become a sweet potion to which the flies were attracted; the sense of female power and prowess seemed to be exuding from every pore of my body, desiring union with a mate, and attracting men out of the woodwork. Fourthly, my lifelong dream of finding my 'one and only' predestined partner had been re-awakened, along with the accompanying longing to share my life with someone. Lastly, I had sold all my belongings, left my apartment, and wanted to continue travelling, open to all the advances being made to me. I longed to settle far from home, to begin a new life according to the exotic fantasy of my dreams and the conditioning I had been fed as a child. Such was the logical (?) perspective from which my predicament had to be viewed.

There was a poem I identified with, written by an Indian woman in the early 1900s, describing the longing a woman feels for a man:

> Alone, O Love, I seek the blossoming glades,
> The bright, accustomed alleys of delight,
> Pomegranate-gardens of the mellowing dawn,
> Serene and sumptuous orchards of the night
>
> Alone, O Love, I breast the shimmering waves,
>
> The changing tides of life's familiar streams,
> Wide seas of hope, swift rivers of desire,
> The moon-enchanted estuary of dreams.
> But no compassionate wind or comforting star
> Brings me sweet word of thine abiding place . . .
> In what predestined hour of joy or tears
> Shall I attain the sanctuary of thy face?
>
> —Sarojini Naidu, "Alone"

I was ripe to respond to Mansour's advances. One way or another, I was simply deluded. Furthermore, I suspected it deeply within. However, my reticence to admit my skepticism allowed me to maintain my innocence. Regardless of the niggling doubt, I wasn't prepared for the drastic fall.

I chose to have faith in his compliments and ardent attentions. He approached me from the heart. His eyes, beautiful in their apparent honesty, matched the words of appreciation he was showering upon me. He expressed a genuine interest in knowing me and beseeched me to stay longer. He talked of a future between us as if he truly believed there was one.

I responded to the sincerity of his speech because he said all the right things, all the things a woman longs to hear. He was offering me the gift of extended relationship and devotion. I wondered how that could be true, but admitted the possibility. At home, no man ever spoke to me in this kindly fashion. Did God have a hand in this? Or Durga? What was really happening here? Was this truly a Divine call for faith, and a full response?

He arrived at my hotel early the next morning bearing gifts. The managers were curious about this suave, finely dressed, silver-haired Indian businessman. They were unaccustomed to seeing men of such means and distinction enter their establishment. I felt honoured when one of them came to my door to tell me that a gentleman had arrived to see me and was waiting down in the lobby. Mansour presented me with a small midnight-blue velvet bag. It contained a delicate white marble jewellery box, finely engraved with lapis lazuli, jade, and garnet in a flowery mosaic design, the same art found inside the Taj Mahal. The artisans of Agra were famous for this traditional craft. I was taken by surprise and touched, being unaccustomed to receiving precious gifts from men.

That morning was spent exploring Agra. We trudged around the remarkable Mughal buildings of the Red Fort, where Shah Jahan had been imprisoned by his son. Standing by the upper wall of the fortress, we contemplated the Shah's situation and appreciated the distant view of the Taj, imagining his sadness and longing for his beloved wife. I was given a tour of India's mecca city. Then we drove to the deserted city of Fatehpur Sikri nearby and walked around the abandoned ancient monuments. They had remained intact and as perfect as when they had been first built. Apparently, the city was never inhabited. Its isolated perfection fascinated me and tweaked my imagination.

Mansour needed to work that afternoon. After he dropped me back in my area, I spent the time being driven around to various shops by the original bicycle rickshaw wallah I had hired on my arrival. He received ten percent commission on everything that I bought; consequently, he was delighted when I purchased my red rug at the Abdul Carpet Factory. We also returned to the emporium to pick up my purchases from the day before. Mansour took me into the back area to show me the work of the marble artisans. Outside on the balcony we enjoyed a mint tea. He hugged me as I left, assuring me that he would pick me up around six the next day to go to dinner. He wanted to take me to a very special restaurant on the river that he owned. It sounded rather romantic. Needless to say, I was favourably impressed and excited by the prospect of our ongoing association.

Aside from an hour listening to a master playing exquisite tunes on a beautifully hand-crafted sitar in a music shop, I spent the better part of the next day preparing for my evening rendezvous with my Kashmiri gentleman. I sought out an aesthetics studio and treated myself to a pedicure and facial. Admittedly, the quality of service didn't match Western standards—sterilizing the instruments was a non-existent process. However, my face was radiant and my toes sparkled with frosty ruby toenail polish. I purchased a new pair of sandals to match the sky-blue chiffon, beaded long dress I had purchased at Ram Jhula, which I intended to wear. A far cry from the ratty-tatty traveller of late.

I sat patiently waiting Mansour's arrival in the rooftop restaurant of the hotel, feeling extremely elegant considering that I had been travelling for almost two months. The ravages of budget travel had, until today, taken their toll on my skin and feet. Reasonably fit for the occasion, I was delightfully excited. A date!

Mansour joined me for tea overlooking the Taj. The sun had set and the stars were out. The anticipated reflection of the full moon rising onto the translucent domes would have created a very romantic setting if we had chosen to stay there and wait. Mansour had other plans.

"Shall we go? I have a table reserved," he artfully suggested.

He escorted me down the precarious steps, resting his hand gently on my back as we descended. It was embarrassing to imagine his impression of the hotel, assuming that such a cultured and cultivated man as he would never consider such meagre lodgings. My insecurity faded as he held the front door open and saw me into the leather seat beside his. It was quite an expensive car, an Audi, giving me no reason to believe he was anything other than what he presented himself to be.

At the restaurant, we were escorted to a table outside overlooking the Jumna River. The setting was perfect, a soft lamp lit, flowers in the middle of a table covered with an evenly pressed linen cloth. His order was anticipated and it wasn't long before we were served a bottle of wine in a bucket of ice. Unheard of in India! He held my hand, chatting about his ex-wife and family in Kashmir. He talked about his teen-age children and I could feel that the separation weighed heavily on his heart, noticing deep sadness in his eyes and voice. I was touched that he trusted me enough to confide in me.

The meal consisted of various Indian delicacies that I didn't recognize and couldn't tell the names of if I were asked. I was in a bubble of love as our eyes met over and over again. The moon rose, reflecting its silver light upon the ripples of the water that ran softly below the balcony. Poetry was made of such beauty. Nothing could have been more perfect.

Afterwards, we went back to my hotel. I wished that it were the Sheraton or Hilton rather than the rustic basic room of a backpackers' budget hotel. The remainder of the evening was written in the stars. Fate played itself out.

The spell was broken by the hardness of the cotton mattress and the simplicity of the room. The overhead light dangled from a cord from the ceiling, casting very bright light onto the stained unpainted cement walls. I felt the enchantment of the evening shattered by the reality of my circumstances. I tried not to think about it as Mansour lay beside me and put his arms around me.

"It's OK, Beauty. Don't worry. We will find a nicer place next time. I will move you to a friend's hotel where you will be more comfortable. I want you to know that I love you," he whispered into my ear as he stroked my cheeks with his sensitive fingertips.

"I want to believe that, but we have just met," I meekly responded.

"Time is not important where love is concerned. The first time that I saw you, I knew that I had to know you intimately. You are a true woman. I have longed to meet a woman such as you for such a long time."

"How did you know that I was the one for you?" I asked quietly.

"When I watched you come up the walk. When you glanced over to me and met my eyes, yours lit up with such a golden smile that reached into my heart and grabbed it forever. I knew that I was lost and that you were the one for me. That is why I stood up to greet you myself and to take your hand. I don't usually spend much time with the customers. You know I'm the owner there and it is not my job to be the salesman. It was most unusual for me to take you around; all my employees were extremely surprised at my behaviour. It was worth every minute to stay connected to your heavenly gaze. You have the most extraordinary eyes, so filled with light and love. I want to bask within their warmth forever." Mansour was so believable, vowing to cherish me always, etc., etc.

I succumbed. I wanted to swim in the glory of his advances, to sail upon the winds of his words and fly with the dream. I did. For all of about five minutes.

Then it was over. He stood up. Zipped up his trousers. Walked over to the door and opened it. Before he stepped out, he turned, looked at me with a cold calculating stare as if it had all been premeditated, and then, sharply and unconvincingly said: "I'll call you tomorrow." He walked out into the dark hallway and left.

I was shocked. I was devastated. I was sick to my stomach. I rushed to the bathroom and threw up into the dingy enamel toilet. I couldn't sleep. The night was spent crying and going over the last three days, incident by incident, word for word, examining the 'turn' of events.

"How could I have been so stupid? Why didn't I see it coming?" I cried out loud into my pillow, over and over again, pounding it with my fists to release some of the frustration and rage that I felt. (But then, somewhere deep inside my heart, I knew I had, but needed to experience my tantrum anyways.)

Regardless, I was mad. "How dare he?"

I didn't wait for Mansour to call or to look me up. I knew that he wouldn't. It wouldn't have mattered because I wanted nothing further to do with the 'rake'. He had dishonoured himself in my view. "No way to treat a lady!" I admonished, thoroughly defending myself. I wasn't really a silly, stupidly gullible woman, was I?

He had had his way, gotten what he had wanted. He was a shark and I had been severely bitten. It would take me a long time to recover from the emotional and psychic wounds his betrayal had left. (Or would it? After all, I was in my fifties and had run around this circle many times before. Nevertheless, I was hurt that the universe had done this to me, yet again, when I had opened my heart to believe.) I left on a southbound train early that afternoon, never wanting to see the man again. My soul, however, remained untouched. My pride might have been hurt, my heart wounded by the deceit, but my spirit remained intact—enough to write in my journal:

Full of wind and wave
The night's conscience
Portrayed life like dream work
Webs of mourning's adventures
Vivid as the spider
Hanging from the fingernail
Up and downward climb
Deciding whether or not
Wisdom spins
Or just unwise desires
To fulfill pleasure's ebb
The river runs
While the insect spins its silence.

This bird had not found her perch—her feathers may have been singed by the fires of lust and passion, smoke may still have been in her eyes, but her vision had not been impaired. As the wheels of the train sped their way back to the loving arms of Amma and respite in the sanctuary of her ashram, she again took flight like the bird in the *Rubaiyat* of Omar Khayyam:

The Bird of Time has but a little way
To fly—and lo! The Bird is on the Wing

And no, I did not get to see the inside of the Taj Mahal. The afternoon that I wanted to go, I stubbornly refused to pay the price. They had hiked it up from 80 rupees to 750 rupees for Western tourists. I felt that it was unfair and decided to spend my money on the magic ruby carpet that now resides on the floor of my bedroom, to remind me of the pitfalls of temptation.

The flip side of that particular coin of memory was the tempting image of the Taj forever etched in my mind, luring me back to enjoy its beauty. I knew I would return to see it again some day.

An excerpt from my journal dated October 25, 2003.

It's now noon. I have been travelling since 5:30 last evening when I boarded the 2AC coach in Agra. Apparently the train is running two hours late. I look out the window to see an ox grazing by the tracks. The country is flat with only a few palm trees. The dirt is reddish in colour and the sky expansive with cumulus clouds, like puffy cotton balls throughout. It looks very hot out there, the air permeated with a heat haze.

It is nice and cool inside this air-conditioned car, although the air is rather stuffy. Not very healthy, being recycled so many times. There are probably thousands of people on this train, everyone vying for the bottom sleeper instead of occupying their upper berths. I treasure mine and hoard my space. I have to watch like a hawk and keep stretching my legs out or lying down to assert ownership. Like peeing on my own territory! The guys seem to understand but the women find me unfriendly. They tend to peer at me underneath their furrowed thick eyebrows with disapproval.

Oh well, I am not here to earn Brownie points. I think that I deserve my privacy after all that I have been through. I want to remain comfortable for my two-and-a-half-day sojourn in this hotel on wheels. I have made better friends with the wandering cockroaches and the tiny lizard that climbs the edges of the compartment walls than I have with the passengers.

I have had a headache since I woke up this morning. And loose running! Talk about being uncomfortable and feeling dirty. There is so little water to wash in and the toilet conditions are abhorrent. To distract myself and to build up my forbearance, I have returned to my Ngondro practice. I've also taken the dysentery medication that I got at the travel clinic before I left home. This is the first time that I have had to resort to using it. Should have known better than to accept the tea and lunch that the wife of the rickshaw driver offered me the other afternoon when I went home to meet his family. He was so happy to be my driver and so thankful when I gave him the $20 to fix his rickshaw. Such a meagre sum. He had five kids all living in the same sooty cement room. I didn't want to insult or hurt him by refusing his invitation. Now I am paying for it. I feel as though there are millions of bugs crawling around inside me. Yuck! My heightened sensitivity and surrealistic paranoia could be due to the anxiety I have been feeling throughout this trip.

Just crossed over a bridge. Saw clusters of people washing their clothes down by the river and spreading them out on the red rocks to dry. Interesting configurations of coloured lungis, and six-foot-long rainbow variables of saris. Nearby, a village of round thatched-roof huts. Everything is so very primitive and basic in the rural areas. Quite a contrast from the cities that have an overall modern flair and attitude. I wonder, since India is a democracy, how the villagers stay informed enough to vote. The Indians seem very committed to upholding their democracy and rights.

A woman herding oxen in the fields, a man shepherding goats over the railway tracks, a bell, a temple on a hill, red dug ditches filled with muddy water, washing strewn about, an old man with a stick crossing over land making his way along the dry, hard muddy paths crisscrossing the fields; a village, a few people waiting on a bench for a local train; more fields, a big herd of cattle and oxen, a stream with indecipherable things swimming in the middle; square irrigation lakes, fields of small tree plantations; a man squatting doing his business; a cross on a grave, a family swimming and sitting by a red muddy pond. Once there were probably wild animals, now perhaps only poisonous snakes and crows. Funny how that durable black crow hops, flies, and caws with familiarity all over the world. Every bit of free land seems to be freshly cultivated. Another Christian grave, another man and his ox, another herd of cattle, another village of round thatched huts. Oxen grazing between the tracks, fields of sugar cane, paddies of rice, working people bent over in the hot scorching sun tending the land; a highway running parallel with freight trucks, buses, and taxis, taking people and products north. A town with clay-tiled roofs and mothers in saris holding children, standing in the streets visiting, belonging . . .

Where do I belong?

A crowd of people on bikes and on foot waiting to cross the track. Within the train, three young men arguing over who belongs to the berth above. A child with a bad cough, a baby crying, and the man carrying the big metal tea container going up and down the isles calling "Chai, chai, chai!" Five o'clock and almost 24 hours into this marathon journey.

A satellite dish! Another train. A father and boys walking barefoot down a dirt road carrying tiffin cans. More thatched huts, clay roofs, rice paddies, and a colourful temple with a painting of Durga riding her tiger. The setting sunlight and rain pouring down to cool everything off.

I sat in the freshness of the open air by the open door next to the toilets, until we passed a factory spewing serious pollution across the skies. More rain. The tail-end of the monsoon. A good time to grow rice.

Approaching a town. Slowing down. Stopping. Standing on the steps wondering how long we will stop. Banana, samosa, chai and water vendors. Think I will buy something. The train's thali last night only made me more sick to my stomach. Some water, some bananas. Here are some rupees. Thank you. I am the only white person in a sea of dark faces. White-black eyes staring at me. I am the stranger out of place and unwelcome in their midst. I disturb the boundaries of their familiarity. Some infantry girls in their khaki uniforms and green-black berets with the red-feathered pompoms in the front, set against their black-bunned hair, dark eyes and shiny white-toothed smiles. Train station beggars pressing towards me with their grimy hands and oozing cankerous faces. Lepers.

The tooting horn, hissing of the wheels in motion, whirring of the motor and off again. Another night ahead. Train travel on the Indian Continental Railway. Nothing like it!

I arrived two mornings later at Amma's ashram. Amma wasn't there. She had gone on her European tour and wouldn't be back until December. The place was so quiet with not much going on except cleaning and repairs. Amma's energy was minimal, not enough to hold me. I took a dug-out boat across the backwater to Vallikavu to visit my friends at the hotel I had stayed at for a few days before Amma's birthday celebration.

The owner from Mysore was there. He had previously invited me to accompany him home, but after all that I had been through, I didn't feel comfortable enough to ride with him alone. I was considerably touchy and didn't really want anything further to do with men. I decided to continue on south to Trivandrum. I could go to Kovalam beach for a few days before my flight, bask in the sun, relax, and pretend that I was on holiday.

Again, excerpts from my journal:

October 27, 2003. Father's birthday!

Kovalam is a beach almost at the most southern tip of India. It is a tourist destination and retirement town for both Indians and English people alike. There are many expatriates here from what I have been told.

I am extremely proud of myself, venturing onto a city bus to get to Kovalam beach. The crowded and stuffy bus stopped in the town square. I followed a cobblestone street down to the beach, stopping only to buy myself a pair of handmade brown, tooled leather sandals for 100 rupees ($3.50). I was thrilled to see the sandy beach. In fact there are two beaches separated by a rocky point and cliffs on both sides covered with palm trees aplenty, and cows grazing on the plateaus. Very secluded, sheltered, and quiet.

I am looking forward to my rest here—some sun tanning and swimming.

Had a bit of a fright when I first arrived. Have to admit I am exhausted with the challenges of the men. Just before stepping onto the beach, I decided to stop for a cup of tea at a restaurant next to it. I wanted to sit on the balcony, sipping my morning tea while watching the people jumping and playing in the water and listening to the soothing sound of the incoming waves. The owner sat down at my table, curious because it was, as yet, too early for the high season. He apparently owned a pleasant hotel across the rice paddies behind the beach. He invited me to come to see it and to consider staying there. I had my heart set on a beach-front room, so hesitated. He offered me a nice a room at a very reasonable price, so I agreed to go see it.

The hotel was new and all freshly painted with some of the nicest rooms that I have seen so far. I was tempted. It was all rather contemporary with lovely linens and interior decorations. We sat outside one of the rooms overlooking the rice paddies, enjoying a glass of cold Coke, and chatted. He told me of the Englishwoman whom he had lived with until recently, when she unexpectedly returned to England. He seemed pretty broken up about it. He asked me if I would consider staying for the winter. I shook my head. He offered me the best room on the fourth floor, saying I could have it for $200 a month.

I was quiet after he made the offer. I wasn't in any mood to consider the opportunity because I knew that there would be conditions. I had no desire to be the Englishwoman's replacement. Before I had time to respond, he reached down to his trousers, unzipped his fly, pulled out his penis and offered:

"You can have this as well, as often as you like for the same price."

I stared with disbelief and quickly patted his leg saying: "No, thank you all the same. You can put it way now."

I assured him that there was nothing wrong with him, that I really was only staying a couple of days, then was on my way home. I couldn't believe the audacity. It's as if they are just young children, their attitudes about their bodies so naïve. So matter of fact and so natural. Sorry, I have had enough.

I'm sitting on the upper balcony of a lovely new room, overlooking the ocean. The tide is coming in; the waves are crashing against the shore. The sun is still pretty hot although it is almost evening. It will be a beautiful sunset. I have my bathing suit on for the first time this trip. How absolutely glorious! I wish that I had discovered this beach sooner. I will have to return here another time. I leave tomorrow to catch my flight. Yesterday and today were wonderful. I couldn't swim in my bathing suit because the traditional dress code is pretty much in place. All the women wear their saris. I wore my lavender shalwar kameez. I really had wanted to suntan but ended up all sandy. I have been up here on the balcony for a couple of hours. I moved one of the single mattresses out and am lying on it. Thoroughly enjoying myself.

This morning I witnessed the cooperative dance of the fishermen as they cast out their nets and pulled them in. The healthy brown bodies with their colourful lungis—all lined up, energetically pulling in the line, tugging, singing, and chanting, all the while establishing an efficient communal rhythm. As the net approached the shore, young boys waded out, splashing about so that the fish wouldn't get out of the net. Then the big net was dragged ashore and people began to fill their baskets, bags, or plastic containers with the hundreds of tiny silver fish. Reminded me of what it must have been like in Jesus's day around the Sea of Galilee where the fishermen, like some of the disciples, cast their nets in such a primitive fashion.

This afternoon I had lunch with an Englishwoman I met, who filled me in on all the expat gossip. There is a whole community of retired people from England here. One thing of interest she told me: She said that middle-aged white women have a reputation amongst the Indians, that they come here only for sex, particularly with the younger Indian men. They can get away with it here and no one will know. At home, it is frowned upon. Maybe that explains why all the men have been so free with me, thinking that I was just one of those women. Regardless, I will be glad to get back to familiar ground. At home I will be able to relax and not have to ward off the continual advances of the opposite sex.

In memory:

On December 26, 2004, the historic tsunami hit the coasts of Sri Lanka and Southern India, as well as the coasts of other South Asian countries. Over a hundred thousand people died, swept away by the tidal waters hitting the coastal regions. Kovalam was not as damaged as some other parts of Kerala but many fishing families lost their homes and boats. I sent Reiki and my loving thoughts to my friends there.

The plane was to leave at midnight. I had taken a room across the street from the Trivandrum airport, planning to easily make my way over to the checkout building around ten. I had intended to rest beforehand. Lying on the bed unable to sleep, I listened to the cacophony of sounds from outside the open window. Aside from all the noises of the various vehicles, I heard people talking and laughing, children squealing, babies crying, dogs barking, cows mooing, horns blowing . . . such an organic mixture of congeniality.

Memories of India. I would miss her ever-changing multifaceted face. Would I ever return? That was a sixty-four-million-dollar question. I had presently had my fill. Full to capacity from the myriad adventures of this trip. I wasn't running away. I was puzzled by the turn my trip had taken, back into the relative dilemmas of my personal existence. My initial intention to expand my spiritual horizons, had it been fulfilled? As I looked back over the time I had been here, I could fairly say that the teachings had presented themselves in unexpected ways. It would take time to digest and assimilate my experiences. I surmised that time and space were necessary to get a broader perspective.

I tempered the tendency towards hasty judgment. Shit happened, as it always did. How was I to know the greater picture? Unable to settle down my mind, I pulled out a book of days by Sogyal Rinpoche that I had been carrying in my suitcase, closed my eyes, flipped to a page dated March 10 and read the following words of Buddha:

> Know all things to be like this:
> A mirage, a cloud castle,
> A dream, an apparition,
> Without essence, but with qualities that can be seen.
>
> Know all things to be like this:
> As the moon in a bright sky

In some clear lake reflected,
Though to that lake the moon has never moved.

Know all things to be like this:
As an echo that derives
From music, sounds, and weeping,
Yet in that echo is no melody.

Know all things to be like this:
As a magician makes illusions
Of horses, oxen, carts and other things,
Nothing is as it appears.

"'So long, farewell, *auf Wiedersehen,* good-bye,' my beloved India. Till we meet again," I whispered into the pungent, tepid, and receptive evening air.

SRI MATA AMRITANANDAMAYI (Amma).

Amma's ashram on the backwaters of Kerala.

Krishna's chariot over the door of Amma's shrine room.

Devotees singing bhajans in Amma's auditorium.

The Little Toy Train to Darjeeling.

The Lotus Blossom Seller.

The Granddaughter Bodhi Tree behind the temple in Bodhgaya,,
under which Buddha sat when he achieved enlightenment.

Wandering sadhu – woman with snake.

Wandering sadhu wearing pashmina shawl.

Sunset over the Ganges at Laxman Jhula.

Boat ride on the Ganges at Varanasi by the burning ghats.

Sacred cows of India wandering in back streets of old Varanasi.

Morning at the bathing ghats in Varanasi.

The Taj Mahal, viewed from behind on the Jumna River in Agra.

2005

Dedication

Milarepa, a Tibetan saint, hid himself in caves and sang:

Hark my sons {and daughters}!
If you want to climb the mountain peak
To enjoy the view
You should hold the Self-Mind's light
Tie (it) with a great 'knot'
And catch it with a firm 'hook'.
If you practice thus
You can climb to the mountain peak
To enjoy the view.

The spiritual quest is an ascension, the paths leading to the summit are many and of diverse lengths, and necessarily so, as men think, understand and feel differently. While the path may be different, the goal is unique.

—Bhumananda, Indian ascetic and
spiritual guide to Guiseppe Tucci during
his expedition to Mt. Kailash in 1935.

There is a story as told by Sogyal Rinpoche of an old frog who lived all his life in a dank well. One day a frog from the sea paid him a visit.

"Where do you come from?" asked the frog in the well.
"From the great ocean," he replied.
"How big is your ocean?"
"It's gigantic."
"You mean about a quarter of the size of my well here?"
"Bigger."
"Bigger? You mean half as big?"
"No, even bigger."
"Is it . . . as big as this well?"
"There's no comparison."
"That's impossible! I've got to see this for myself."

They set off together. When the frog from the well saw the ocean, it was such a shock that his head just exploded into pieces.

Was I ready for my head to blow into pieces? It most certainly needed revamping. The Dalai Lama had said that all humans were equal in their ability to achieve happiness, that there was equal potential for all to transform the mind, to transform one's mental ability. He had emphasized at the turn of the millennium that humanity needed this transformation to achieve peace and harmony amongst all. It was my responsibility then to continue my quest and adhere to the *je ne sais quoi* that fuelled the motor of my spiritual drive.

My activity in the relative world seemed ineffective and redundant, centred upon the roles of mother or companion. Becoming increasingly uncomfortable confined within the cage of my limited understanding, my greater self, no longer convinced by my minimal efforts to grow and expand, wanted reflection and active expression. If a means of self-expansion and expression were not found soon, I would burst like the frog, but not from new vision, rather from lack of it.

Possibly the power and awareness generated by my meditation and Ngondro practice were the cause of my discomfort, or the experience and unidentified knowledge gained through my travels. My awareness seemed out of the box of all the structures I had previously created for myself, craving something more intelligent and true. Inactivity felt stifling and stagnant. Having disengaged from social responsibilities and feeling inhibited by familial ones, I needed and wanted to make some definite changes in my life, once again integrating myself into the collective society.

Encouraged by the Dalai Lama's words to do my part in creating peace and harmony in the world, I applied for and was accepted into graduate studies, with spiritual and cultural vision the focus of my inquiry. I had had an epiphany the winter following my return from India. It looked as though my services were still needed at home, at least temporarily and intermittently. (As a single parent of a two-year-old, my youngest daughter needed my presence and support.) Going back to school would provide mental grounding and establish a way to channel future travelling through a research focus, and to realize yet another item on my 'list of dreams'.

"Good idea!" responded my efficient and innovative mind.

The river was bound to flow smoothly, re-routing to circumvent obstacles, its intention stronger through its course. I was determined to progress towards my goal. Infinity or bust!

Still suffering from the aftermath of single-parent burn-out, I felt the overwhelming need to develop compassion. How could I reboot the program? My 'mother-love' well had almost run dry. Who was here to fill ME up? Only me, myself, and I, and a little help from my spiritual friends . . . When I heard that the Nyingma dharma group was doing the Chenrezig practice every other Wednesday, I committed to going. That October, my friend Nana and I went over to Vancouver to attend a weekend teaching and empowerment of the Red Chenrezig practice given by Venerable Thrangu Rinpoche. Rinpoche, on tour in North America, was a Tibetan living in Kathmandu, Nepal. As a revered and accomplished Tibetan Buddhist Master, he had been selected by the Dalai Lama to oversee the education of the young Karmapa, the head of the Kagyu lineage of Tibetan Buddhism, who had fled Tibet as a child and was now in his mid-teens, living in Dharamsala in the monastery that the Dalai Lama had built with his Nobel Peace Prize monies.

The local centre was of a different lineage, led by a lama from Bhutan. However, Bhutan had in the past been part of Tibet, so the religious practices were similar. The centre specialized in the Rainbow Light Dzogchen teaching. I had previously received my Ngondro practice from there; however, other practices were carried out during the week that helped prepare a solid foundation for its reception. Most of the people had had the *abhisheka* (empowerment or initiation) to the Chenrezig teaching, rendering it more powerful. I wanted to have the full experience of this practice to develop compassion. When the opportunity arose to go to Vancouver, I was delighted and eager to attend.

The Dalai Lama had said he thought compassion would be the religion of the new millennium. How was it possible to generate it? According to the Tibetan Buddhists, compassion was the characteristic of the bodhisattva Chenrezig; therefore, the esoteric teaching coinciding with him was necessary to develop this quality. They also believed that there were two components, compassion and wisdom (skilful means), necessary for enlightenment or the realization of the true nature of mind. This was symbolized as the *yab-yum* or union of male and female often depicted in Tibetan art as a man and woman (deity and consort) in the gesture of intercourse. By using the skilful means of this Vajrayana teaching, one then acquired the compassion necessary to complete the union—resulting in completion and realization, growing into the embodiment of Chenrezig, a compassionate bodhisattva, living one's life for the betterment, happiness, and enlightenment of all.

Albert Einstein had said something very similar to the Dalai Lama:

A human being is part of a whole, called by us the 'Universe,' a part limited in time and space. He experiences himself, his thoughts and feelings, as something separated from the rest—a kind of optical delusion of his consciousness. This delusion is a kind of prison for us, restricting us to our personal desires and to affection for a few persons nearest us. Our task must be to free ourselves from this prison by widening our circle of compassion to embrace all living creatures and the whole of nature in its beauty.

If such great men were advocating selfless service, and Amma, whom I very much respected, said the same, then maybe it was time to pay attention and give up my selfish ways. Not that I hadn't been trying to help my fellow human beings. The difference lay in the motive underlying my good intentions. How much of my loving action towards others was a means to give myself identity and to feed my ego? I cared about others because it gave me a *raison d'être* and a sense of place in the world. Not that I would be doing anything different, but I would be doing it from a completely different perspective. There was nothing more important in life to do but "love others as oneself," as Jesus had said. However, I wouldn't be doing so because my ego was in survival mode, I would be doing it because otherwise life was meaningless, without any true value.

The Dalai Lama has also said that 'compassionate action' is a means to overcome one's own suffering. Deliberating on one's personal suffering results in being completely swallowed up by it, leading to contraction, withdrawal, separation, paranoia, and ultimately violence. Firstly, it is violence against oneself because human beings are social creatures who need to trust each other. By thinking of another's suffering, we step outside our personal dilemmas, opening our minds and hearts, expanding in the process. In turn, we open to love, placing the needs and feelings of others before ourselves. The magnitude of our suffering shrinks to less than nothing; we become unaware of it. As compassion for the other takes priority, we open to feelings of kindness and generosity. That is how human beings work. Buddhists believe that this is an antidote and remedy for anger, depression, and most of the world's ills.

We are most happy experiencing our natural state—Love. It is important to understand the nature of ourselves as human beings. Other animals do not have such an unlimited capacity or awareness to serve others. If our actions are to have any effect upon the evolution of this millennium to counteract the growing effects of terrorism, we urgently need to refocus our attention away from our personal problems and selfish needs onto the needs of the greater whole. It is imperative. The Dalai Lama travels the world saying: "Practice compassion and kindness towards others always."

I love that man. He stands as a beacon upon the horizon of global consciousness. Exiled and countryless, he continues to serve not only his own people but also every citizen on earth. I hold him up as my model.

The nature of my personal suffering centred around feeling overwhelmed by the needs and suffering of those around me. How could I step out of myself to take care of others when I felt so abandoned and in need of love? Was it possible to cultivate and grow the flowers of compassion and kindness? I most certainly was willing to find out. The Tibetan Buddhists seemed to think so and had the support of their most beloved bodhisattva, Chenrezig, in the form of the Dalai Lama. Who or what was this being? I resolved to find out. Having heard it was possible, I wanted to experience the compassion of Chenrezig through the meditation practice.

This would be stretching the perimeters of my Christian conditioning. I was no Mother Teresa. I had been trying but felt myself a failure. Even my youngest daughter was beginning to rebel at my attempts to help. She felt that there were always strings attached. Her psyche was more attuned than my own. As she began to push me away, I began to feel extremely panic ridden. Going for communion regularly at the cathedral helped, but I still felt an empty well in my heart, unable to escape my own personal anguish.

I had previously taken refuge and bodhisattva vows, which had lain dormant for years. Deciding to re-activate them and commit to the Vajrayana teachings, I began with the Red Chenrezig, with Thrangu Rinpoche as my root guru. I wanted to experience for myself the dynamic effects and reality of the Tibetan Buddhist way, possibly acquiring the pristine clarity of mind that I had intuited in the minds of the Tibetans in Dharamsala. I wanted to improve my life so that I would be able to be of service to my family, humanity, and the planet: truly desiring to participate in creating global peace and harmony following the Dalai Lama's instructions.

It was a privilege to receive the Red Chenrezig teaching from such a qualified master. In order to support my practice, I submitted a proposal to my education supervisor to research the teaching of Compassion through this practice, and to go on a journey into the heartland of Tibetan Buddhism to more fully understand the context from which it evolved. My proposal was accepted.

After finishing most of my courses I booked myself a ticket to India, with the intention of heading up to Nepal to 'stake my claim' on my pot of gold—to realize my intended goal—in front of Mount Everest! I had also made a list of all the places that I wanted to see before I died; Mount Everest was first on that list. Why not go to the highest place in the world to state my highest intention—to realize the truth of myself and get a master's degree in the process?

I was to depart at the end of October. My youngest daughter had just discovered that she was three months pregnant. I told her that I wanted a few months away before the baby was born, assuring her that I would be back well before her due date. I packed my camera, notebook, hiking boots, warm jacket, along with my trusty friend the Lonely Planet guidebook for Nepal, and set off.

Years ago . . .

I was travelling on a Gray Line bus north along the Vancouver Island coastline towards Port Renfrew. Dozing in my seat, I shook myself awake to enjoy the lovely view, noticing a silver-haired middle-aged man stand up in the front and start walking to back towards me. It was my father! What was he doing here? The bus stopped and he said:

"Let's get off."

I was shocked to see him but also delighted. He was supposed to be in Calgary with my mom. I got out of my seat and followed him off the bus. We found a café across the road to sit in. He started talking to me in the most earnest fashion. Just like in the old days when I was a teenager. He would wake me up at night with a barrel of Kentucky Fried Chicken and we would have lucid conversations about the meaning of life.

He reached across the table to take my hand in his and said very softly but firmly:

"Dorothy, I need you to listen to me. It is very important."

He took me on a journey. I wasn't sure if it was a vision or just a story. Dad held on to my hand and led me outside and up into the hills. We began to climb a small mountain. He seemed very intent on the direction. Straight up. It was a difficult climb but at last we reached the summit. The sky around us was blue and expansive. It was glorious to look at the world from up there.

Then suddenly, he pointed down to the bottom where we had started. I saw a group of people gathered there, men, women, and children of all ages. My family! What were they doing there? I squinted to make sure it was really them. My vision couldn't have been clearer. As Dad pointed to each and every one of them, he walked me through their strengths and weaknesses, one by one.

Then he very intently said:

"Now dear, I want you to go down and bring them up so that they can see this view, so that they can see all that we can."

I nodded, agreeing to his directive. Then the lights went out.

I started and opened my eyes. I was on a bus heading towards Sooke. I had been dreaming. I got off the bus in Jordan River, headed to the nearest coffee shop and wrote the story.

A few days later, back in Victoria, I was staying with a friend named Gloria, a psychic who read palms and tarot cards. I had been travelling with a crystal ball that had been handmade in England. It, along with my flute and Israeli carpet bag that I had made from a red velvet carpet purchased in the Medina Bazaar in Jerusalem years before, accompanied me on all my journeys. I asked her if she would look into my crystal ball to shed some light upon the possible meaning of my daydream. She consented.

We took the perfectly polished ball and laid it out on the woven tapestry that it was usually wrapped in. Gloria studied it for a while. Then suddenly she said:

"Put it away."

She brusquely got up and left the room. I was extremely puzzled but did as she told me, leaving it at that. Later that evening, as I sat watching *Jesus Christ Superstar* for the first time (it had been filmed in Israel when I was there in '72) and had come to the part of the story where Judas hung himself, there was a knock on the front door. I opened it to find my aunt (Dad's sister) and uncle there. They looked upset. I led them into the front room and sat them down.

"Your father died today," my aunt said sadly.

Her hands were trembling as she reached for mine.

"He had taken your mom and youngest brother, Stephen, to Hawaii. They arrived yesterday. Today they did all the things that he loved to do—snorkelling and hiking. They went to a beach to swim and his heart stopped as he started up the path to go home. We are so sorry, dear."

That happened in October 1976, twenty-nine years ago. Now my sister Carol was on the phone pleading with me:

"You've got to take some of Dad's ashes with you. Take them

up the mountain and throw them off in front of Mount Everest. He said that he wanted his ashes spread all around the world. I have faith in you, Dorth, you can do it!" She continued with excited encouragement.

"I'll send them Express Post this afternoon and you should get them in a couple of days. You don't leave until Monday, which is three days away. You'll have them by then."

Carol sounded certain, but I had my doubts. I wondered why no one in my family ever called me Veda. I had officially changed my name years ago. Oh well, some people refused to admit change. I left it all up in the air.

If the ashes came, they came. If they did, I would take them with me, crossing my fingers that no one found them while I was going through security. I hoped that it would be easy and I could just find a bus to take me to a hill where I could see Mount Everest in front of me. I was forty menopausal pounds overweight and very out of shape. I had long since stopped doing yoga and had hardly been walking since I started university last year. I'd just have to take my chances and hope that meeting my commitment to the family wouldn't prove too difficult.

I was to eat my words. The ashes arrived in the post the next day. The task of taking them to their final destination took a lot longer and a heck of a lot more work than merely going to the post office and putting them in the mail.

I love to go a-wandering, along the mountain track,
And as I go, I love to sing, my knapsack on my back.
—Frank Weir & Henri René

"Not yet! Not yet! Hold your horses, Veda," I 'whoaed' myself down. "There's something you need to do before you take to the hills," I tempered myself out loud.

Having just woken up and feeling 'hot to trot', I rubbed my eyes and looked at my surroundings. I was in my favourite Delhi budget hotel in the old market area of Paharganj, embraced by freshly painted pink walls. What a change from the dingy, dirty, pale grey with mouldy stains. Hmm. The place had had an upgrade, as emphasized in the Lonely Planet guide.

"The hotel managers, those two helpful brothers, must be doing well," I continued to muse. One of the things I do when I am travelling is to keep myself company with an ongoing audible conversation. At home one might think that I was crazy, never hesitating to answer myself.

"I must ask them about cheap flights to Nepal today," I reminded myself. However, I still hadn't decided whether or not I wanted to go the long way by train and bus to see some countryside *en route*. I'd have to think about it some more. I went for chai and breakfast to do just that.

The thing that I needed to do *first* was to get a blessing for my trip and my research project—the perfect way to begin a new venture. Framing my project with blessings from realized beings seemed an auspicious enterprise and a correct way of doing things. The Dalai Lama was in America. It would be futile to go to Dharamsala for his blessing, although I could approach the Karmapa. I decided that I wanted to find Mindrolling Trichen Rinpoche, the one who had become head of the Nyingma lineage at the request of Penor Rinpoche (Sogyal Rinpoche's brother). It seemed pertinent, since I had been studying the Ngondro, the preliminary practices of Dzogchen, the Rainbow Light teaching. I wanted to know if he really thought one could dissolve into rainbow light at death or whether he thought he would be able to do it. I had vowed that I would spend this trip going around asking people if they knew anything about this teaching. It continued to hold my fascination. I would seek the Karmapa's blessing at the conclusion of my research. Sandwiched in between the intentions of two of the world's most spiritually enlightened beings according to the Tibetans. Not a bad idea!

I had discovered Mindrolling Trichen Rinpoche in the March 2005 edition of the *Shambala Sun*, a Buddhist magazine that I subscribed to. He stunned me by his direct, incorrigible gaze. I wanted to meet his eyes, never having encountered anyone who was that seemingly present, and to match his face to the picture. I valued his words outlined in the article:

The essence of Dharma lies in being true to oneself (one's innate nature) and in exerting great effort to be courageous. When truth and the courage to walk on the path of truth are joined with mindfulness, a practitioner truly begins to practice the dharma. Until these qualities of truth and courage are generated, we will be vulnerable to our own pretences and fabrications.

Wasn't that what I was trying to do? Would he be my Dzogchen teacher? I was still seeking a master to lead me through the Dzogchen process. I had heard that it was imperative to find oneself a teacher of great virtue and kindness, as the process involved could lead into insanity if one didn't have the proper guidance. I wasn't about to take that risk, so I would continue my preliminary practices until I had found the right teacher. If it were my destiny, I would find one. If not, I would have an interesting time searching one out.

"This is your stop. You need to get out here," the minibus driver advised me.

"Is this Clement Town?" I asked.

"Yes, Mindrolling Monastery is just down that road," the driver replied, pointing to his left.

It was mid-afternoon. Hot. The road was dusty. I was all dressed up for the occasion in a beautifully embroidered long gown that I had purchased in Ram Jhula the day after I had arrived in India. I had taken a night bus, and ended up in the Swiss Cottage Hotel there to recover from jet lag and get my bearings, being once again in Asia. It had been Diwali and I didn't want to be in the big city. I had heard that it would be very noisy and a bit dangerous. Tourists were always targeted during festivals.

I'm glad that I did. Rishikesh (remember my favourite places Laxman and Ram Jhula?) was on the way to Mussoorie, where I had heard that Khandro Rinpoche, Mindrolling Rinpoche's daughter, had a centre for nuns. I had wanted to approach her about her father, to arrange a meeting with him, thinking that the proper protocol might be to approach her first. (Khandro Rinpoche is a very popular teacher in the West, with a centre in Virginia. I had seen a picture of her in the *Shambhala Sun* magazine.) However, I had been unsuccessful, having gone to Mussourie and asked about, with everyone replying that they had no idea who she was. Consequently, I headed back down to Dehradun, took a hotel room close to the train station, cleaned myself up, and boarded a minibus heading in the direction of Clement Town, the location of Rinpoche's monastery.

I walked in the direction that the bus driver had advised me and came to a local post office. In front was a man sitting at a rickety wooden tea stall. I decided to have a small cup of chai and adjust myself to my surroundings before I entered the monastery compound.

Standing under the shade of a Neem tree, I was delighted to see women and children dressed in Tibetan clothes.

"Ah, yes. The Tibetans," I whispered to myself. I loved to be in their midst and wondered why. Had I been a Tibetan in a previous incarnation? I knew Christians weren't supposed to believe in more than one lifetime but I chose to believe in rebirth and reincarnation because it made sense. I had heard that in the 4th-century Emperor Constantine had begun the process of a Christian 'reformation' which included condemnation of reincarnation.

I emptied my little plastic cup of chai, threw it in the rusty garbage barrel, and set off to my right, down the road towards the monastery gates. I passed many houses and shops with Tibetan artefacts and accoutrements needed for their religious practices. I had stopped to gaze at the wares in one of them, when a young monk sidled up to me. He was European.

"Do you need any help? May I be of service?" he asked politely. "My name is Hendrick. I am Russian."

I took a few seconds to scrutinize the maroon-clad Western fellow in front of me, and to peruse the surroundings, snatching some time to digest the moment. Everything seemed ultra-quiet. And so clean. Not at all like India. The Tibetans were such a different people, exhibiting qualities and virtues not found amongst the Indians. They seemed able to maintain cultural identity regardless of the fact that they were living in a country other than their own, this having a lot to do with their religion being their way of life, I supposed.

"Actually, I am looking for a kata. I want to meet Mindrolling Trichen Rinpoche and have a blessing. I hope it's possible."

"We may try," Hendrick responded. "But there are no guarantees. He's had a mysterious sickness for many years now. I will take you to his house."

"Thank you. You are being so helpful."

Hendrick asked the woman for a kata which I purchased for 10 rupees (30 cents). Making our way through the overarching gates into the monastery compound, I noticed the familiar golden wheel with two deer on each side that usually sat on top of Tibetan Buddhist monastery gates or shrines. It represented Buddha's 'turning the wheel of the dharma or law' for the first time at Deer Park in Sarnath, near Varanasi—a place to visit at some point on my research journey.

As we passed under the gate, everything seemed to change; it became obvious that we were walking upon hallowed ground. To the left, through another smaller gate, stood a towering golden standing Buddha, whose right hand was held up, palm facing outward, and the left extended out with palm upward. I thought the hand gesture was the teaching *mudra* (sacred hand position). The gate itself was beautiful—the two identical pillars were painted red, with large silver-grey vases holding the pink lotus topped by the wheel, three of the eight auspicious Tibetan symbols. The top of the gate was Chinese-like with upturned corners to ward off ill-intentioned spirits. Again, on the very top of its roof were the two golden deer and the golden Wheel of the Law.

The 'eight auspicious emblems' (relating to the major premises of the religion) are widely depicted in Tibetan tradition and found everywhere in the art, architecture, literature, and materials of the culture. There is the parasol (protection from suffering), wheel (the Dharma), endless knot (the truth of dependent origination), victory banner (triumph over ignorance), fish (liberation from the sea of *samsara*), treasure vase (endless spiritual jewels), lotus (compassion and purity), and conch (proclaiming the Buddha's awakening).

The artistry of the monastery was superb. In front of me in the distance towered a gigantic white stupa again with a golden Buddha standing in front of a painted Buddha, under an arch of brightly painted peacock feathers. It was stunning and spellbinding, emanating victory and glory. A large area of lawn stretched in front of the building with a huge statue of White Tara sitting on a brightly coloured rainbow lotus seat in the foreground, filling me with awe and appreciation for the quality and beauty of the whole setting.

More impressive was the atmosphere of quietude and sacredness. It seemed to permeate every cell of my body, inspiring reverence and having a very peculiar effect upon me; I felt purified and worthy just by being there. The energy around emanated beauty and bliss. Feeling those qualities within myself, I was filled with gratitude knowing that my search hadn't been in vain, glad I had made the effort to come.

Hendrick veered me towards a red metal fence with closed doors. He opened them and we entered the driveway of a Tibetan-styled house, yellow stucco with wooden window frames painted with bright Tibetan designs like those found around monastery windows, doorways, and rooftops. It was Rinpoche's house. We knocked on the brass knocker of the red wooden door. A nun answered; she and Hendrick conversed quietly and then he turned to me and said:

"We are in luck. Rinpoche will see us. We must wait here on the bench along with the others. He will see us after them."

There were a few other people lined up on a wooden seat along the front wall of the house, obviously Tibetan. They were wearing ethnic clothing and the women's hair was braided with colourful silk tassels dangling from the ends.

When it came our turn, we were asked to remove our shoes and to come in quietly. Hendrick elected to wait outside. I entered the hallway and passed through a cotton curtain hanging at the entrance of Rinpoche's room. It also had some auspicious symbols on it made of yellow, blue, and red silk. I entered the room, stooping a little with hands folded in prayer position in a gesture of respect.

Rinpoche was lying on a bed with his eyes closed. A woman, presumably his wife, stood beside him holding his hand, as he seemed asleep. She took the kata from me and touched it to Rinpoche's hand and then placed it around my neck. Then she took my hand and touched it with his for the blessing. For some reason my eyes filled with tears: I was touched. Even though he was not conscious, Rinpoche's spirit filled the room.

He may as well have been awake; such was the effect the blessing had on me—profound and powerful. My mind immediately became very calm and quiet. Extremely humbled, I admitted being in the presence of a great personage. I quietly backed out of the room without turning my back to the Rinpoche, as one is supposed to do as a matter of respect. I passed once again through the curtain, leaving my offering within a white envelope in a basket at the door to his room, and left the house to sit down on the bench outside for quite a while afterwards, with tears streaming down my face.

Of course, it hadn't been quite as I had planned. I didn't get a chance to talk to him. I was not clear about his secret illness because nobody seemed to talk about it. It was disrespectful to do so, according to Hendrick. Apparently, he was not truly ill. He was in a sacred state of dreamtime where he was flying in another dimension with the bodhisattvas and *dakinis* (female beings living in higher dimensions of consciousness). How long he would remain in that state no one knew. Did he come out of it to eat and sleep? I wasn't clear about his daily routine and it didn't feel appropriate to ask.

No point considering him as my teacher. Disappointed but not unhappy, I was touched by the blessing and felt I had accomplished my original goal. My research project had officially begun!

A bit later, I had the privilege of a half-hour interview with Khandro Rinpoche who very graciously agreed to see me and answer my questions. She verified with certainty the actuality of the Rainbow Light teaching, advising me though to study the basic Buddhist philosophy and practice my Vajrayana teachings. This would lay a solid foundation for the Dzogchen practice. She suggested I have lunch with some of her students from France and then join her afterwards for a tour inside the stupa. I gratefully accepted her generous offer.

Khandro Rinpoche also invited me to her centre outside of Mussoorie to do a six-week contemplative retreat. I thought not. It would be getting cold after my intended Nepal journey and I didn't want to sit meditating in freezing temperatures under austere conditions. I knew that few places in India had indoor heating and pretty certain that hers wouldn't either. I never went there to find out. Life had other plans for me.

(A few years later, upon receiving a final blessing from the Karmapa at the conclusion of my research project, I returned to the Mindrolling Monastery. The Karmapa was there, presiding over the death puja of Mindrolling Rinpoche who had passed a few days before my arrival. I guess Rinpoche had finally decided to go join his friends in higher realms. It was then that I received blessings and an empowerment of Amitayus Buddha, the Longlife Buddha, from the young Karmapa, along with thousands of Tibetans on the grass beside the marvellous white stupa. Interesting that my journey had begun with the passing of Papaji and ended with another death, that of Mindrolling Trichen Rinpoche, as well, auspicious that it had commenced with the Hindu celebration of Papaji's samadhi and concluded with the Buddhist puja of passing though the various bardos of Rinpoche's afterlife journey. Who, if anyone or anything, was orchestrating this?)

Before I had left for this trip, I had opened my mailbox and, instead of finding the million dollars that I was sure would arrive one day, I found the September 2007 edition of the Shambhala Sun.

"Oh, glory!" I said to myself as I excitedly took it out of the slot.

I headed down the hall to the patio sundeck, laid out my towels, took off my sundress, and set myself down to bask in the sun, in my new two-piece bathing suit from Thailand. I sat there with my tea, and quickly ripped off the dusty plastic wrapping, opening it up to the index page to see what was in store for me this month. I sipped and browsed.

Lo and behold, an article just for me! How apropos. Wonders never ceased. The New-Agers called it synchronicity. I tended towards the interdependence of all things, even if I *was* weaving the shape of my own knot—back and forth, weaving the present into the past. My awareness into my past experience . . . a karmic coincidence? What I had sown in the past had resulted in the arrival of a brilliant idea—that I could most certainly refer back into the avenues of my past to explain my present. Did that make sense?

I wondered if that was what the Buddhists referred to as the inter-connectedness of all things? Someone out there was listening to my tale. And thus, the article ("Grandmother Mind" by Susan Moon) spoke to me:

> Zen master Eihei Dogen, founder of the Soto School of Zen in 13th-century Japan, told his monks they should all develop "grandmother mind." He said, "You can understand all of Buddhism, but you cannot go beyond your abilities and your intelligence unless you have *robai-shin,* grandmother mind, the mind of great compassion. This compassion must help all of humanity. You should not think only of yourself."

Now, returning to my story . . . I was sitting in a degenerated Nepalese bus, cramped into the corner of a window seat with a drunken, unsavoury Indian man beside me who kept trying to feel me up. Who in the bus would care? I had to look after myself. I knocked his hand off my leg.

I had been thinking about my lovely little three-year-old granddaughter, and the new baby yet to be born. Who would this little one be? My granddaughter had told me a story while visiting one weekend the June before. She said:

"Grandma, I talked to my baby brother!"

"What do you mean?" I replied.

"I'm going to have a baby brother. He told me he was coming. I said to him that it was OK; he could come now," she answered with a very knowing voice.

At the time I thought how very interesting that was, considering my history of talking to the babies in the family before they were born. I wondered if she had inherited my gift. I told her, "That's great! When you go home tell your Mommy that Grandma said it's OK."

When I mentioned the story to my daughter, she adamantly refuted the possibility: "I'm not pregnant and not going to be, NOT any time soon!" she argued. It turned out otherwise. She had a pregnancy test three months later, which came out positive. She must have just conceived around the time of discussion. Now that was pretty exciting! My granddaughter knowing about it, I mean.

The baby was supposedly to be born early that coming February. I wondered if it would be a boy after all? (Incidentally, it was a girl.)

My mind meandered to a children's song by Raffi. I loved Raffi. I had listened to him with my kids and now with my granddaughter. The child within me still lived on. The bus ride was tedious and I found myself singing his bus song:

"The wheels on the bus go round and round, round and round, round and round. The wheels on the bus go round and round, all around the town.

"The people on the bus go up and down, up and down. The people on the bus go up and down, all around the town."

Funny how the mind worked making associations—my mind spinning, bouncing in and out of thoughts along with the rhythm of the wheels traversing the miles and knocking its passengers about over the potholes. Speed was as much an addiction with the Nepalese drivers as it was with the Indians.

I wondered about my relationship with my children and if I would be able to open my heart as much to the new grandchild as I had with my first, and how my daughter would manage with the new baby coming. My ability to be compassionate seemed to be limited by my fear. A friend had once said:

"The difference between sympathy and compassion is that sympathy is fear based. Compassion stems from one's deep understanding of the ideal of suffering."

I wondered at the time what he meant by "ideal." Maybe I was only making sympathetic offerings to my children from a base of fear, trying to keep the suffering at bay, or at arm's length to protect myself. Or was I?

What was I doing travelling about the world when needed at home? Was it more of an act of compassion, getting on with my life? I was seeking blessings for all my children every time I solicited a blessing from a 'high' being, wasn't I? What more could a mother do for her children? Piddly amounts of money couldn't match the value and worth of these blessings. I was helping to purify their negative karma, the effects of their past deeds. I had heard that one blessing from a realized master washed away the effects of hundreds of lifetimes of negative karmic accumulation. I was truly acting compassionately by trying to shed 'light' onto their lives, working with them the best way that I knew how. Or was I simply justifying my fear through escapist activities? Was seeking the divine an act of escapism, as suggested by my friends?

These thoughts perpetuated the whirling wheels of my own suffering. *Samsara.* The relative world. Always one drama or another. Was there a way for it to end besides death? Buddha said yes. The way out of suffering was to know the 'true nature of the mind'. Beyond all the thoughts of right and wrong, good and bad, there was an awareness of neutrality, where things never changed. Like the blue expanse of the sky—the ordinary thoughts and the ordinary dramas were merely clouds, marring clear vision. Behind the scenes of my life, I was anchored in the assurance of untouchable infinite awareness of well-being.

So, as Jigme Lingpa stated in his Bodhicitta Prayer:

Ho! Mesmerized by the sheer variety of perceptions, which Are like the illusory reflections of the moon in water, Beings wander endlessly astray in samsara's vicious cycle. In order that they may find comfort and ease in the luminosity And all-pervading space of the true nature of their minds, I generate the immeasurable love, compassion, joy and equnity Of the awakened mind, the heart of Bodhicitta.

May I, too, generate the faith and wisdom of the true 'heart' of awareness and compassion?

The bus ride, instead of taking the ten hours that was scheduled, took twenty. The bus driver decided to go home for the night and left us in the middle of a large parking lot. We had left the Nepalese border at six in the evening with a stop for dinner around eight. After the bland thali meal that was served at a roadside makeshift restaurant (which looked so unappetizing that I hesitated to eat it for fear of 'loose running') the driver drove for another half hour, stopped, stood up, said something in Nepalese, which of course I couldn't understand, and then walked out of the bus into the dark. I had no idea when he would return.

I spent the next eight hours squirming in a small space next to the window trying to keep my legs from cramping. It was so stuffy in the bus that I kept the window open. However, all sorts of men seemed to be milling about, often stopping underneath my window trying to peer in. I was the only white person in the bus. Some families were near the front with the children snuggled in blankets on the aisle floor. I was surrounded by snoring, stinking men who inevitably woke and lit up their raw Nepalese or Indian *bidis* (cigarettes) in the back near me.

I was more concerned about the men outside. I had heard that Nepal was in the middle of a smouldering civil war, with the Maoists (supported by the Chinese government) controlling the rural areas. They used weapons and were also renowned for hassling tourists for money to fund their initiatives. I had heard that some tourists had previously been kidnapped and harmed. Consequently, I was extremely nervous about the men hovering around the bus, particularly near my window.

I didn't sleep a wink that night. I was not impressed with the quality of the local bus service.

When the driver finally returned, light was beginning to appear over the hills. As the sun came up, I absorbed the loveliness of the green countryside and the quaint designs of the houses. They used a lot of brick since there were brick factories sprinkled all over the valleys. The soil was very red and was obviously clay. Nepal seemed quite different from India, fewer people and cleaner.

I was dropped off near the famous Swayambhunath Temple on the hill overlooking Kathmandu, the capital of Nepal. A decent young man from the Blue Horizon Hotel met and escorted me to my lodgings. I had inadvertently bought a combination ticket—bus and first night in hotel. I wondered what I had gotten myself into, especially the night before when the bus driver had taken off. However, the hotel was clean and centrally located in Thamel, the old part of the city. According to the Lonely Planet guide I couldn't have chosen a better location. The gods were kind since my choice seemed to have been made for me.

I set myself to the task of investigating the quickest and cheapest way to the Himalayan hills—my mission. I needed to see myself gloriously standing on terra firma in front of Mount Everest, boldly stating my intention and casting my father to the winds without further ado. I could see it in my mind's eye so very clearly. Yet it did not prove to be as simple as a quick bus ride out of Kathmandu to a nearby mountainside, as I had previously imagined.

"I recommend that you go trekking to the Everest Base camp, at least up to Namche Bazaar. It would only take you three or four days," Pam said. "You could do it on your own. The path is really well laid out and there are loads of lodges along the way."

Pam, a sixty-year-old Australian intrepid adventurer, was sitting on my hotel bed encouraging me to trek solo up into the Himalayan hills!

"Are you kidding? I've never done anything like that in my life. I've hardly been walking around the block for exercise. I'd never make it; I'm so out of shape!"

"Sure you would. I'll help you. We'll get you decked out with all you need from a rental equipment store I know, and I'll see you off to the plane. You just need to take your own time and do it your own way. Just take it easy. You really could do it, no problem. Guaranteed."

Pam sounded so certain that I stopped arguing and began to embrace the idea. Surely, if she could do the trek, I could. Pam had been a trekking guide for twenty-five years, partnering up with a Sherpa fellow she was in love with. She had given it up because of bad knees, so must know what she was talking about.

"All right, tell me what we need to do first," I replied a bit unsurely.

"We need to get you a down sleeping bag and down jacket for starters, a hat, some sunscreen, sunglasses . . . I'll take you to my friend's store."

She headed out the door, back to her room. I followed, fully trusting that Pam knew what she was talking about and that I could do it if she said so.

Later that afternoon, we had everything laid out on the bed—the equipment, the clothes, and the medication. Pam had taken me to a pharmacy and loaded me up with all the necessary medications that I would need if anything happened, including Diamox for altitude sickness and some dysentery and Giardia pills.

"All you need to do is take half a tablet morning and night of Diamox, and you shouldn't suffer from altitude sickness. Start today, since you fly in tomorrow morning and Lukla is almost three thousand metres up."

Pam was quite certain I would only need to climb another thousand metres to get a good view of Mount Everest, so I should be OK if I took it easy. I hadn't even thought of altitude sickness.

"I mean it. If you just go slowly, taking your time, you will have plenty of time to adjust to the altitude. If you have severe symptoms, just go back down a bit and acclimatize; the body will get used to the thin air and then you can go on. But, really, you aren't going all that high. Just go to Namche and then a hike up to the Everest Hotel.

"There's a great view of the mountain from there. That's all you need to do. Namche is a pretty village with a wonderful market. Lots of Tibetans come over the mountain pass to trade, particularly on Saturdays. Stay for that if you can." Pam was beginning to get quite excited about her new protégée.

I took everything she said into consideration and stuffed it into my mind, along with all the things I was packing into my rented knapsack. The question remained, would I really be able to make it up the mountain with all this stuff? I wasn't a backpacker. I hadn't carried a pack since I went to Europe when I was twenty. I figured the pack weighed about ten kilos. I tried it on and it didn't feel all that heavy, especially if I kept the belt snug. I'd just have to ride on Pam's confidence in me and of course her awareness of the trek. If she said I would be OK, then I would.

A taxi picked me up at 5:00 a.m. the next morning to take me to the airport for the 6:30 flight on Yeti Airlines. The hotel had arranged the ticket for me, while all I had to do was put it on my credit card. So simple; just follow the course from now on.

I wasn't so sure, however, when I saw the plane. A tiny little bird! From the outside it didn't look like it would hold even ten people, although there were sixteen seats inside. The Lonely Planet had said to make sure I got a place on the left to assure a good view of the mountains on the way in.

We would be flying to Lukla. Sir Edmund Hillary, who was the first man to climb Mount Everest, had established the Hillary Foundation, subsequently building the airport and a town. He, however, had trekked in from Jiri. Apparently, one could take a bus to Jiri but it would add a few more days to the trek. Now it was much easier. I would be following the same path that Hillary's group had forged—Lukla, Phakding, Jorsalee, Namche Bazaar, then up a bit farther to the hotel, four days tops. It really was pretty exciting, my learning curve stretching each step of the way, and I hadn't even started walking yet! What was in store for me? I truly had no idea.

Once I got up to the Everest hotel, I could toss Dad's ashes over and really get on with my life. Or, wasn't THIS my life? Well, anyways, I was on my way at last!

Come away, oh human child!
To the waters and the wild,
With a faery, hand in hand . . .
—W.B. Yeats

With thanks to William Butler Yeats and Loreena McKennitt, I was singing the few lines that I knew, while the Irish part of me picked up the mood.

"There's magic and mystery in them there hills," I mused to myself, looking out the plane window at the fairyland to my left.

The snowy-white powdery peaks of the Himalayan range stretched across the way, separating the sky from itself—past eruptions from the bowels of the earth touching the glorious tips of heaven with their shining crests. The morning sun sprinkled sparkles of fantasy upon their peaks and tipped my fancy over the edge of my usually rational reality.

I felt on top of the world. I was higher than I had ever been in my life! In more ways than one. Not that I felt all that secure in this little tin-container of a plane. There was not all that much separating me from the sky and the ground below. They had just pointed out a place where one of these planes had crashed: a small plane filled with eager, anticipatory, slightly anxious people like myself. I had never been in a small plane before and this was a little too close to the fairground rides that I *never* (except that once on Magic Mountain) went on! So far, there hadn't been too many unexpected dips or tosses in the turbulence. It was all very clear sailing. I was lucky since I had heard that it could be otherwise.

"God, please stay with us. I do really love you so much and trust that you will keep me safe and sound!" I whispered faithfully under my breath so that the passenger across the aisle wouldn't hear.

There remained the question of true faith—did I believe in God in such precarious times? However, this time I really could not help myself if I didn't. Resting in God's loving arms without that trust would make me quite nervous. I preferred having my two feet on the ground rather than on the floor of a small metal bird.

"Look over to your left, everyone. There's Mount Everest."

The guide to the group I was travelling with was standing up front doing his job and I was beneficiary of his expertise. They all looked rather seasoned and prepared. I was the only one wearing a long skirt. I had forgotten to bring a hat and gloves, let alone a scarf.

The scenic view was truly marvellous. The Himalayas! The most beautiful, miraculous structures of nature. I was in love! I soared to the highest peaks with my heart as a filter to my vision. Completely rose tinted. Airbrushed. Naïve. I had no idea what was in store for me. All I could think of was that these peaks just might be the abode of the Gods, as everyone in Asia believed.

I would be walking in their midst, bowing at their feet. I was being introduced to the 'wild' in the height of glory. Would I pass this test? My father was with me. He was kin to nature. He had spent his life walking the rivers and streams of the Canadian Rockies, fly-fishing. He would make sure that he had his last fantastic send-off, soaring the skies about the mightiest mountains in the world. He couldn't have asked for more. I had no doubts I would succeed with Dad on my side! And before I threw him off the side of the mountain, we would have one last chat and enjoy the view together.

"Sitting on the top of the world . . ." Wasn't there a song?

Did I have the courage to meet the test? I had heard once that courage wasn't being without fear; it was being aware that one had choices. I had made the choice. I would do my best to stick to it.

Three hours later, I found myself sitting at the base of a mountain waterfall agonizing over my poor aching feet, which incidentally were soaking in the icy water. 'Stumbling my toes at the feet of change'—a good name for a poem or a book. Hmm, maybe I wasn't cut out for this sort of thing. My boots certainly weren't. Why they called them Timberland hiking boots I didn't know, as every sharp stone and bump underfoot jabbed my soles, with my toes slipping back and forth against the tip, knocking the big toenails against the hard toe of the boot. Poor things, beginning to look rather purple, not weathering the bumps and bangs very well. I would be lucky if they didn't get infected, and then what?

There were no hospitals in the valley and I had no antiseptic cream with me, one of the few things we failed to purchase at the side-street pharmacy. One could have gotten anything over the counter there. The quality of the drugs, however, was questionable, probably contraband stuff. I hoped my Diamox was going to work.

Looking up, the mountain tips caressed the skies; the path zigzagged its way towards the billowing clouds invitingly. From the perspective of a novice trekker, however, it seemed daunting. I was feeling rather discouraged. Taking a second look around, I closed my eyes and basked in the late morning sun, letting peace subdue my trepidation. Temperatures were rising, but the water felt extremely good on my feet, cooling and refreshing. I could take off my leggings and jacket and put them in my pack before I started up again. This really was something. Who would ever have imagined I would undertake such a venture? Certainly not my family or friends. Completely out of my urban character. I again felt encouraged by my sense of adventure and bravery.

When I had climbed out of the plane around 8:00 a.m., it had been surprisingly cold. I could see my breath! Walking up the cobblestone path from the airport through the village, I had noticed there were already people selling wares in stalls along the way. I purchased a hand-knitted, rainbow-coloured wool hat with earflaps and tassels and patterned gloves to match. The people were famous for their beautiful, traditional, hand-knitted things.

Apparently, Sherpa people, descendants of the Tibetans who

had migrated over the mountains from Tibet hundreds of years ago, inhabited the valley. They had been driven south by the Mongol hordes or the warlike people of Kham in eastern Tibet. They spoke a dialect of Tibetan and practiced a form of Tibetan Buddhism. I had already spotted a couple of monasteries on the hills and noticed the prayer beads and quiet chanting of those who had passed me along the way. The Tibetans never failed to touch my soul for some reason. I loved their broad faces, rosy cheeks and bright eyes. The Sherpas seemed very similar, reminiscent of the Tibetans I had seen in Dharamsala years ago. Somehow, they had managed to preserve their culture even in the Nepalese hill country.

Once I had left the town of Lukla, I walked for about an hour up the hill, down the small mountain about half way, and then around a bend. There I stopped for some breakfast. Pam had told me to be sure to eat porridge each morning, as it would hold me through the day. I never ate breakfast but followed her instructions. I later regretted my obedience, vowing never to do that again because my stomach felt heavy and uncomfortable.

However, at the little restaurant where I stopped and sat outside eating in the early morning sun, I met an old man and his granddaughter, who let me take some pictures of them. As I was about to leave, the old grandfather started to get quite excited, pointing to his hand and the ground; then he went off running down the hill a ways, kicking up the dirt behind him. I was surprised at the speed of such a wizened old fellow. A few minutes later, he returned with a whittled walking stick in the shape of a capital T in hand. It was thin, a good length for my height, with a crossbar on the top to hold and rest upon. It was similar to the ones that the Sherpas, human carriers bearing inordinately large baskets and other huge loads of goods, walked with and sat against. Theirs were thicker and shorter but I was sure the T part of mine would serve the same purpose, useful to sit or lean upon.

Which I did a lot. I hadn't yet realized just how good a friend that stick was to become. The path ahead crisscrossed the mountains up and down, up and down, up and down . . . on and on. I was going to need the help of my newfound friend. Definitely an oversight on Pam's part. I had no idea how important a walking stick was to a trek; every step of the way I was supported by the strength and security of this hand-whittled piece of tree.

I couldn't have made it to this waterfall without my precious stick. The path had been riddled with stones and steps, not an easy walk; not an inch of it could have been traversed without it. Thank you once again, whoever was overseeing my journey. God? The angels? Jesus? Buddha? Whoever. THANK YOU!

Just around the bend from the restaurant, two army attendants had stood at the stone gate entrance to the valley. The men in their camouflaged khaki uniforms held long rifles and gave me very serious looks. I had felt a moment of fear. Then I determined to put them at ease by smiling and saying something funny as I passed by. Surely this middle-aged woman walking solo with rainbow cap, stick, long skirt, small pack, and without guide or porter was not an average trekker. Definitely an odd occurrence. They looked rather dubious, probably questioning my ability. My determination and stick could surmount any obstacle, I was certain. I unwaveringly stared back at them, slightly defiant and cheeky, projecting: "I CAN so; you'll see!" as they turned to each other and chuckled underneath their gloved hands.

I remembered the war situation and appreciated the army's presence, sincerely hoping that I didn't encounter any Maoists *en route*. Information was that the rebels didn't have a presence in the valley, but I still wondered. Maybe it was just under control with the army surveillance.

"At least there aren't any leeches," I said out loud to no one in particular, as I rubbed my sore purple toes and inflamed toenails before I put my socks and boots back on. I had heard that the other trek, the Annapurna, was plagued with the repulsive critters. Since there was no one around, no one heard me shootin' words to the breeze.

"Yuck! Bloody little things!" I added, shivering at the thought. One was advised to pour salt on them, but I really didn't relish experimenting to see if the remedy worked.

I was again sitting, feet in water at the foot of yet another enticing waterfall, watching all the trekkers (particularly the Japanese) pass over the bridge, single-mindedly and collectively forging ahead, trying to get to the next lodge before the sun got too high. A to B and no stops in between.

"That's the mindset of the *true* modern-day trekker. Whatever happened to the happy wanderer?" I questioned with chagrin, everyone in too much of a hurry to hear.

No need to rush. Pam had suggested not to. I really had no inkling where I was. I knew that up the way were some lodges, and it was recommended for the first day of the trek to stop at Phakding. Didn't look too far on the map. The woman at the restaurant suggested that I go to the Namaste Hotel, owned by her cousin. Considering the plan to head to that place when I arrived in the village, I continued to bask in the sun, listening to the water tumbling off the mountainside—a wonderful preoccupation for a Himalayan cat (my sister had three of them).

"Maybe I should just curl up here for the rest of the day?" I said to my stick, my companion. "Too cold at night, though," I added, assuming a listening ear. No response. I took that as an agreement, stood, and picked up my trusty friend. "Come on, fella," I said, bemused and smiling as I did so.

It had been a long while since I had been completely alone. I was glad and thankful that I wasn't with a group; people got in the way of my solitude. I stepped out of myself somehow when I was around others. It was a delicious feeling to know that it was solely me, myself, and I. Having no one else to bother with, I wasn't obliged to consider anyone else's wants or feelings—walking sticks not counting.

"Halleluiah! Halleluiah! Halleluuiaaaah!" I belted out Handel's refrain to the waterfall as I turned to climb up the clay-packed hill back onto the path.

I had had no idea how much I would love being out in nature. Doing my own thing—relating to the rocks, trees, and streams—was very idyllic and soothing to the body, mind and soul. Moreover, there were no dangerous animals. Except the yaks on the path!

My first encounter with the yaks, apart from seeing them grazing complacently in the fields, was on the way down the other side of the Lukla mountain. Three of them were heading up the trail towards me. The incline was steep, the path narrow. I heard the tinkling of their neck bells well ahead of seeing their approach, so had a few minutes to ponder my strategy. Not much choice. I was forced to go up the side of the hill face with only a few inches to spare. The stubborn beasts didn't budge an inch to give me any room. I was afraid that they would butt or knock into me. They really were beasts of burden, and so much dust they kicked up as they passed, right into my eyes and face! The little Sherpani woman in her brightly coloured scarf and striped apron gave me an apologetic look as she passed, trailing behind her charges with her little switch. My first encounter with what was to be an ongoing occurrence. Yaks were the freighters of the Himalayan hills, along with the Sherpa men with their peculiar baskets—all laden with heavy goods on their backs destined for the neighbouring villages.

I overestimated my strength and perseverance, while underestimating the effects of the hot blazing sun on my head, as I strove to get to Phakding. I should have stopped at the preceding village but I had ignored my intuition and came to regret it. The last hour of the first-day trek was agonizing. It hadn't looked that much farther on the map. The perpetual up-and-downward climb became unbearable, with the growing weight of my pack, the constant knocking of toes into the ends of the boots, the extreme weariness . . . I was overjoyed when I saw Phakding in the far distance.

By the time I reached the entrance to the town, I had serious doubts as to whether I would be able to continue the trek. Being run over by a truck probably felt about the same. I had completely overdone it, seriously abusing myself in the process. Instead of stopping at the bottom of the hill at a lovely riverside stone hotel surrounded by lush green grass, I stubbornly continued up towards the centre of the town to find the Namaste Hotel. Gasping for air and limping as I came upon the courtyard of the place, I was sure I looked a sight with my hair all mussed and face covered in dirt and sweat.

I entered the front door to inquire about a room. I had had to pass a group of travellers all freshly scrubbed and laughing, sitting at a picnic table out front. It was about 2:30 in the afternoon. My feet were killing me and I thought I was about to die! After getting the key, I very slowly and painfully made it up the last ten wooden steps to the second floor.

As I passed down the hall, I heard a young male British voice say: "One thing I can't stand is all these overweight, middle-aged people who think they are trekkers. I don't know who they think they are. They should just bloody well stay at home. They shame the reputation of the rest of us."

I hissed to myself, "Who the hell does he think he is? The pompous . . ." I was too tired to think.

I opened the wooden door of my room and surveyed the primitive surroundings. The wooden walls had a quarter of an inch of space between each board; the bed was simply a narrow wooden slat the length of the wall with a thin plastic mattress on it. I laid out my Thermarest mattress and down sleeping bag, took off my boots, and climbed in. I didn't even have the energy to wash. I would do that later. I HAD to rest.

I was extremely upset, thinking I could go no further. I felt as though I had been seriously beaten up, that it would take me days to recover. I would have to head back, admit defeat. I could throw my dad's ashes into a stream below a waterfall, which would just have to suffice. I fell asleep assuring myself I had done my best. I had come to the limit of my trekking capability. Period. Full stop.

"Sorry, Dad. You'll just have to give up the flying and settle for swimming up and down the Himalayan streams," I sobbed into my pillow just before I dozed off.

I woke up singing. "Early one morning, just as the sun was rising, I heard a maid singing in the valley below." Not quite, but I was feeling very chipper. I COULD go on! I could continue. I felt much better.

I had slept for a few hours the preceding afternoon, then rose, washed, and headed downstairs to the main dining room. There were long wooden tables around the edges with seats covered with earthy Tibetan carpets. In the centre of the room was a rusty barrel stove with logs burning. The cold air was permeated with the heat streaming from it, so there was a curious mixture of heat and draft. The walls had spaces where the cold air came through. As above, so below! No insulation. No drywall. A typical trekking lodge.

I had on my down jacket and Sherpa rainbow hat. I was not the only one dressed in this fashion. At least I didn't look out of place. However, they all appeared to be professional seasoned trekkers. But then, they weren't on a mission to throw their dad's ashes over the mountain like I was. I had a vision; its wings would have to carry me wherever I needed to go because the strength of my conviction was wavering. I still did not know whether or not I would be able to continue.

At least there was a glimmer of hope. I felt much better. After the hearty hot thali meal, I headed straight back to bed and slept the night through, snug as a bug in a rug. My sleeping bag, for all its thinness, was sufficient. I had purchased a fleece suit that I wore to bed along with some thick woollen socks. The next morning, I felt refreshed and surprisingly fit to begin the second day of the Everest trek.

A completely different rhythm. Not long after I started walking, I came to a village along the path, up from the river. There were children hanging about, on a wall across from their rustic houses. They were laughing and singing a lovely folksong or children's melody. I stopped to listen to them and asked if I could take their picture. They were delighted, giggling with glee.

Some of them were dressed in their school uniforms, a bit dishevelled yet ready to go to school. The little ones remained in their pyjamas. They all had runny noses and some of them still had sleep in their eyes and dirt on their faces. They seemed very happy, welcoming my participation, and tried to teach me their song. One of the fathers came out and nodded his approval. I was glad and touched.

Inevitably, a group of Japanese trekkers came past. As they did so, we counted them in English. The kids started clapping and laughing but the school-aged ones counted along with me. Then the group stopped to take pictures and a couple of the ladies started to wipe the noses of the little ones, who of course resisted. The Japanese women reached into their jacket pockets and gave the children some pencils and papers. The children were excited but then started to ask for money. The father came out and shooed the kids away.

One of the disastrous effects of the trekking reality was that of making beggars and opportunists out of these lovely people. I felt disgusted at the group of trekkers and turned to put my pack back on, leaving with distaste and disdain in my mouth. However, the experience with the children prior to the group's arrival had been magical and memorable.

A bit later on, I came upon an astonishingly tall waterfall that gathered in a huge pool at the bottom. Water droplets magically leapt off its face, dancing like platinum stars in the air. Enchanting. I crossed over the short wooden bridge and stopped at a teahouse on the adjacent side of the hill, ordered some chai, and rested with the owner on the patio. What more to life than enjoying the rushing sound of the waterfall splashing, revelling in its dance, the heat of the morning sun's rays upon my back? The wind coming up from the river valley was refreshing. It was already getting hot and only 9:00 a.m. I most certainly was taking it easy, pacing myself much differently than yesterday, situated in my own life, on my own trek, wandering at my leisure amongst these deliciously fragrant mountain hills.

Nepal was a stunning country, the scenery so completely untouched and beautiful. Luscious trees and shrubs, and bushes that reminded me of the rhododendrons back home. It would be wonderful in the spring with the hillsides a mass of pinks, reds, and purples. I longed to return to see it in bloom. The hills were bedecked with other wild flowers and delightful wild strawberries, which I had stopped to eat for breakfast earlier.

The owner of the teahouse was very congenial. He spoke English quite well. "I used to be a trekking guide as well as a climber."

"Did you ever climb Everest?" I asked.

"Many times. I have reached the summit eleven times," he replied proudly, beaming from ear to ear. "Now I am looking after my two sons. I bought this land and built this teahouse. I have a campground in the back."

"Why did you stop trekking?" I asked curiously.

"My wife left me. I was away so much. She went off with someone else. I had to stay to look after my sons." He seemed very sad as he spoke the truth of his life.

"Is it common to divorce here?" I wondered if I were being too personal but he seemed quite responsive to my interest and concern, seemingly eager to share his confidence with me. I wondered if many people stopped to talk to him. His establishment was not in a very strategic position along the path, an hour into the second-day agenda for most people: too early to stop, too far to carry on from the day before.

"Yes, the women are now leaving the men. We want to make more money for our families but the expense is too high. Most people here are extremely poor. Trekking provides an opportunity for us to lead better lives. But we must leave our families for so many months of the year. The women don't like it. They would rather have the men at home and struggle without any modern things."

"I'm so sorry to hear that. It must be difficult for you."

"Would you consider staying here with me and helping around the place? You speak English and could help me. We would be good together. I like you."

I felt touched and appreciative that he trusted me enough to consider me. He had such a sincere face. I looked into his eyes and honestly said, "I'm sorry, I can't. I have to see Mount Everest. I have something to do there. I also have children at home and must return to my country, Canada."

We talked a bit more and sat listening to the waterfall, mutually enjoying the beauty. Then I set off, after taking his address and promising to return sometime. To him, it all seemed so simple. Things were so much more complicated at home in the West. Here it was simply "man needs woman, woman needs man."

The only way to learn about the inhabitants was to take the time to stop and communicate with them. I had heard about the friendliness of the Sherpa people. I wondered though, if after all, they might be becoming jaded with the thousands of trekkers that so obviously bypassed them without recognition or regard, all the while changing the face of their reality—possibly, in the long run, not for the good.

"*Om Mani Padme Hum, Om Mani Padme Hum, Om Mani Padme Hum, Om Mani . . .*" I chanted along the mountain path. The Red Chenrezig mantra and chant of all time for the Tibetan people. Soliciting compassion. Just what I needed to cushion the duress of this craggy, jagged, rocky climb. Without my mantra, I wondered if I would be able to carry on. As I repeated the phrase over and over again, I seemed to be filled with a sense of lightness and bliss, my mind protected from the frightening thoughts of the formidableness of the trek and the pain . . .

My feet continued to bother me. If ever I trekked again, I would get proper boots. My back was OK, surprisingly enough.

"One step at a time. Don't look up, just at the step ahead. Keep my mind on the chant, not on the difficulty of the climb. Keep going, keep going, I can do it."

I continued in the same rhythm. Sometimes I even sang the chant to a lovely melody I knew. Sherpas understood as they proceeded ahead, counting their prayer beads as they went. They didn't sing though. Probably thought it expended too much air.

It was early afternoon. I was making good progress, hoping to reach the next lodge within the hour—up one side of a mountain, down the other side, and again, and again. Where exactly was I? I stopped to stand still, leaning on my prize stick, gazing appreciatively around the Solu-Khumbu valley region. Below, I saw the rushing waters of a milky green river, the Dudh Kosi, quite high up but only halfway up the valley walls. Across was a lush forest, above the towering crests of forested mountains. Every once in a while, I would make a turn on the difficult path and be surprised by a snowy peak in the distance, never failing to astonish this weary trekker and lift her spirits with its beauty. The clear, bright blue sky acted as an inspiring backdrop.

The trail had been arduous but thrilling. Many times I had crossed the gushing waters of the winding Dudh Kosi. I had stopped a couple of times to soak my feet and soak up the sun, taking my time, absorbing the beauty and fresh mountain air, reminding myself of Pam's advice. I was enjoying the winding paths and quaint wooden bridges, an approachable adventure for a shy inexperienced hiker. I had just overdone it yesterday; I ought to have stopped at Ghat, the village before Phakding. No point looking back. Onward and forward.

The days were still so warm, although it was mid-November. Tomorrow would be my daughter's birthday. Twenty-three and 'almost' mother of two. I wondered how the baby was doing. I hoped well. I had been out of contact for a few days. There was no Internet access in the lodges so I would have to wait until Namche and hopefully there would be some there.

I had heard that the Maoists had cut all the telephone and

electricity lines, so there was little access to the outside world. The schools had no use of modern technology, let alone tape recorders and TVs. How would Nepal ever come up to par with the rest of the world?

Huddled over a rusty tin stove, rubbing my hands together to get warm, waiting for my dinner to arrive, I looked across at Nawang Thrawpa.

"How did you get such serious arthritis?" I asked quietly.

There was no one else in the dining-cum-social room of the Jorsale Stone Lodge. So far, I was the only registered guest. I had ordered Tibetan noodle soup and some rice with vegetables, not having eaten all day except for a few wild strawberries and a large carrot purchased at a table stand located near a significantly huge grey 'Mani stone' healing rock, which was covered with the mantra *Om Mani Padme Hum* in white-painted Tibetan script. The old stall man had had a broad smile and a twinkle in his eyes.

What was actually going on here, I had asked myself, wondering what miracle had happened in the past, or what famous saint had rested there, because a makeshift wooden healing bed had been built on the other side of the rock. There were so many stories concerning Milarepa, Naropa, Marpa (Buddhist practitioners who had achieved enlightenment in their lifetimes) and other Buddhist saints wandering the Himalayan hill country. All had walked these fabulous mountain valleys, meditating in caves on the various mountainsides. Was I walking on the same ground as Milarepa? Did he rest under the shade of that rock? If so, miracles probably had transpired there.

I had bought my large carrot and munched on it, walking and musing over the possibility of sacred coincidence, all the while hoping that Giardia bacteria weren't being ingested along with the badly needed vitamins and minerals of my newly acquired fresh vegetable diet. Usually I didn't eat fresh or raw while travelling in Asia. Need I mention why?

Would I possibly meet an enlightened master along my trek? If I did, how would I know it? I had walked with a local Abbot who was going up past Namche to visit a colleague at a monastery. He wore a remarkable, embroidered silk vest that I commented upon and rather coveted for my own wardrobe. Would I ever give up my attachment to beautiful clothing? We had chatted for a bit. I wondered how far along 'the path' he actually was. Was it possible to measure the progress towards enlightenment?

I again looked at Nawang, waiting for his answer. There was no other heat in the lodge, save this little stove which he fuelled with pine cones every once and awhile. When I asked him why only pine cones, he replied that we were in a National Park where cutting down trees was prohibited.

"I got arthritis in school in Kathmandu. High school. There was no heat in the winter. It was very damp and cold." He spoke hesitantly, choosing the English words carefully. He looked so serious and very much like an old man, rather than his youthful twenty-two years. My heart went out to him.

"I had to stop my schooling four years ago and come home. Now I can hardly walk and am not even able to get to Lukla, so will never be able to get back to the big city." He sounded so sad and defeated.

"This is my older sister's place. She raised me from a child after our mother died. Her husband is away leading mountaineering groups. It is the height of the climbing season. He is a very famous climbing guide. He has been to the top of Mount Everest many times. Look over at those pictures."

He pointed to the wall at the back of the dining room. I saw lots of photo-shots of men with their arms around each other, standing beside poles with flags on the top of mountains. Surely I was in another dimension here.

"He will be coming back for a few days next week," he continued earnestly. "My nephew, my sister's son, runs the trekking company in Kathmandu. He is a Reiki Master like you, very interested in healing. He learned from the most famous Reiki teacher in Nepal, who learned from people in India. Reiki is very popular here. I would like to learn it but my brother is too busy to come back to teach me. Would you teach me?" he hopefully inquired.

I couldn't believe my ears. Reiki way out here? I had no idea it was so popular in Nepal.

"Yes, of course, if you'd like me to. I could start after supper and give you your first lesson; then tomorrow morning before I go, I'll give you another initiation and show you how to treat yourself. It'd help to relieve your discomfort." I was pretty excited at the prospect of teaching Reiki way out here in the Himalayas.

"When I come back down from Namche Bazaar, I could finish the last two lessons with you. How does that sound?" I knew he'd have no money to exchange. If he helped the people around his village, that would be commitment enough for me. Commitment through service was as valuable as a financial exchange.

We began after dinner. It was an incredible experience. He was a good student, eager and attentive. He seemed to understand everything that I said. He mentioned that he had read a few books on Reiki; consequently, we did a lot more hands-on practice than I usually did the first lesson. I taught him how to give a head treatment on another person as well as himself.

Miraculously enough, the village had heard that there was someone in town who did healing. There was a knock on the door and in walked a Tibetan man right out of *National Geographic*. He smelled like he hadn't bathed in a year. He wore a sheepskin jacked turned inside out, very dirty. His hair was long, matted, and strung with turquoise and yak bone. His face ruddy, with the deep red of the sun emblazoned in his cheeks, broad cheekbones, extremely good white teeth, and bright sparkling eyes. He explained he was a trader just come over the Nangpa La Pass with goods on the back of his faithful yak. He had had to come by moonlight, because it was now illegal for Tibetans to trade in Nepal due to the new tax laws. The famous market was no longer in existence so the traders had to secretly go from door to door selling their imported wares to the expectant buyers. It appeared rather 'hush hush' but understood by all concerned.

Nawang Thrawpa translated his Tibetan. "I broke my foot last year. I went to a Tibetan doctor. It still hurts very much, hard to walk over the pass. Could you heal it?" he asked plaintively.

He pulled his foot out of his felt boots and took off his sock. His feet smelled pretty nasty. I took a look at the foot, covered in round scars from the hot iron poker that the traditional medicine men used for healing. I had read about it—something like using moxibustion, the heating of acupuncture points using burning mugwort in traditional Chinese medicine.

So there we were, in the front room, treating a little Tibetan trader—Nawang Thrawpa at the head and me at the feet. The little girls of the family were watching through the panes of glass in the dining room door, and people from the village were outside poking their noses against the window next to me to see what was going on, everyone looking fascinated. I was amazed to find myself in the middle of such a unique experience. Wonders never ceased to amaze me.

The little man complained that it seemed to be hurting even more, but by the time the treatment was over he seemed very satisfied. A grin spread across his broad face and he began chattering with Nawang and his sister. Then he went out into the moonlit night, back into the far reaches of Himalayan time where eternity never ended and clock time never began.

Nawang seemed content with his new skill. Being exhausted but happy, I decided to go to bed, leaving him next to the stove practicing the head treatment on himself.

My first night in Namche Bazaar. I was sitting on a plastic chair outside the door to my room looking up at the midnight-blue sky, full of light from the reflection of the full moon. Across the way, looming overhead, were huge mountains shining their glistening silver faces towards me. The air was freezing, crisp, and biting cold. Looking at the sky I was reminded of a few lines of a poem by George Meredith:

> Sharp is the night, but stars with frost alive
> Leap off the rim of earth across the dome.
> It is a night to make the heavens our home . . .

My sentiments exactly. What was it with these poets that they could capture the beauty and fullness of the moment so gloriously and so succinctly? I wished that I had that talent. I had never felt so significantly insignificant. Alone in the night. Yet within the expanse of life, I felt an intense sense of equanimity, having a place in the greater scheme of things. The mountains were so overwhelming, all knowing, peaceful, and calm. I could sense their magic and felt it playing itself out upon my soul. If ever I had experienced the spirituality of nature, it was at that moment. Who would ever want to return to the despairing tedium of everyday life? This was where I wanted to remain, a place where life assumed a greater purposeful meaning.

It was a brilliantly clear night. I could have remained under the twinkling stars forever, except that I eventually became too cold and tired, taking to bed for warmth and comfort. The day had been extremely long and arduous. I still couldn't believe I had made it all the way up here, an inexplicable feat considering my lack of physical condition. I must have climbed over a thousand metres—six-and-a-half hours STRAIGHT UP!

The morning had begun around six o'clock, with tea and a Reiki lesson. I remained the only visitor at the lodge in Jorsale. Nawang got up early as well. Without other guests, we were able to resume Reiki instruction and practice in time for me to get an early start on the last leg of the journey to Namche Bazaar. I left the lodge with friendly farewells and a promise to return on the way back.

Like family, they saw me off—Nawang, the girls, the adult son, and the owner. I was touched when the sister (the owner of the lodge) came out to present me with a colourfully striped Tibetan apron. I tied it around my waist over my long teal-blue skirt. She nodded her approval and raised her two palms to her heart and said: "*Tashi Delek,*" meaning the same as *Namaste,* the Hindi salutation of greeting, honour, and spiritual recognition.

Although I wasn't wearing a *chuba* (Tibetan dress), with the paisley-patterned purple scarf tied around my head to cover it from the blazing sun I looked very much like a Sherpa woman. In fact, along the path, the people passing me either coming or going greeted me:

"*Namaste,* Sherpani Didi!" Didi meant sister.

Passers-by seemed quite amused and rather delighted, smiling broadly and showing their wonderfully white teeth as they did so. I felt honoured and included—one with the people of the land, closer to being part of the earth. Walking its face as if I too had a rightful place on it, wandering the hills confidently and safely as a global inhabitant, I had never felt so human and true.

I was so excited that when I came to the Swiss suspension bridge that crossed the Bote Khola River a hundred feet above the rushing waters I was undaunted. I waited for the yaks and Sherpas to cross before I attempted to walk over the metal slats swinging in the wind. The railings were covered with white and yellow blessing katas, as well as the colourful prayer flags that people had tied to the metal cords, all rather marvellous and unique. Stunned by my courage, I confidently crossed over and began the final ascent.

It seemed that the Sherpas *en route* took care of me and watched out for me. At times I was only able to go twenty feet or so before stopping. I tried to pace myself with them but often fell short.

Carrying their heavy loads, they too stopped frequently. One time I counted thirty steps between stops. They had very unique and particular whistles for signals. By the end of the day I was able to decipher which whistle was for stopping, which for going, as well as the various lengths of the stops.

The strength and endurance of the Sherpas amazed me. At one point, one passed me with his basket loaded with huge bags and on top of it all—two wheels! I wondered why one would want a bicycle up in the mountains? It was far too steep and treacherous to ride the trails. A while later another Sherpa, followed by a young European woman, approached me from behind. I stopped to let them pass. On his back was a young woman seated in the basket. She was a paraplegic, unable to walk, and the wheels were for her wheelchair!

She was manifesting her dream to see Mount Everest! Touched by the sight, I stood crying as they went on ahead, marvelling at the determination and strength of the human will to realize its potential.

Of course, we were passed many times by various hyperactive trekking groups racing towards the top. The final destination, Namche Bazaar, was the most important Sherpa settlement in the Solu-Khumbu (or Everest) region. It was situated within the U-shaped mountainside and served as a transit point for both trekkers and local villagers. In the past, a grand market was held on Saturdays. People from all over the region, as well as Tibetan traders coming over the Nangpa La Pass, 18,000 feet high, had gathered together to sell and haggle over trinkets, pots and pans, clothing, turquoise, jewellery, yak butter, eggs, food stuffs, etc. It apparently had been a great social occasion and would be sorely missed by both villagers and visitors alike. I sincerely regretted having missed it.

However, later that afternoon, I noticed yaks bearing goods and Tibetans all about the town; so some sort of trade was about, even if it was contraband happening underneath the government's nose. The whole scene was fascinating and full of energy. Despite the cold, all sorts of activity seemed to be going on. As an outsider, I would only be able to interpret the surface comings and goings. No matter, it was proving to be extremely interesting. After I completed my mission and fulfilled my filial duty, I would take the time to loiter in the streets and visit with the local inhabitants. I truly was looking forward to it.

Thinking back over the trek up, I was astonished at the triumph. Many times while leaning over my faithful stick, bawling my eyes out, I had felt discouraged and almost resigned to defeat. However, it had been ridiculous to think of turning back after managing to get as far as I had. In the heightened awareness brought on by the necessity of remaining in the moment, as if in walking meditation, I sensed I was either being carried in my father's loving arms or on the back of angels' wings. The Chenrezig mantra was helping terrifically. Maybe the bodhisattva Chenrezig was carrying me? The mantra repetition certainly seemed to protect me from the onslaught of negative thoughts, as well as bolster the lightness of my being. As long as I kept chanting (with eyes on the path underfoot, resisting the impulse to look up to measure the distance of the unrelenting climb ahead), I was able to maintain my confidence and go on.

Only once did I almost slip. Not paying attention to my step, thinking about my children, I forgot to notice where I placed my walking stick, which became unstable and slid off the rock it was supposed to be secured on. I subsequently began to teeter backwards. I quickly assessed my situation—the cliff on my left stretched downwards thousands of feet! I couldn't afford to topple over it or roll backwards down the mountain, so instinctively threw myself forward with all the force I could muster, counteracting the loss of balance and rectifying my position. Whew! That was close. I almost fell off the mountain, Shirley MacLaine! Being consciously present in the moment was imperative, or else, game over. After that, I paid much closer attention to each and every step.

I couldn't help wonder just how many steps it took to climb the mountain. I stopped when the Sherpas stopped, resumed when they did. We criss-crossed each other all the way up. When I leaned over my stick, gasping and crying as they passed, I was sure they must have been concerned about me.

They did beat me to the top, deposited their wares, and began the descent down, passing me on their way, as I had stopped around the last bend to have a 'spot of tea' and regard the entire situation. The village stretched gloriously in front of me. I wanted to take it all in and get my bearings before I headed into the hustle-bustle of the town. The Sherpas laughed and waved good-bye, heading down home for the night and probably taking less than an hour to get to the bottom. Amazingly, some of them were only wearing rubber flipflops on their bare feet!

When I finally did reach the entrance to the town, I stopped at the first hotel and had some boys take my picture. What a sight! There I stood in the height of my glory: a middle-aged grandmother decked in seemingly ethnic clothing, leaning on her Nepalese whittled walking stick; dusty, dirty hiking boots on her feet; khaki sun hat tucked into her knapsack belt, smiling crookedly at the onlookers, extremely proud of herself for almost reaching the summit of her vision. Just one more day! Today Namche Bazaar, tomorrow Everest. Eat your heart out, people! I had passed the initiation, truly a Himalayan trekker now, regardless of my eccentricities and quirky ways. I probably would lose my toenails as proof but would face the prospect with pride.

"Lovely Lady, Lovely Lady, you made it!" a male voice cried out in the dark. I looked down the narrow cobblestone street of Namche Bazaar.

"Veda Mata! Veda Mata! Look at you!" I recognized two young Nepalese men approaching me excitedly.

I was standing on the granite steps outside of the Internet café across from the German bakery in Namche, having just emailed my older daughter and a few friends at home that I was safe and sound. Forced to limit the extent of my ecstatic boasting because the price for use of the computer was outrageous (400 rupees per hour [$10.25], as opposed to the 25 or 30 in Kathmandu!), I had been overwhelmed with resistance to give them so much money for so little. However, because it was very difficult to get Internet connection so high up, it was inordinately expensive for the owners of the café. There was a price to pay for being so far from civilization.

After finishing, I had stepped outside to ponder the evening and listen to the blaringly loud but lovely chant *Om Mani Padme Hum* being piped into the surrounding air. I stood absorbing the enchantment of the village streets as the melody and words wafted out over the hills and into the dark valley, like incense to the wind. I wondered how far it would be heard? Very beautiful and moving. Caught in its trancelike drift, it was then that I heard the voice calling out my name.

Ah, yes . . . Raj and Tashi, the two fellows I had met at the Blue Horizon Hotel in Thamel the night before I left Kathmandu. Pam had introduced me to them. We had dined together at the outdoor restaurant next door, where I was introduced to the group of Japanese women going to Gokyo Lake on the Everest trek, for whom they were to be the guides. I had seen them all pass on the trail when I was sitting yesterday, at the little teahouse by the tall waterfall. We had exchanged greetings and agreed to meet up at Namche.

I carefully stepped down the steps and into the street. I hadn't gone far before Tashi threw his arms around me as if I were a long-lost relative, extremely pleased to see me. Curious. We hardly knew each other. I had noticed that the Nepalese were very friendly and affectionate. However, I wondered whether these guys were stoned or drunk because they seemed to have indulged quite a bit during the supper we had shared. I suspected that they did drugs. (Later, I learned that they were heroin addicts.)

"Where are you staying, my lady?" Tashi asked.

He was a hotel owner in a small village, Nagarkot, outside of Kathmandu. Taking a couple of weeks off, he had agreed to accompany his friend on the trek with the Japanese ladies. Raj had a small school with a few Nepalese orphan children. He had asked if I would make some sort of donation to his school after my trek. I consented, telling him that I had some art supplies he could have.

"I just arrived about an hour ago. I thought I'd look at my Lonely Planet guide over a cup of tea before I made any decision. As yet, I'm not booked into a hotel," I responded.

Tashi jumped at the opportunity to include me. "We got here this afternoon. It's one of the ladies' birthday today and we're going to the German bakery to get a birthday cake. Why don't you come to our hotel by the monastery and stay there? Then you could come to the party!"

I was a bit hesitant, reluctant to break my solitude, but Tashi took me by the elbow. "Come, we'll take you there. Follow us," he encouraged, bending his head towards the other side of town.

Raj looked as eager as Tashi to have me accompany them to their hotel. I relinquished my previous plan and nodded that I would follow. I went inside to retrieve my pack.

Although it was only 6:45, it was extremely dark and cold. Coming out, I could see my breath. I'd put on the down jacket Pam had had me rent which felt and looked rather awkward and bulky as I slung my pack onto my back. I tied the tassel strings of my rainbow hat and pulled the woollen gloves up over my bare wrists. It must have been below zero, yet had been so warm during the day. I was a bit puzzled by the rapid temperature drop, although I had been warned it got extremely cold at night. As for the conditions at the hotel, I suspected there would be little or no heat, so didn't get my expectations up.

We wound our way through the uneven streets of Namche Bazaar, up towards the other side of the U-shaped mountain, then farther up the incline by some unevenly carved stone steps. It was difficult and I felt short of breath, tiring very quickly from lack of oxygen.

"Almost there," Tashi, the spokesman, said.

I wondered why he was always the one of the pair to talk? They were carefully carrying the cake and party favours for the evening. I was becoming rather excited myself but huffing and puffing pretty heavily by the time we arrived.

The hotel was a newer one, made of the usual granite blocks that I'd seen men chiselling down by the river. It must have taken an incredible amount of work and effort to make enough blocks for all the buildings, since the town was composed of many such structures, which I assumed were the Tibetan design. Windows and doors were framed by brightly coloured, painted wooden boards. The monastery was recognizable by the religious painted designs around the roof, windows, and doorframes. I loved the style of the architecture here—solid, strong, and unique, standing the test of time and the extremity of the weather conditions.

I entered the hotel through a cream-coloured curtain door, noting the bright silk patterns of the auspicious symbols—a conch and a pink lotus in the centre, with dark blue knots in the four corners. It seemed the Tibetans liked to hang curtains on their entrances even though there were also solid doors. The owner, Tsering, was a relative of Sherpa Tenzing, who accompanied Sir Edmund Hillary to the top of Everest. There were photos on the varnished wooden dining room walls. Towards the end of the big room stood a large wood-stove, the only heat to the place, where we immediately headed. We all sat down around one of the large wooden hand-carved tables, reminiscent of the mountain lodges in the Yukon I had visited in my mid-twenties (when I travelled up the Alaskan Highway with my friend Helen), and ordered tea.

Tsering, along with his wife and two adult twin daughters, managed the hotel. The rooms ranged from $5 to $20, with the more expensive ones out back along the hillside, overlooking the valley. As a reward to myself, I chose a more expensive room, deciding that I could afford $15 for a few nights. There would be a full moon tonight and it was my daughter's birthday, justification enough to celebrate—the birth of my last child, as well as the fact that I had managed to climb up to 12,000 feet were pretty good reasons! I prayed I didn't get altitude sickness because I intended to get up to the Everest Hotel in the morning, rather than being rushed out by helicopter back to Lukla, having heard that that was often the case.

As it was, one of the Japanese women was suffering from altitude sickness, preventing her from continuing the trek. Her friend was staying back with her. It seemed pretty serious. Tsering, arranging for medication from the hospital in the next town over, offered his limited supply of oxygen at $200, but the woman refused any medication or help, preferring only herbal remedies. I wondered if she was just being cheap resisting the steep price, or if she was another health food fanatic risking her life for her principles. Dangerously foolish regardless. Tsering's wife was trying to cope with the situation by getting the sick woman to drink an herbal tea, but again, she refused saying it made her nauseous. (Of course, nausea was one of the main symptoms!) The guidebook said it was imperative to drink lots of liquids. She was only asking for trouble, acting so stubbornly. People died from the altitude up here; didn't she realize that? Tsering and his wife were very concerned, at a loss as to how to cope with her, knowing that as hoteliers, they had her life in their hands.

My room being right next to hers, I offered a Reiki treatment. Her friend, sitting on the step outside, said she would ask—tomorrow possibly. I left it at that and went in to get cleaned up. I was looking forward to the shower; there was HOT water, a luxury

I hadn't enjoyed since I left home! (In the end, the Japanese lady made it to lower ground, recovering enough to trek to Lukla and take the little plane back to the city. The last I saw of her was a week later in Kathmandu, stuffed into a Land Rover with the others of the group, plus luggage, heading to the airport to catch a plane, all packing individually remarkable stories to tell their friends back home.)

The birthday party was full of *bonhomie*; we were a lively group drinking the barley *chang* and eating and eating. Lots of food and drink! We laughed heartily, thoroughly enjoying ourselves. Raj and Tashi really knew how to throw a party. The Japanese women seemed rather shy but friendly. It was hard to understand them, but they were very polite. Tsering was very obliging, having the cooks prepare dish after dish regardless of whether or not it was on the menu. Tashi knew many different Nepalese dishes, which he wanted us to try. The vegetables and food seemed much better than those of the other trekking lodges; Tsering was catering to a higher quality of traveller.

I surmised he was probably one of the elite of the town, more than likely one of the more wealthy people of the region. He and his wife had a rather aristocratic demeanour, more refined than the average Sherpa—confident of their position, which was apparent in their self-assurance and respectfulness, honouring their guests. I was glad I had chosen to come. (Not that I am a snob, but I don't mind enjoying the fruits of those a few cuts above the typical backpacker!) Besides, I was paying extra for it.

The night was quiet and serene as I sat on the plastic chair outside my room, wondering about the morrow. I felt contented: accomplishment, friendship, vision, certainty, unusual circumstances—fantastic! The moon, full and sensational, shone down upon the village.

Not an ordinary view to be sure. The mountains looming across the way spoke of greatness and grandeur. Their presence struck the creative imagination with unlimited possibility. My placement in it all seemed so unbelievable yet appropriate. I, along with many visionaries, strove to accomplish the extraordinary, stretching the predetermined limits of the masses. It was a phenomenal sensation to experience an idea become reality, the journey in between most certainly worthwhile. The beauty before me and the truth of the moment struck me with awe.

"To bed, to bed, sleepy head. Tomorrow's another day!" I chuckled, as I rose from my plastic chair, reached towards the large appliquéd midnight-blue Tibetan knot of infinity on the hanging curtain, spread it away from the frame and walked in.

The warmth of the bed welcomed me. The manager's wife had placed a couple of hot-water bottles beneath the covers! This lap of luxury felt pretty darn good. Blissed-out and cozy, I drifted off to sleep with a smile on my face, undoubtedly heading into sweet dreams.

"OK, Dad. Here we are!" I said to the small plastic vial container that held my father's ashes.

I had pulled it out of my daypack, placed it on the ground, and sat down beside it looking at the marvellous view in front of me.

"Mount Everest, Sagarmatha, Chomolungma—Goddess Mother of the World! Oh, glorious mountain of heaven, here we are!" I exclaimed, proclaiming our successful arrival.

I had just spent the last two-and-a-half hours climbing up the hill behind Namche Bazaar, over the flats of the helicopter field, past a herd of yaks and again up and over the next hill where a hotel was situated. I turned the bend and there, stretched in front of me, was my first sight of the mightiest mountain in the world. There I stopped.

This then would be the place. The notorious place of 'casting off'. Perfect.

"Now, Dad, this is it. Our final farewell, after thirty years of grieving. Please take a hike, a flight; ascend, or whatever. However, before you do, let's talk. Did you know how much I valued your gifts? You gave me vision. You inspired my spiritual view. You interpreted my identity and reflected my greatness. You, above all people, showed me the way, the way towards liberation. You opened possibilities, expanded my scope, extended my horizons. You were my mentor. For you, I committed myself to the quest, the search, the journey towards the One. The Truth. You believed and passed your belief on to me—that there was a sense of perfection, something more, greater than the small mind. You suggested awareness, introducing another view of the 'nature of reality'. I recognized your greatness and acknowledge it within myself—not that I know anything in particular, or feel that I am better than anyone else; just different. I strive to be a truer human being because of you.

"I thank you for ALL that, Father. I miss you, but I must finally let you go. So must all the others. Each and every one of us is crying because you are gone. It's now time for all of us to get on with life and realize our dreams and potential. Having said that, I must now cast you to the winds, throw you over the mountain! Good-bye, Dad. I'll try my best to realize your dream, for it is mine."

I lifted myself to my feet, plastic container in hand and took off the lid. I boldly tossed the remains into the empty space before me; Mount Everest stood as my witness. The ashes flew out of the vial and swished up into the air. Illuminated by the mid-day sun, they dropped like firecracker sparklets in front of my eyes. They inevitably fell to the earth, along with my long overdue tears.

Somewhere, somehow, I knew we would meet again to resume our communication. For the time being, I had a mission to accomplish and a project to finish. I whispered to the wind and to my father one last time, lines from one of my favourite poems:

> Whilst, burning through the inmost veil of Heaven,
> The soul of Adonais, like a star,
> Beacons from the abode where the Eternal are.

"Such was the nature of your soul to me, Dad. Even Percy Bysshe Shelley would have been delighted to have had a father like you!" I proudly admonished.

Turning, I bent over to clasp my precious walking stick. I deliberately grasped its handle and set the tip firmly into the grassy soil. Standing directly opposite the mighty mountain, I emphatically made my statement and proclaimed my rightful heritage:

"I intend to realize my True Potential and the Ultimate Truth of myself. I claim my Dreams and my Happiness. I state this not only for myself, but for my family, friends, and all of humanity!"

I banged my stick three times upon the earth.

"Hear! Hear! Hear!" I simultaneously exclaimed to ground the intention.

Tickled that I had successfully accomplished an exact replica of my imagined drama, I gladly resumed the walk along the grassy mountainside path and plain towards a grove of pine trees in the distance. There, hidden from view, was the famous Everest Hotel now owned by a group of Japanese entrepreneurs. Needless to say, the panoramic scene that stretched out beyond the hotel was spectacular. I did my most favourite thing in the whole world on the 'top of the world'. After I took pictures and had pictures taken of me, I sat on the veranda enjoying the view and sipped a cup of tea.

"Why is it that the pendulum of life always has to swing from one extreme to another?" I asked myself plaintively.

I had just opened my email and received some bad news from my oldest daughter. The title of it read: "Don't Panic, Mom, But . . ."

I had only had three hours to revel in my triumphant joy—not nearly long enough. I deserved so much more! I felt like filing an official complaint but didn't know who to email it to.

Damn. The problem was that my youngest daughter had gone into premature labour and had been hospitalized, rendering me needed at home immediately. As if that were possible, unless I took the helicopter for an exorbitant price—money I didn't have! Of course, my oldest daughter, Oriole, encouraged me to think about it and not come home unless I felt I needed to, to take care of myself first. Definitely not an option. How could I be happy now that I knew there were serious problems at home? My daughter was about to have a baby: it was my duty, as a mother, to be there.

I was sitting at a table in the dining hall of my hotel with two tall English brothers, who were doing the Everest trek as a birthday celebration. I think they were turning forty.

"We were born prematurely, and look at us—healthy and strong," one of them reassuringly said to me, trying to be of comfort and relieve me of my worry. He looked over at his brother who was nodding and they both smiled lovingly.

"My twin daughters were also premature and they are just fine. That was here in Nepal without all the fancy hospital stuff that they have nowadays," Tsering added. He had been standing beside the table, waiting to take our dinner orders.

I wasn't sure that I felt reassured. "No one in my family has had a premature baby. I'm not familiar with this sort of thing, not sure how I'll be able to cope or help my daughter," I admitted honestly.

"You should just get there as quickly as you can, to be by her side. That's what she needs. Everything else will follow," Tsering said positively. "I'll have a porter help you down with your things early tomorrow morning. OK?"

I sighed and nodded, resigning myself to the situation, not wanting to depart because tomorrow was Saturday. I had wanted to wander around to see what trading was going on and what the Tibetans had to sell 'under the table' so to speak. Maybe I could pick up a few things on the way out of town, like a pair of those hand-knitted socks that were so beautifully crafted.

"After supper, my wife has a surprise for you, Veda. Some of her friends are coming over for the evening and want you to join them. Would you like that? You could talk with my wife further about her experience with the twins."

Tsering was being particularly kind to me. I couldn't have asked for a better friend and I had only known him a couple of days. It all went along with being the host and owner of the hotel; his job was to keep his guests at ease and help them in any way he could.

The Japanese woman had had to be taken back down the mountain that afternoon while I was at the Everest Hotel. Her altitude sickness hadn't gotten any better. Unwilling to cooperate with the help that was being offered from the doctor, Tsering or his wife, she wouldn't take the medication and was unwilling to pay the expense of the oxygen. Admittedly the price was pretty steep. The rest of the group had gone on ahead, making their way to Gokyo Lake. I knew that Tsering was worried about her and that the responsibilities of his guests weighed heavily upon him. My predicament had added to his list, so I gladly responded to his kindness.

I had also hoped to see Raj and Tashi again. Since they would also be returning to the hotel in Kathmandu, I'd have to leave the art supplies for Raj there. Petty details were the last thing I cared about at the moment. So worried was I about the situation at home, I had to keep reminding myself to repeat my Chenrezig mantra because the mounting terror was driving me crazy.

Later that evening Gyen, Tsering's wife, smiled and looked over the table at me.

"Try this on," she offered, as she slid what looked like the most delightful black silk chuba across the wooden table we were sitting at. (The same one the group had sat at for the birthday party, right beside the wood stove shedding light and warmth into the big dining hall.) I was sitting with a group of female Tibetan descendants from the village, gathered for their weekly chin-wag over Tibetan butter tea, all dressed in their ethnic clothes, each with a different-coloured striped apron. I raised my eyebrows in surprise and smiled shyly as I thankfully accepted the small pile of clothes.

"It's our ceremonial dress. Tsering said you wanted one. There's also a blouse, jacket, and apron there that goes with the chuba. We always wear our antique jewellery that our grandmothers wore before us. Maybe you could get some beads and make a necklace yourself."

"Why don't you let me help you with that?" she added, as she stood up from the table of Sherpa women who were all gazing at me with bemusement. It was quite unusual for a foreigner to take such an interest in things. They also looked quite expectant. How could I refuse?

"All right," I said.

We headed into the back room behind the traditional curtain. It was the kitchen area but no one else was there. Gyen helped me out of my things and into hers. "There!" she exclaimed, looking quite satisfied as she made the last adjustments to the apron, tugging it in place exactly.

It had been quite a complicated process, folding the collars and cuffs just the right way, with the blouse underneath the jacket, underneath the chuba. After putting the final touches to the ceremonial striped apron with silk on the top corners, she said: "Turn around and let me look at you. Then go look in the mirror over there." She directed my gaze to the back wall.

I was curiously surprised at how well both she and Tsering spoke English. When I asked her, she responded that they went to America every year to visit relatives and do business. Then she went back out into the main room to get something.

Although I was much taller than Gyen, I was about the same size in breadth. I didn't look too bad! I smiled with satisfaction at my reflection in the mirror. As I was looking at myself this way and that with vanity and pride, she reappeared through the yellow curtain, holding a curious royal-blue silk hat, quite stiff, with four turned-up fur-trimmed edges.

She plopped it on the top of my head, adjusting it over my forehead just right, then laughed and clapped her hands with satisfied approval. I donned it with amusement. Except for my colouring, I could easily be mistaken for a dressed up Sherpani or Tibetan mama!

"Let's go in and surprise the others," I eagerly suggested, anxious to show off my extraordinary attire. We exited the kitchen giggling and holding hands, like schoolgirls about to pull a trick on the teacher.

I proceeded to parade around the dining hall filled with guests, proudly modelling Tibetan women's ceremonial dress. Everyone seemed reasonably impressed! I was pleased that such a show was welcome. Quite a handful of male trekkers from Europe, as well as a few North Americans, were at least tolerating me. The table of Sherpa women loved it. They sat 'oohing and aahing' as I circled their table, making the moves of a Parisian model. Laughing and clapping, everyone appeared to be having a good time with me as the evening entertainment. It swayed my mind away from my present dilemma. Tsering stood me in front of the bar to take a picture for posterity.

Furthermore, I fully intended to wear the outfit when I made the final presentation for my master's degree. I felt that the Tibetan ceremonial dress would put the finishing touch on the most remarkable endeavour I had ever undertaken in my life.

"Halleluiah, Amen!" I internally declared to the universe.

My trek back to Lukla was highlighted by an invitation to join my Sherpa family from Jorsale, whose members were heading there to meet the plane from Kathmandu, which was transporting their beloved husband, father, and grandfather. The Reiki Master son from Kathmandu was also arriving and they wanted me to meet both men. I felt touched by the invitation, very aware what an honour it was to be received by a native family, so included into their reality.

I had arrived back in Jorsale by ten o'clock the previous morning. The porter had been instructed to leave my backpack at the lodge there. I was sure it only took him a couple of hours to go down and back again with what he would have considered a 'light' load.

Tsering and Gyen had seen me off with a yellow kata draped around my neck as a gesture of friendliness and offering for a safe journey. I tied it onto the Swiss swinging bridge at the bottom, stopping there to throw the last remaining ashes of my father into the rushing river. I had thought Dad might like to swim the Himalayan rivers and streams along with the Nepalese fish, so had saved a bit of ashes for the return journey. Just his sort of thing.

I completed the Reiki teaching with Nawang Thrawpa, who had seemed quite keen, practicing on himself the whole time I had been up the mountain. He was eager to continue and finish. It went well. I hoped to return with his certificate someday, there being no mail delivery so far out in the valley. I also encouraged him to share his newfound gift with family and friends, to help relieve their suffering as well as his own.

What had taken me two days on my inward journey took only one on the way out. The family stopped for tea and for lunch, making it quite a family outing. I, along with the other women, was wearing my striped apron—only married women, widows, and divorcées like myself wore them. No longer a stranger in a strange land was I.

Surprisingly, I was able to keep up quite well. My feet had adjusted to the rocky pathways. In fact, what had proven torturous on the way in was more like a foot massage on the way out! It felt quite wonderful. I could have walked for days at that point, having really progressed in dexterity and perseverance. Two days more and I could have walked barefoot, throwing my Timberlands over the mountain edge, such was the condition of my soles! My purple toes and big toenails, however, were another matter.

I wished that I could keep up the trekking back home but it would be the start of the winter season and, of course, I was a city dweller. I also assumed I would be quite busy with the baby once he or she arrived. There would be a two-month stint ahead in the hospital, where I would need to go every day to hold and give my precious new grandchild Reiki. Such was my intention. My relationship with nature and trekking would regretfully have to be put on hold.

We arrived in Lukla around 4:30 that afternoon. The family told me not to worry, that a flight out the next day would be arranged. I had a ticket, just needed confirmation of a seat. The family put me up in a separate room at the luxurious Lukla Hotel beside the airport, most impressive. The daughter-in-law had been the manager there, along with her husband, until the year before when she returned home to have her second child. Her five-year-old, accompanied by his uncle, had walked out with us to begin with, but went on ahead in order to meet his father (the present hotel manager) sooner.

The older woman, Nawang's sister who had given me the apron, was eager to meet her husband. It was curious to watch the two of them greet for the first time in five months. As per custom, they sat at the same table but did not acknowledge each other or look at each other for the first hour—odd and made no sense to me. Cultural tradition often didn't to outsiders. I had assumed she would rush into her husband's arms with lots of hugging, kissing, and joyous exclamation. Not so. It wasn't until dinner that they sat together and participated as a loving couple.

The flight out was scheduled to leave at 6:30 a.m.; however, it was foggy. Consequently, all the planes were delayed and the passengers were advised to wait inside the terminal building until the sky cleared.

After I checked in my belongings (including the Nepalese walking stick, sticking out of the end of my back pack!), I had time to study the airport that Sir Edmund Hillary had helped build. It was a singular building perched on the side of a mountain. The runway went up the mountainside and ended at a wall built into it. I hadn't noticed the peculiarity of the runway coming in, too excited about the forthcoming adventure. We had landed on a runway that ended directly at a solid cement wall! Had I known, I would have been apprehensive about the airplane running into the barrier. The short runway provided a landing and take-off strip mainly for small airplanes carrying in climbers, trekkers, locals, and freight goods for the surrounding villages. Taking off was merely a matter of starting the engine and moving forward until the plane dropped off the side of the mountain, an easy and certain take-off; the landing, however, was rather chancy and precarious.

I had my last reluctant view of Mount Everest on the way back. The sky had cleared and I procured a seat on the right-hand side of the plane for good viewing. I wondered whether I would ever see the special mountain again. I folded my hands at my heart, nodded reverently, and quietly whispered: "Thank you, Solu-Khumbu. *Tashi Delek*."

The next evening, I was luxuriously lounging in a lawn chair underneath the bamboo awning of a bungalow veranda, sipping cold coconut milk, listening to the evensong of the jungle birds, and gazing at the fiery pink sky of the Terrai region of southern Nepal. How had I so quickly traversed the entire length of this varied country and ended up here, instead of on a plane heading back to India and on homewards?

It was quite simple actually. Aside from the fact that I had promised my granddaughter that I would ride an elephant and write her a poem about it, my speedy flight out of the country had been stymied by a difficulty in getting a flight to Delhi. I was scheduled to leave in a few days. Consequently, I jumped at the opportunity to realize another dream on my 'to do' list. The hotel manager booked me into a three-day tour package to the Terai jungle region.

Although I wasn't actually in the middle of the jungle, my hotel was situated on the edge of it, in what was known as the community park area. Apparently, elephants, rhinoceroses, crocodiles, and sometimes tigers ventured across the river and into the villagers' fields. We were close enough as far as I was concerned. I would be happy to ride an elephant and see a rhino or two.

The tropical flowers and fauna were delightful. As I sat there sipping my coconut drink, my eyes meandered to the tops of the palm trees. An old man was perched underneath the branches of a very tall one, retrieving coconuts for the guests. I had watched him scurry barefoot up the trunk in what I thought a phenomenal attempt to mimic a monkey. Left me wondering about our actual primate heritage; I could almost believe in the theory after watching him. He must have been well over seventy! Aside from the trees, my eyes feasted on the hibiscus, ginger and birds of paradise flowers in the well-manicured garden stretched out in front of my bungalow.

I had travelled by bus down from Kathmandu to the nearest jungle town and had been picked up by a young man on a motorcycle, who helped hoist my bags (and me) onto his two-wheeled vehicle and sped off back over the muddy clay flats to the river's edge, where many of the tourist bungalows were located. I amused myself during the ride watching my skirts flap in the wind, wondering what the locals thought seeing my bare legs. Most unusual; women in Nepal, like India, covered themselves from head to foot, barely showing their ankles.

After settling myself into a rather dirty bungalow and noticing a few bugs on the stained but clean sheets, I joined a group of travellers and the hotel manager for a tour through the local village and to catch the sunset over the river. Then, after watching a few tourists help wash some elephants, I elected to return to my room to enjoy the evening transition—darkness slowly falling like a blanket over the jungle terrain, comforting in its depth and stillness. The others had stayed to have a drink at one of the restaurants strung along the river's edge or to frequent the local PC room to tackle their emails. I relished the quiet and solitude.

I found tourist group excursions rather tedious and boring. One of the young women had become quite upset at the condition of one of the local cows that was bleeding from both ends. It obviously was seriously sick or had a severe case of parasites. Regardless, she kept stroking and comforting the poor thing which I thought extremely foolish, at the risk of infecting herself with something. She didn't heed any recommendations, so we left her behind to succour the animal, proceeding on with the tour. We noticed a crocodile on the far side of the river slither and slide into the rippling water after having spent the latter part of the afternoon basking in the baking sun.

I was enjoying the heat and looking forward to a night without freezing temperatures. I had noticed the mosquito net hovering above my bed and anticipated other inconveniences such as the monotonous buzzing of the pests. Without malaria medicine, the threat of mosquitoes was a risk. I had decided to forgo taking the medicine this time after the psychotic fiasco of my last trip. The net was a necessary precaution that assuaged my worries a little.

Early dawn: mist rising from the river and enveloping the grassy plain across from the entrance to the jungle forest. A group of us trudged towards the standing group of elephants lined side by side in front of the tourist shack. We climbed some steps and queued up on a platform, waiting our turn to board the back of the huge pachyderms—one to each corner of a square board with railings, perched on the top of the animal's back. The elephant mahout rode barefoot on the head, using his feet to guide the animal. Whenever he gave a direction, he gouged his foot behind one of the flapping ears and said something in his tribal dialect. The beast seemed to understand and followed directions accordingly.

I thought of a poem I had written once long ago in my twenties. I had never thought, then, that I would see myself riding into the jungle on the back of an elephant.

Tails to trunks to tails and on
The elephant parade marches past
Our souls have met and are gone
To join the circus just for fun.

The caravan to glory shines
Its light upon my face
And yours leads me past the gate
And out into beyond
Night's end.

We march and sway
Praying we'll meet others
Along the way.

Frivolity and solemnity. Were there any others here seeking something beyond a glimpse of a tiger or a rhinoceros on their travels? Looking for wild animals was exciting, interesting, novel and exotic. Whether or not the beasts thought the same of us

I didn't know. They probably had their ways of avoidance just like people did. I was glad that I was taking this time to play and explore. It was well on the tourist route so I didn't expect much. Even the spiritual pursuit had become a tourist route of its own, with various gurus and lamas charging fees for a peek at the divine through various blessings and ceremonies. Maybe the real goods couldn't be bought.

It was hard not to feel disappointed or discouraged that everything was being infiltrated by consumerism. There was a time when travellers in these parts were respected for the interest they had in the culture and religion, or valued for what they brought from the outside world. Now with mass media and intercontinental travel, most travellers were regarded as tourists wearing the same face—the dollar sign. I wondered if there was any authenticity or honesty left in any of it.

Was it possible to have spiritual experience in India or the Himalayas anymore? For that matter, was it possible to have a touch of the authentic wild either? Most tourists didn't really care; as long as they got a picture shot of some sort of animal that they didn't have at home, they were happy. I didn't consider myself a regular tourist. Maybe that was my mistake. Maybe, in fact, I was—to them, at least.

We plodded our way through the forest on well-worn paths to the rhythm of the elephant's gait, swaying along with its rear end and tail. At one point we did come face to face with a huge rhino. It was exciting. He stood camouflaged by the tropical forest, lazily munching on the deciduous leaves and branches without taking any notice of us. He was the first of three that we were to see that morning—a strange beast, a remnant of the prehistoric age with his tough armour-plated skin and nose horn.

My pictures would act as proof that this grandma had actually encountered a rhinoceros on her travels, while riding an elephant! Something to talk about when I tucked the children in at night.

It was time to go home and recount my tale.

My experience in the wilds of Nepal lay deep within the hidden recesses of my heart, to pull out in the privacy of my most introspective moments, to cherish and hold as spiritual nuggets in the treasure chest of my realized dreams. Well on my way to fulfilling my innermost longings, my experience in the Himalayan hills had grounded me in a way that I had never expected. I left the country with a newfound confidence and sense of worthwhile direction. I was not finished with my quest or my research project, just temporarily stalled, to continue after I had taken care of business at home.

Then I would head up to Tibet, the heartland of the Buddhist religion. I sensed that there was something there waiting for me to unearth, be it literally or within my psyche or soul. I pledged to return to Nepal and then make my way north across the border into the land of Chenrezig and his people.

Mindrolling Monastery, Clement Town – Gate with Deer and Wheel of the Law.

White Tara statue.

Tibetan woman with prayer wheel and mala.

Mindrolling stupa with gold Buddha statue.

Author Veda entering Namche Bazaar at approx. 12,000 ft. after a 6½-hour climb.

Mount Everest on the left in the far background.

Healing 'Mani stone' with Om Mani Padme Hum mantra in Tibetan script.

2006

Advancement

There is a story of Buddha.

Buddha was walking alone down the middle of a dusty road. He looked up to see a frightened elephant charging towards him.

His first response was fear.

"Oh, my! What to do now? If I value my life, I'd better think quickly." He saw no place to go to get out of the elephant's way.

His second response was anger.

"How dare this animal threaten my life!" he thought. "I must do something to stop it."

Of course, Buddha's first reaction was to protect himself. He looked around for something to use for his defence. There was nothing effective enough to stop the raging bull. Nor could he run as fast as the beast.

He thought deeply for a moment and chose to simply stand there. Still.

He watched as the angry and terrified animal quickly descended upon him.

Buddha wondered what could be wrong with the elephant. Maybe he was encroaching upon its territory. Maybe there were young ones nearby and the elephant was protecting its own. Maybe there was something else the matter.

At that moment, Buddha realized he was no longer afraid for his life. In fact, he was more concerned about the animal. Not wanting the elephant to think him a threat—there to harm it or its family in any way—he wondered how he could communicate his willingness to help.

He held his right hand up to direct the animal to stop—to stop being afraid, to stop acting in fear. Then he extended his left hand, palm upward and open, towards the elephant, beckoning its approach, offering it gentleness and love.

The elephant slowed down to a stop. Curiously, hesitantly, it approached close enough for Buddha to pat its forehead.

Somewhere between the refractions of black and white lay the truth. I had just bought myself my first pair of reading glasses, but suspected that not even they could help me to decipher things any more clearly. Maybe there was no definite answer as to what it was 'exactly' that I was seeking.

I was certain I wanted to continue my quest. Did I really have any choice once I had begun? Was there any turning back? No, I had made my pledge years ago. Now it was time to move on again towards . . . Heaven only knew. The 'for sure' thing was that deep within my being, I felt there was *something* to find and there was nothing more important than pursuing it—not even staying to love my grandchildren. They would have to wait for me to come home once more. Grandma was taking to the road once again!

When people asked me why I wanted to go to Tibet, particularly since the Chinese had so completely taken over, I could only say:

"I feel I have to go there, pulled towards my destiny. I can't explain it in words." They continued to look dumbfounded.

"Of course, it's part of my research project for university, you know," I added, feeling as though further explanation would strengthen my credibility. Only then did they nod, considering it a worthwhile expedition of research. People didn't seem to share my interest or inclination towards Tibet at all.

In this day and age of reason and material consumerism, no one did anything for 'no particular reason', especially if there was no financial benefit to it. I was beginning to feel a 'stranger in a strange land' at home in my own country. Oh, oh. I just might find myself a misplaced person in my own life if I persisted with my quest. Such was the ever-present risk of continuing on the spiritual route. The further I got along the path, the further away from friends and family I seemed to be getting. Remembering my elephant poem, I prayed that I would meet others along the way.

Most of the people I knew didn't even know where Tibet was, or that it even existed, in spite of all the 'Free Tibet' demonstrations that occurred in front of the Parliament Buildings in Victoria. Of course, my family was worried about my going so far away, to such strange territory. (Later, as the world approached the 2008 Olympics and the Tibetans came to the forefront in the news, they understood even less my penchant towards this country and its amazing people.)

To me, the other side of the Himalayas still held mystery and mystique. Maybe I would find the secret to eternal youth as I travelled beyond the view of the 'lost horizon'! If nothing else, I would satisfy my longing to be with my beloved Tibetan people again.

I had made preparations. I had completed the prerequisite one hundred thousand repetitions of the Red Chenrezig mantra and followed it with the meditations necessary to bring it to fruition. I felt an affinity with the compassionate self. I had discovered with great surprise that the primary focus of the teaching was to receive compassion towards my own self. Of course, only then would I be able to offer it to others.

I was reminded of a story I had heard long ago about Mahatma Gandhi:

One time, a mother brought her young son to Gandhi for help. She told him how her boy wouldn't stay away from the sugar bin, that he seemed addicted to sugar. She wanted the beloved guru to admonish her son, telling him to keep away from the sugar, not to eat it any more.

Gandhi told her to come back in three weeks. The mother was disappointed but took her son away. Following his instructions, she returned in three weeks and when she appeared in front of the master, Gandhi had no trouble telling the boy not to eat sugar any more. When the mother asked Gandhi why he hadn't said that three weeks ago, he replied:

"I hadn't stopped eating sugar myself at that time. Now, as I don't eat it any more, I am in a more honest position to advise your son not to do it."

Things had not been easy since I had arrived back from my last trip. My family situation was problematic, as was my personal life. My effectiveness as a parent and friend was shaky. I questioned my ability to extend love and compassion to others, since I was barely able to feel it towards myself. My well seemed to have run dry.

The Red Chenrezig teaching and practice anchored me in my 'sanity' rather than my fear. Having faced the edges of my personal terror and travelled beyond its usual limitations, I came to realize the subtle and delicious world of compassion; the secure foundation that it offered; the respite and refuge that it encompassed.

There was no denying that this quality existed, with inherent aspects of healing and well-being. I began to understand why compassion was one of the two necessary components of enlightenment—that and the skilful means with which to acquire it. Together, the two rendered one free of the ongoing onslaught of suffering: a solid comfort and assurance that there was a way off the wheel of karma into the basic space of awareness, the true nature of oneself. The practice had given me a glimpse of the infinite possibility of liberation.

I had accomplished the greater part of the practice during the Lenten season, if that made any sense. The remaining thirty thousands mantras were repeated and integrated as a requirement for the last course of my master's degree. In an effort to move towards enlightenment and accrue merit, I completed the first stage of the practice and wrote a poem about it, before starting my research.

Ever hopeful that I was moving closer towards freedom from the causes and effects of the daily patterns of my own suffering, I continued with the practice. I had no doubts that it had become my 'best friend'! A skilful means to help break my addiction to suffering –an addiction that felt familiar and safe. I now wanted to change that pattern. I wanted my mind to blow to pieces so that when they all came back down to earth, they would fall into a new pattern, a program for happiness. I wanted to be happy. I wanted to be an effective mother and friend. I was tired of always living in fear. I wanted to be like Buddha and get past my own obsession with suffering. If Buddhism could help me, then I wanted to pursue its teaching.

The practice of the Chenrezig teaching had developed and integrated compassion within my self. I now felt ready to continue my journey into the 'Land of the Snow', the land of the compassionate bodhisattva, Chenrezig, the father of Tibet.

On my fifty-fifth birthday, I booked a ticket to India with intentions to continue directly on to Nepal to join a tour over the Himalayan passes into China's most contentious province—the Tibetan Autonomous Region, or TAR. I was to depart on August 22nd, less than three months away. My last university course finished, I would be ready to continue the next leg of my research project and the course of my soul's intention.

Kathmandu . . .

It had been a drenching night—gallons of raindrops bouncing off corrugated tin roofs and winding their rivulets of sound through my restless sleep and liquid dreams. Each time I awoke, I wondered how I would make my way through the muddy streets in the morning on the way to the monastery school. I hadn't brought the right shoes!

I finally woke up to sounds of a wailing baby and the dogs' incessant barking. Dreams of monks, Tibetans, and lots of colourful activity. As I rose from the depths, the face of a very old woman turned to look at me. With a soft penetrating awareness of fragility and closeness (awareness that nothing in the material world is of any value, and awareness of the preciousness of this impermanent life), she looked at me. It was the knowing face of an ancient one. A nun and my grandmother at the same time, for her look was that of my grandmother the last time I saw her, before she died. That time when all she wanted to do was to look deeply into my eyes and tell me how precious I was. This little nun's message:

"To walk with humbleness amongst these my people," she had quietly directed.

To walk with humbleness.

Now the cock was crowing. People were stirring into life. Night darkness was beginning to leave the sky as the light of dawn crept in. The long horns, blowing messages from the monasteries, were sounding and resounding the morning pujas. Preparations were permeating the atmosphere with reminders that all was not as it seemed, that there was a way through the trouble and muddle by turning to Buddha with offerings. By turning and returning each moment to awareness rather than to the thinking process, to watch rather than to look, and to perceive rather than receive.

The sounds. The sounds of the life of a culture were what remained in the memory long after departure. It was the layers and harmonies (or discordant melodies) of sounds that filled in the gaps of thought or stirred the body to rise and respond to their invitation to engage. How I had missed the sounds from my last visit and never knew it.

The question: Would I engage? Or would I remain closed as a voyeur absorbing the sights, to leave once more with merely mental pictures rather than experiential knowledge? How to open, to receive, and to respond? I was so full of my own arrogance—another face of my fear. My affluence protected me and yet, in reality, I was not so very far away from poverty, homelessness, and unemployment. And yes, I was afraid—afraid to let go and to join these people in life. What to do?

What was my business here? I had followed the messages of my knowingness, followed my heart's longings and leanings, and now, I was back in Kathmandu. However, this time I had stationed myself with the Tibetans in Bodhnath, rather than near the royal palace and the Durbar Square in Thamel, the old city, like last time.

It was not what I expected. There were no open spaces, clean, with monasteries in the distance or on the hills as pinnacles of integrity. Rather the place was cramped, teeming with activity—people, families, animals, artisans, all occupied with business pertaining to their individual intentions, moving in and out of each other's lives whilst maintaining their personal initiatives.

Bodhnath. The streets were narrow, hilly, windy, with buildings joined coupled up against each other on both sides. The area was congested with no seeming order—rather complex and, I supposed, understandable from an insider's point of view. The muddy streets were full of holes and bits of bricks (or whatever material they once were made of), broken and rubbly. The taxi had quite a bumpy time of it bringing me in. I had no idea what I was getting into. Now I had no clue how I would get out of it and I meant that in the most analogical sort of way!

My plan had been to stay a few days and move on to Lhasa. I didn't think so! This was far too interesting. I wondered what sort of puzzles and configurations I could find myself involved in if I just let myself be. Maybe this was the exercise? To just let myself BE here. Well, the day was here now. No sun yet but I could see, between impending rain clouds, bits of clear sky. I heard birds chirping, as well as an underlying rhythmic pounding of something. I didn't think it was the drumming of regular drums, but could have been the resonance of the little hand-drums that accompany the repetition of the mantra at morning pujas.

Cocks continued to crow in the distance as people were stirring, coughing, clearing throats and talking over breakfast. Odd, listening into the intimacies of people's lives, as there was no glass in the windows. Lots of activity seemed to be taking place out in courtyards and spaces behind houses. Looking out, I could see a man washing his body from the pump outside his house. A dog was sniffing his feet and chickens were wandering around, while smoke from the fire in the back kitchen wafted out the door into the little scene.

It was an Asian version of the same morning rituals that took place in more private and sterile suburbs where I lived back home. Here, though, everybody's business seemed to belong together, stirred and absorbed into the collective public arena in precious ways that were not found in the West. I kept reminding myself that I was in the midst of the capital city of Nepal, not a tiny village in the heartland of the Himalayas, although there were many similarities that had been maintained, despite the impending and obvious technological revolution of present civilization that was beginning to permeate this culture.

Regardless, the baby was no longer crying and I could hear cars making their way through the streets. Business had begun and, as Cat Stevens had sung:

"Morning has broken, like the first morning . . ."

Famous stupa in Bodhnath, Kathmandu, Nepal.

Tibetan Wheel of Life.

Large bell in front of temple by Bodhnath stupa.

Old Tibetan woman in traditional clothing.

Hanging thangkas of auspicious symbols and mantra Om Mani Padme Hum in a thangka shop.

HIS HOLINESS THE 17th KARMAPA (left) and HIS HOLINESS THE 14th DALAI LAMA.

THE VERY VENERABLE 9th KHENCHEN THRANGU RINPOCHE.

SHAKYAMUNI BUDDHA

BUDDHA IN GLORY

Centre of all centres, core of cores,
almond self-enclosed and growing sweet—
all this universe, to the furthest stars
and beyond them, is your flesh, your fruit.

Now you feel how nothing clings to you;
your vast shell reaches into endless space,
and there the rich, thick fluids rise and flow,
illuminated in your infinite peace.

A billion stars go spinning through the night
blazing high above your head.
But *in* you is the presence that
will be, when all the stars are dead.

—Rainer Maria Rilke

EPILOGUE

October 8, 2007.
The anniversary of my father's death.

Three pink roses now growing in the brown clay pot. The auspicious number three. My three children and their extension of my life towards immortality? One way to think about it. The prevalent Trinity. No matter which religion I've looked at, the triple deity spins itself around and within the formations, arousing speculation and archetypal meaning.

The roses seem much darker now that summer is approaching its end. The foghorns blow their way audaciously through the mist and over the choppy waves. The wind is cold. I find myself shivering in my gliding rocker, looking out to the balcony and beyond, while perched beside the bamboo birdcage listening to the finches' chirpy honks. Little geese! Miniatures of the ones flying overhead and south for the winter.

And the dragons chasing around the bottom of the pot? Less challenging now that I am telling my story (which incidentally is not over yet. "That's not all folks!").

It has been recommended to me that this would be a good place to pause. Leave the rest for another time, another book. Take a breather. Regroup. Have another 'cuppa' of my favourite tea blend, PG Tips. And rest.

The story will continue as will the journey. There will be time to pick up the threads and tie up loose ends.

I guess that one can never really completely let go of the dead.

And every girl has to deal with her father issues. Somehow, through birth and all the childhood and adolescent conditioning, parents seem to transpose the visions of their souls, and the products and fruits of their unfinished business and karma, onto their children. Soul or cosmic legacy, I suppose.

In my case, my mother's shoes finally became too small and my father's too weary.

In my mind, as I stand barefoot on the soothing sands of time facing a resplendent crimson-lavender dawn of a new day, I ponder my future fully aware that I am standing still in the eternal present. No longer the youthful untarnished Kouros standing on the razor's edge of time. My edges are like those colourful pieces of precious beach-glass or tidbits of shells one finds on the ocean's shore—some smooth, some blunt, some a bit jagged. Myriads of shapes moulded by the tossing and turning of the water's energy and momentum ebbing and flowing in its own natural rhythm and time.

Until the end of my time, like the ocean waves, I will continue to flow in and out of experiences, knocking off bits and pieces of my fear, restlessness, reluctance, resistance, and egotistic attachments. Letting go and letting in.

I have been the dutiful daughter observing filial piety, honouring parental motivations, and living out their visions for me. At this middle point, however, as I drink my tea "surveying the situation" of my life so far, and this particular spiritual journey that I have undertaken, I find myself no longer willing to carry my parents' burdens. Basically, no longer energetic enough to carry any burdens! Taking time to rest before I hold up my cup once again to ask for "More, please!" (Remember little Oliver?)

The exercise of striving for the Ultimate is like paring an apple with multiple skins—when you get to the core there are just seeds for more fruit. Cyclic existence. The never-ending knot.

And the truth? Am I any closer to it? I tend to adamantly wear the dream of enlightenment and its promised revelations on my sleeve, just as I carry the longing of its possibility in the deepest recesses of my heart. Like a dog, I gnaw on the bone of freedom, refusing to believe that the nourishment is lost once the meat is gone. My life effort may be a drop in the bucket, but at least it has been true and will continue to the end because I believe in its potential.

In conclusion: I saw my father one last time in a vision two months after he died. I was sitting on the couch in my mother's house, hand-sewing a red velvet fairy costume for the annual Christmas Craft Fair, held in an old brick fire-hall down by the Bow River in Calgary. It was 1976. Remember those days? I was the Craft Fair Christmas Fairy; my job was to weave a circle of light, love, and magic around the occasion. As I was sewing, I inadvertently switched into a vision where I saw my father sailing on the South Seas, standing on the prow of a ship with the wind blowing in his hair. He was standing tall, his head back, his hair streaming behind him; he was laughing and laughing.

"Dorothy!" he shouted. "I'm happy! I'm free! I've found my peace!"

And then, the vision was over. I relocated myself back on the couch, sewing.

I believed him without a doubt. My father had found his peace and freedom in death.

I truly believe that I can find it in life. I will continue to pursue this *way* until the end.

OṂ GYA GYA GYA

May all beings be happy.

REFERENCES

Allix, Simon and de Vilmorin, Benoït. *The Rivers of the Mandala.* Thames and Hudson, New York: 2004.

Amritanandamayi, Sri Mata. *Lead Us To The Light.* Mata Amrita Centre, San Ramon, California: 2000.

Ash, Niema. *Flight of the Wind Horse, A Journey into Tibet.* Rider, London: 1990.

Baum, Frank L. *The Wizard of Oz.* Grosset & Dunlap, New York: 1900.

Dobrée, Bonamy. *Rudyard Kipling: Realist and Fabulist.* Oxford University Press, London: 1967.

Erickson, Barbara. *Tibet, Abode of the Gods.* Pacific View Press, Berkeley, California: 1997.

Gentleman, David. *India.* Hodder & Stoughton, London: 1994.

Gettelman, Nancy. *The Himalayan Journey of Buddhism.* Procrustes Press, Wisconsin: 1989.

His Eminence Chagdud Tulku, compiled by Jane Tromge. *Ngondro Commentary.* Pilgrims Publishing, Varanasi, India: 1995.

His Holiness The XIV Dalai Lama. *Ethics For the New Millennium.* Mystic Fire Video, New York: 1998.

His Holiness The XIV Dalai Lama. *Commentary on the Thirty-Seven Practices of a Bodhisattva.* Library of Tibetan Works and Archives. Dharamsala, India: 2004.

Hopkins, Kenneth. *English Poetry.* Phoenix House Ltd., London: 1962.

Keats, John, and Shelley, Percy Bysshe. *The Complete Poems of Keats and Shelley.* The Modern Library, New York: 1983.

Khayyam, Omar. *The Rubaiyat.* Gramercy Books, New York: 1992.

Kingsley, Peter. *Reality.* The Golden Sufi Centre, California: 2003.

Mitchell, Stephen. *The Selected Poetry of Rainer Maria Rilke.* Random House, New York: 1982.

Osho. *The Book of Wisdom, The Heart of Tibetan Buddhism.* Element Books Inc., Boston, MA: 2000.

Peacock, John. *The Tibetan Way of Life, Death, and Rebirth.* Element Books Ltd., London: 2003.

Rinpoche, Patrul. *The Words of My Perfect Teacher.* Shambhala Publications, Boston, MA: 1998.

Rinpoche, Sogyal. *Glimpse After Glimpse.* Harper San Francisco: 1995.

Scales, Sandra. "Sacred Voices of Nyingma Masters." *Shambhala Sun.* Padma Publishing: 2004.

Shantideva. *A Guide to the Bodhisattva's Way of Life.* Library of Tibetan Works and Archives. Dharamsala, India: 2007.

Singh, Sarina, Barkhordarian, Arnold, and Harding, Paul. *Lonely Planet India.* Lonely Planet Publications Pty, Ltd., Oakland, London, Paris: 2005.

Veda Mata continues to pursue the course of self-mastery, treading along the footsteps of her inspiration and the path of her intuition. Vancouver Island remains her home as that is where her heart lies and her family resides. Enlightenment has not quite been realized, yet its clear possibility dwells in the forefront of her vision. Rainbow lights and yellow brick roads still appear frequently in her dreams.

This is her first book. The sequel is bursting the seams of her consciousness—memories of Tibet beckoning to be revealed. Veda can be contacted at knockingonbuddhasdoor@hotmail.com. She welcomes your responses and hopes you will share your journey with her as well.